# LOVE THEM DO:

## The First Book of the Beatles

Ian Croskell

First published 2025
by Rowanvale Books Ltd
The Gate
Keppoch Street
Roath
Cardiff
CF24 3JW
www.rowanvalebooks.com

A CIP catalogue record for this book is available from the British Library.
ISBN: 978-1-83584-067-2
eBook ISBN: 978-1-83584-068-9

# Contents

# Prologue
## A Gift from God

A gift from God. That is the meaning of my name, according to the One True Religion. It also means 'God has been gracious'. My name is John. I am blessed by the name John. John, the Father, is one of the Holy Sextet. The Father, the Sons and the Holy Spirit. A doubting type might suggest that surely we are all gifts from God, that a righteous God would not have favourites. But the one true story, the Greatest Story Ever Told, tells us He had four favourites and He sent them to earth as a blessing to us all.

Like all prophets they were dismissed by many at the time, not taken seriously, their message of peace and love derided. It was only after humanity emerged from the Dark Times, after centuries of conflict that had virtually destroyed the planet, after wars had raged within nations and between nations and hatred ruled, that humanity sought a different path. The reasons for the wars were many and varied. They fought over their different gods, they fought over their claims for sacred lands, they fought to keep people out of their own lands, they fought because they thought their own kind was somehow better than those they were fighting, encouraged by leaders who benefitted from the hatred.

And along with the self-inflicted harm of continual war, humanity continued to cut down forests and build on the land which had once been inhabited by other species. And this led to the deaths of many of God's creatures, diminishing the biodiversity of the planet. And the creatures that survived these encroachments, such as rats and bats, were most likely to host dangerous pathogens that jumped to humans, which led to frequent outbreaks of plagues and diseases that also, along with the never-ending war, laid waste to humanity. It seemed that God had blessed His children with free will and cursed them with a lack of wisdom. Humanity seemed set on a collision course with oblivion.

And then a few men and women started to emerge from the rubble and the chaos, who looked at the perpetual war that was going on around them and made the heretical statement that maybe there was another way. And they all had something in common. A love for a group of men who had come before and brought joy to the world, had brought smiles to the face of humanity for a brief but ecstatic moment. And the other way, which they whispered at first, was a simple way. It was based on the premise, after centuries of war and killing and hatred, that maybe we should give peace a chance.

And what started as a whisper grew louder and louder until it became a Shout. And it said that after all the years of hate that perhaps all we needed was love. And slowly the idea took hold. After so long, after so much killing and hate, it was difficult for people to grasp the concept of peace. But the four prophets, the four gods, had provided a simple tool and it was called our imagination. All we had to do was imagine. And so it became our prayer, our Lords' Prayer. And this prayer imagined a world in which there was nothing to kill or die for. And the prayer goes on to admit that the Lord may seem a dreamer, but He was not alone and that His fervent wish was that we should join Him and when we did, the world, united in love, would be one.

And slowly, as the word spread and it spread that the word was love, more and more people did indeed want to join them. And the movement began to grow. From small acorns mighty oaks may grow, and in this case there were said to be fifty acorns tied in a sack all growing into mighty pillars of a new religion.

# Chapter One
## Flaming Pies

---

We are taught from a young age that the world is made up of four basic elements, fire, water, air and earth. We are also taught that our Saviours, sent to save us by an exasperated God in heaven, each represented a different element. The passionate, energetic, creative element of fire was personified by our Lord John. He taught us that honesty was always the best way to live, however brutal, however insensitive to the emotional sensibilities of others. Diplomacy was to be found elsewhere in the religion. I am a novitiate in the Order of John the Father, and the more I read about him in the Scriptures, the more I get the impression that to be in his presence was to run the risk of being burned.

Today we are discussing the origin of the Beatles. According to Scripture, from the very mouth of John, the Beatles were born of fire. Our tutor, a middle-aged man, a Lennonist monk for twenty years, put on his round glasses and peered at the words in the Holy Book that told us the official story of the Greatest Story Ever Told.

"And John said," he began, ""Many people ask what are Beatles? Why Beatles? Ugh, Beatles, how did the name arrive?" So we will tell you. It came in a vision – a man appeared in a flaming sky and said unto them "From this day on you are Beatles with an 'A'." "Thank you mister man," they said. Thanking him.' As you can see, it was a heavenly visitation that marked the beginning of our story, *the* story, the *Greatest* Story. Are there any questions?"

I had been here long enough to know that he did not really expect any questions. He was one of those believers that took the words as sacred. It was not really open to debate. But I could not help myself; I was born curious and had the unhelpful habit, in a strict religious order, of reading too much, including those books which the brotherhood frowned upon. I put my hand up. Brother John turned towards me, his face taking on a wary look when he saw who the hand belonged to.

"Yes, John?"

Eight faces turned towards him, including my own. John was a popular name. There were nine of us in the class, nine being a sacred number in the order. John was, of course, born on the ninth day of the ninth month and he himself proclaimed the number to be lucky. The other novitiate was Johann, a German exchange student from the Holy City of Hamburg, a place that famously contained two cathedrals close to each other on the holy sites of the Indra and Kaiserkeller.

I nervously cleared my throat. I knew he was not going to like my question.

"Thank you, Brother John. I was just interested to hear your opinion on how in some versions of the Scripture the man is said to have appeared on a flaming pie not in a flaming sky."

Brother John snorted. "And does that make any sense to you?"

I managed to bite my tongue and not give my opinion that a lot of things did not make sense to me, that a lot of the things we were taught seemed nonsensical, and instead tried to talk in a language he would understand. "We are taught that our Lord is a fire god, full of energy and creativity, but also part of that element is a fierce wit. Is it not possible that he was being playful?"

"No, it is not possible. And can I ask where exactly you have read this heresy?"

"In a book."

"From our library?"

"No, it's…" I paused. He had neatly laid a trap for me. The book was mine, bought in a second-hand bookshop called

Samizdat that I frequented. A strange name, Middle Eastern sounding, though when I asked the genial owner, he had smiled and said no, it was a Russian word. I had paused because I was about to say, no, it was my book, that you would not find anything of interest to read in the library here in the Lennonary. The trap was to get me to admit it was mine. That would mean it was my possession and, of course, in this strictly orthodox religious order we followed his suggestion of imagining no possessions by having no possessions, although when I was occasionally summoned to the office of one Brother or other, usually for a mild berating about something I had said, they seemed to be full of possessions. Books and maps and various trinkets lined the bookshelves, decorated the walls and filled the heavy oak desks that they sat behind. It seemed a stark contrast to the bare dormitory which I shared with eight other apprentices of the order. I could only imagine the splendour of their sleeping quarters.

"I borrowed it from a friend," I corrected myself.

"Perhaps you ought to reconsider having this person as a friend. You must see that the heavenly visitation of the man, one can only assume he was an angel, a messenger from God, appearing in a flaming sky underpins the holy nature of the Beatles story. The links between the Beatles and heaven are many and varied. Were we not, just the other day, talking about their use of the musical instrument, the celeste? An instrument whose very name means heavenly! To suggest it was a man on a flaming pie is to reduce it to simple nonsense!"

Yes, I thought but did not say. "Sorry, Brother John. I will endeavour to have a serious conversation with my friend and if he does not see your point of view, I promise to end the friendship."

I arranged my face into a portrait of humility, though in truth it was only an impression. There was, of course, no friend. He was a veritable nowhere man, living in his nowhere land.

# Chapter Two
## A Dilemma

Listen, do you want to know a secret? Do you promise not to tell? It is just that I do not seem to be able to believe everything I am told. It is 2330. The world has emerged from centuries of wars that left whole continents flattened. The last war was the worst of all. It lasted ten long years and laid waste to half the planet. It ended a hundred years before my birth, and so we have lasted one hundred and twenty-two years without a major war. There has been the odd skirmish here and there and continuous battles between areas who have not taken on the One True Religion but they often give up and join us. This is the beauty of the religion. It never conquers by force but simply waits patiently for the non-believers to tire of their endless fighting and, seeing the example of the apparently peaceful bliss that we live in, give up and ask to be taught our secrets.

Therein lies the dilemma for the sceptics; therein lies *my* dilemma. A suspension of disbelief is perhaps a price worth paying for a century and a quarter of peace. To give you a sense of the religion, the Nine Commandments start with the first commandment imploring us to Give Peace a Chance and the second commandment tells us that All You Need Is Love. The other commandments all emphasise the need to help each other and not to be too concerned with the material things in life. It was part of our training to understand that each Beatle influenced different commandments, with John, our heavenly Father, being the inspiration for the first commandment, and all four being responsible for the second. Number seven, for example, is Peace Will Come When We Learn to See Past the Illusion of Our Differences and Come to Know That We Are One and clearly originates from George, Lord of the Weeping Guitars, and the final exhortation in the ninth commandment to Don't Pass Others By is said to be the only commandment to come from Ringo, Our Starr in Heaven.

There was some concern that given the seemingly tribal nature of human beings that because there were four gods to follow, this would eventually lead to infighting, with each faction claiming supremacy over the other. To combat this potential threat to the peace of the new movement, it is taught from an early age – indeed it is hammered into us from the moment we are able to learn – that although it is inevitable that some may want to follow more closely one of the Beatles that it was only as a whole, when the Beatles themselves were in perfect unity and harmony, that the world was made perfect and the magic was able to happen. When any sign of conflict arises there is a decree issued to Stop and Smell the Roses, to remind us how much we have achieved by unity. There is a rumour that there is a secret chamber in which are kept examples of what can happen when that unity of purpose is challenged. It is said that if a member of any of the four factions starts to espouse the supremacy of their own god, they will be "invited" to this secret chamber of disharmony and played some examples of what can happen when a faction wishes to go off and start on their own.

So far, this seems to have worked. It does not happen very often but there are pictures of shaken-looking individuals taken shortly after their return from the chamber, professing never to speak of breaking away again and mending their ways and muttering darkly about how drumming was their madness and stopping and smelling the roses had taught them an important lesson about the dangers of going solo.

Some still question this approach, arguing that in some of the gospels it is made clear that there was disharmony between the four gods towards the end of the Golden Time. The religious leaders reply that this may well be true but serves to show us the way, that even if we do not get on, if we work together we will achieve more and get better results by our common endeavour than if we worked alone, that if we work through our conflicts instead of giving in to them, not only will we achieve more, we will be less likely to end up fighting in the real sense, and therefore this lesson helps underpin the first commandment to Give Peace a Chance. They would add further dark warnings threatening to make those who did not agree listen to a Chorus of Frogs.

I suppose some might ask, if I am so sceptical, what on earth am I doing in a strict religious order? What is important to understand is that I love John the Father largely in spite of what I am taught here in the Lennonary. I love him because of the things I have read about him in the books that are not officially approved. Along with the other Beatles he provides guidance against racism, for tolerance, for feminism and for peace and love but the thing I most revere about him is his *irreverence*. Indeed, from all the books I have read that are forbidden by the church, I get the distinct impression he would be laughing his head off at his elevation to a god. I therefore try to tell myself that I am carrying on his tradition in my own little rebellions and can therefore justify my presence here. I do not, for example, as almost all my fellow Johnnists do, have a chain around my neck that has a small replica of a .38 Special revolver, the revolver that is said to have been used in the assassination of our Lord John in the year 1980. We are taught that John had to die, that he was killed so that we may be cleansed of our sins. There is much debate as to the reasons for his death, with some suggesting it was preordained, that he was given four decades on earth to do his works and that his violent death was a warning of what was to come in the next centuries in terms of war and destruction. In our brotherhood it is whispered that he was killed because God the Father was keen to have his wayward but favourite son back by his side in the eternal heaven where he still resides. This is never spoken out loud as, of course, officially there are no favourites, but there are a few Johnnists who whisper, with a smirk on their face, that is the reason why Ringo lived until he was a hundred and twenty-four.

And so I loved John and my devotion was plain to be seen, which, I suppose, was one of the reasons my little rebellions were tolerated. I also refused to wear the little round glasses that were so prevalent amongst my fellow novitiates. I had nothing against them; it was just that there was nothing wrong with my eyesight. This did not stop most of my colleagues wearing them as a sign of devotion despite their twenty-twenty vision. I suspected they were something to hide behind. I like the story told by Paul, when after a verbal blast from John, the God of Fire, remember, he would remove his glasses, grin and say, "It's only me," revealing the love behind the gruff, rough surface. Also, I am a practical man and in these modern times there is no separation between church and state and although, once entered, the expectation was to remain in a religious order, to devote your whole life to the study and worship of the four gods and particularly, in this order, of the study and worship of John the Father, it did a person's career prospects no harm to have a devotional background and I had no intention of staying cloistered in this order for the rest of my life.

I came from a good family and the tradition had grown that if one of the usually two children either showed signs of intense devotion or intense ambivalence about a career, they would be sent to a religious order either to indulge their religious devotion or give them another three or four years to think about what they wanted to do with their life and in the meantime undertake studies that would hold them in good stead for a later career in a world saturated by the One True Religion. My sister, the Paulist in the family, had become a vegetarian at the age of six and had also shown an interest in becoming a veterinarian from an early age. As I had no clear idea of what I wanted to do, it meant that I was expected to take the religious route, a route I put off for as long as I could. In the end I was faced with the prospect of upsetting my family and getting a dead-end job or spending four years in a religious order studying the Beatles, John and the meaning of life. It was not a difficult choice.

And although the majority of my fellow learners in the brotherhood were devout and unquestioning, there were a few others like myself, there for reasons other than religious piety, to keep me sane. Indeed, there were a lot of "good" families, because out of the rubble of the continuous wars came a society that was not only based on the principles of peace and love as espoused by the heavenly fathers but a determination to not make the same mistakes that had led to the centuries of wars. The needs of the whole of society and the needs of other nations were now to be taken into account in order not to give people reasons to fight each other. The new constitutions were therefore a mix of the Nine Commandments of the One True Religion and the desire to promote equality between citizens and nations. We therefore lived in democracies, but the democracies were extremely narrowly defined. Political parties had to act in a way that would lead to similar goals. They therefore differed only slightly in the solutions they offered, and certain directions were not allowed and extremely frowned upon. One example was the manufacture of weapons. This was extremely closely regulated by the government and they were distributed only to the small armies that each state maintained in case of threats from the barbarians who did not follow the One True Religion. The closest that most people could get to a real revolver or a rifle was by visiting a museum.

NUSA, the New United States of America, a country that had risen from the ashes of what used to be called, rather ironically, given that it was riven with division, the United States of America, had even enshrined the non-use of arms in their constitution. They had a second amendment which stated that "An unarmed population being conducive to a peaceful, unbloodied nation, the use and availability of weapons will be severely limited." This was an amendment that was zealously supported by the NRA. There was much controversy over the growth of this powerful lobby group, the National Reading Association, commonly known as the book lobby. They had set up local book clubs all over the vast country and were so influential that it was said that without their backing no president could ever get elected. They were said to have fingers in many pies, and their main objective appeared to be to get citizens to have as many books as possible in their homes and on their bookshelves. They also encouraged getting together and discussing the books and generally encouraged discussion and debate, not only about the book of the month but about all aspects of life. There were some grumblings from some quarters about the power of the book lobby, but in the end, apart from when the choice of book was controversial, it seemed to have a beneficial effect on society.

What made a book controversial? Unsurprisingly, the most controversial books were those that contradicted, opposed or even simply questioned the teachings of the One True Religion. An example occurred just last week when a man gave an interview to his local newspaper in Coffee County, Alabama. The newspaper had a small circulation of less than a thousand but because of the controversial content it was picked up by the nationals and a frenzy of indignant debate followed. The man had introduced a book called *The New Testament* to his book group, and although most saw it as a work of fiction, an entertaining tale of the son of a carpenter who ended up dying a horrific death at the hands of the Roman Empire, this man insisted that not only was this book true, but that he predicted that soon the main character, a man called Jesus, a man he stated was the true son of God, would soon be more popular than John.

Well, you can imagine the furore. Sales of this little-known book rocketed as people lined up to buy it in order to ceremoniously burn it in mass book burnings around the country. Although I was not surprised, I thought this was a tremendous shame, the burning of books being a symbol of intolerance. The commotion eventually died down when the individual issued an apology, saying, "I was not saying Jesus was better or greater than John or comparing him with John or God as a thing, I just said what I said and I was wrong, or it was taken wrong." Some took that last part, "it was taken wrong," to mean that he was not sincere about the apology, that it was the ignorance of the listener rather than the words themselves, but most people accepted it as just another crazy fad that would be forgotten about within a short space of time.

And so the world outside the Lennonary walls trundled on in its own sweet and peaceful way. There were the occasional demonstrations for a more conflictual way of life. The young will rebel against what their elders tell them because that has always been the way of things, so occasionally demonstrations would flare up, organised by groups of young people who came to be known as warniks, who gathered together to shout their rallying cries about how war was not such a bad thing while holding up placards that had slogans such as "Build the Bomb" and "Make War Not Love", but they were not well attended and because the attendees were seen as young and foolish they were fairly well tolerated. The toleration worked because without the heavy handed use of the police, the excitement of attending these events was minimal and most of those involved soon grew up and settled down into lives of peace and love. When asked their reasons for wanting war, most of them shrugged and said life was a bit boring. Those that persisted were taken to the Give me Love, Give me Peace on Earth Ministry and shown footage of the reality of war, and most of them came out in tears saying that maybe boredom was not so bad. When asked what they had seen, they would just shake their heads and be heard to mumble words that sounded like faraway places, such as Hiroshima and Belsen.

# Chapter Three
## St Ivan's Day

---

We had returned to class from our one-hour lunch break. The food on offer was cheap and healthy, based on the macrobiotic diet as espoused by John the Father. It consisted of wholegrains, fruit and vegetables, and beans and bean products with the occasional addition of meat and fish. Indeed, there was some controversy amongst Lennonists, some of whom pointed to his proclamation "I don't think animals were meant to be eaten or worn", while others saw this as a particularly Paulist attitude and therefore not to be taken as a strict requirement, referencing the texts which suggested that although John was sympathetic to vegetarianism he always went back to eating meat. I was not overly enamoured by the macrobiotic diet and Seaweed Tuesday was always something of a trial for me but there was usually something for me to eat on the menu. I would sometimes forego lunch and sneak out in the evening and visit a pizza place or, even more heretically for our order, enter a curry restaurant which were seen as the preserve of those who closely followed our Lord of the Weeping Guitars, the Georgists. This lunchtime I had wolfed down my lunch, an action which actually went against the macrobiotic diet, which was seen by some as more than merely a diet but also an actual lifestyle with various lifestyle recommendations such as only eating when you were hungry and also chewing the food until it was pretty much liquified before swallowing. But I was in a hurry to get away and read up on the afternoon's subject for discussion and so, as surreptitiously as possible, I had quickly finished my macrobiotic stir fry with vegetables and brown rice and made my way into the peace and quiet of the Lennonary grounds and found a secluded bench with some shade from the trees against the bright glare of the July sun.

The Lennonary itself was a sacred site. It had once been owned by John the Father. At that time it was called Tittenhurst Park, a large Georgian, though apparently not that George, mansion set in seventy-two acres, which as well as the mansion included cottages that now served as the homes of those high up in the order. They were men we would rarely see, Lennon scholars who would spend their days reading the official religious texts, concentrating on those that involved John the Father, occasionally making proclamations, like the announcement of a new saint, the criteria for which was, in theory, very strict, but in practice just seemed to be people that had been close to John.

I settled down on the bench with a pleasant view of the lake which John was said to have not only made magically appear one night but to have occasionally walked on. As with most aspects of the religion, there was some controversy with the choice of site for the Lennonary, as it was believed to have been not only the home of John the Father but also of Ringo, Our Starr in Heaven. For some, mainly outsiders, this made the site doubly sacred, while for others, such as those in the Brotherhood of John, although they would not say it out loud, it meant that the place was tainted. John's stay was said to be brief, but long enough to build a chapel, or studio as it was known at the time.

It was a place I used to love wandering around, always with a feeling that I was treading in the footsteps of John and sometimes sensing his spirit, especially in places he was known to have spent time in. I wondered if he too had sat on this very bench and looked out over the lake. The place was seen as especially sacred as it was known to be the site where he had written the Lords' Prayer, or "Imagine" as it is sometimes called. In it he exhorted us to imagine no possessions, which I often thought, though did not say, seemed a little ironic given that he seemed to own quite a big house. I particularly loved spending time in the chapel, the space he had had built, which he had called a studio. Tittenhurst Park was, unfortunately, eventually bought by someone who did not understand the sacred value of the place they had acquired, and many of the features related to our Father were torn out. The chapel was therefore a facsimile, as imagined by the Brotherhood of John, of what had been there originally. I loved sitting in the pews, not praying, just contemplating what had been done in that place many centuries before, and gazing at the strategically placed sacred relics, guitars, pianos, drums and a little room with a large console in it.

In these surroundings, luxuriating in the midday sun, I looked around to make sure I was alone and got my book out of my satchel. It was one of those books frowned upon by the brotherhood, and I opened it up to where the story all began on this very day over three hundred years ago on July 6th, 1957. I was reading what had become known as the Gospel According to Mark, an apostle of the Beatles who had lived at the same time as them and who was said to have written many millions of words about their story. The problem that the modern religious leaders had with this gospel was that, although there was clearly much adoration of the subject, it was written as if the Beatles, although amazing, talented, even geniuses in their field, were actually merely mortal men like you and I, with no suggestion of their divinity. This was too much for the church hierarchy and so the bits of his gospels that had survived through the chaos of the centuries of wars were forbidden texts and I was risking expulsion from the order by merely carrying a copy of part of the gospel, never mind actually reading it.

It was occasionally pointed out that most of the contemporary accounts of the Golden Time seemed to similarly treat the Beatles as mortals, not mentioning their divine status, and that their elevation to celestial beings only occurred long after they had left this mortal coil. The church hierarchy, ever ready with an answer to these difficult questions – a process they even had a name for, the Fixing a Hole process – replied that the Beatles existed on earth under the principle of Divine Modesty. Of course they would not reveal their divine nature, the church argued, knowing that it would become obvious to those who were wise enough to see the truth. I found this a typically neat, if unconvincing, religious reply to a difficult question, suggesting belief meant wisdom and presumably non-belief meant stupidity. Indeed there was a small religious group who called themselves Unitarians, who worshipped the Beatles but did not believe them to be divine. They did not believe in the Holy Sextet and instead believed that there was only one God and the Beatles were human. Despite it being a major heresy, it was tolerated because they still loved the Beatles and followed the teachings of John, Paul, George and Ringo. Indeed they mirrored the main religion by having sects that followed different Beatles more closely. I quite liked the sound of them, and they were known as a liberal example of a church, with their stated goals being a world community with peace, liberty and justice for all, and most appealingly to me, they placed a high emphasis on *reason* when interpreting gospels, histories and Scripture. I had even toyed with the idea of joining them but in the end I knew it would break my parents' hearts. They had always given the impression that they were strict followers of the faith, unquestioning in their devotion and even loving each Beatle God equally. Plus, at the back of my mind was the practical notion that, although tolerated, Unitarianism was still frowned upon and would close a lot of doors in my future career.

And so here I was, back in the classroom, slightly breathless. I had been so engrossed in my reading that I had lost track of time and was startled by the sounding of the bell that signalled classes were due to begin. I had had to hurry back to the main building, the former mansion, hurriedly putting away my illicit reading material. There was a buzz of excitement in the classroom this afternoon as this was Saint Ivan's Day. Saint Ivan the Much Vaunted, to give him his full title. Not only would we be discussing him this afternoon and his role in the Genesis of the Beatles but there would be a variety of celebrations later on in his honour. In religious circles there was some discussion as to whether Ivan was a saint or an angel sent down by God to guide Paul to a meeting with John all those years ago.

Saint Ivan holds a special place in the hearts of the One True Religion's devotees. He is the patron saint of meetings and bridges. He was the bridge between the two heavenly bodies known as John and Paul. Some Johnnists, heretically, so secretly, believe that Paul was only an angel, as he is said to have later been often seen with Wings. An angel sent to help John spread the gospel and spur him on to ever greater and greater heights. But this is a heresy only whispered by certain Johnnists who secretly believe but dare not say that God had only one son. I expect the orders of the other three gods also think something similar about their own chosen one, although I find it hard to imagine Ringo as the only son of God.

Angel or saint, Ivan was so special in the divine narrative of the Beatles that Paul, god or angel, wrote a holy tract about him simply called "Ivan". In it he revealed the hand of God in the fact that they were born on the same day. "Two doors open, on the eighteenth of June, two babies born on the same day, in Liverpool, one was Ivan the other me." He also referred to the event that Saint Ivan, whatever else he did in life – for that was the fate that befell anyone who touched the golden aura of the Fabulous Four, to be forever a footnote in their story – was celebrated for. The reference was casual, some say a mystical allusion to the sacred meeting, others, less devotional, interpret it as a coy, amusing line because he did not need to mention who he met. "He introduced to me a pal or two," he wrote, using words as John the fiery wit might have said.

Brother John was talking to us about fate. The simple idea that some events are outside a person's control and are seen as predetermined by a supernatural power, in this case God. The official story is that Ivan was visited by an angel from God one night before the fateful meeting of John and Paul and told, "You have found favour with God, He has chosen you for a special purpose." Ivan was said to have been initially terrified by this visitation but, after recovering his nerve, timidly asked, "What is this purpose?"

"You have two friends. They will be Great and will be known as the sons of God."

"Who do you speak of?" he asked, wracking his brains for two friends that might fit this description but unable to find them.

The angel smiled. "The Holy Spirit will come on you. You will know when the time comes."

"I am the servant of the Lord," Ivan said and the angel was gone.

"And so on that fateful day," Brother John continued, "July the sixth, 1957, Saint Ivan, though simply Ivan at the time, woke up with the feeling that he was infused with the spirit of the Lord. He did not realise it in those waking moments, but this was the day for which he had been put on earth, to act as the bridge between two celestial stars. His initial feelings when he woke up were of vague excitement as this was a day of celebration, a day of fate. He would be going to the sacred site of Woolton in the Holy City of Liverpool, to see, amongst other attractions, his friend who was due to perform with his disciples of the time, a group of young men he had called the Quarrymen. Saint Ivan had asked another friend, a young man named Paul, whom he had met at the school they attended, to accompany him.

"It was a bright and sunny day, a fact not to be ignored, because bright and sunny days were an uncommon occurrence in this country in those days, especially in the North and especially in Liverpool, which was no stranger to the wind and the rain. It was a further sign that this day was to be perfect, a further sign that the hand of God was present on that day of days. Paul and Ivan arrived at the celebration and could immediately hear the sounds of the Quarrymen drifting across the field so, ignoring all the other attractions, they made their way across to where He was playing. The young Paul was immediately struck by the presence of the leader of the group and felt at once that this was someone He simply had to know. They were singing a prayer called 'Come Go With Me', which Paul felt was directed at Him, asking Him to go on a journey down a long and winding road. And so fate had brought the two young gods together."

I could not help myself. I had just been reading about this event and so, seemingly against my will, my hand went up. "Is it not true, Brother John, that the celebration was actually called a fete with an e, an old English tradition that included competitions such as three-legged races and the selling of people's old rubbish and jam, and in this case providing entertainment?"

There was a hushed silence as the other Johns and Johann looked expectantly at our teacher and I waited for the usual frosty reply. But for once our esteemed tutor looked pleased. "Yes, it is said that the sacred meeting took place at a fete in the grounds of a church. What more proof that the hidden hand of God was behind the events of that day? It was fate that they would meet, and they met at a fete! Even God has a sense of humour."

I nodded. My point was that the obsession with fate had got mixed up with the simple fact that they had met at a fete, essentially another name for a fair. But he had, like all good religious devotees, interpreted this as another sign. Maybe it was. Sometimes it was difficult not to get caught up in the continual orgy of worship and unquestioning belief.

But the fete was held in the grounds of a church, a fact that is now given to mean the meeting was a divine event, but little is said of the religion of that church. There was, after all, no Beatle religion at that time. I had read it was Saint Peter's Church, that the Saint Peter was different to any of the saints we know of that name today. Today, for example, one Saint Peter is the patron saint of unions and marriages, who the Scripture says called to say (to John the Father), you can make it okay, you can get married in Gibraltar near Spain, signalling the union between John and his Lady Yoko. The origins of the old Saint Peter have been obscured with time, and the study of other religions, ancient and modern, is not encouraged by the church hierarchy. All I know of the faith of Saint Peter's Church in 1957 is that it was something called Anglicanism, which was part of the Church of England.

It is an idea that seems quaint now, that you could have a church that was related to a single nation, unlike the One True Religion, which covers the whole planet and beyond. As the Scriptures say, the religion starts where you are standing and continues on across the universe.

Brother John continued with the official story of the Meeting. "And so Paul listened to John, who seemed to be saying to only Him, 'Yes, I need you, Yes I really need you, Please say you'll never leave me, Come go with me.' There is of course the famous picture." Brother John turned to the wall behind him, which was covered with pictures of John the Father in various stages of his life starting with this one, aged just sixteen on that famous day in July 1957. "As you can see, John, our Father, is looking right at us, letting us know this is a holy day, and if you look closely He is the only one in clear focus, no matter how hard you look He is the only one you can really see.

"Saint Ivan was nervous as the Quarrymen came to the end of their performance. He had introduced friends to John before and he knew he had to be careful, had to be sure the new boy would be acceptable to the fiery John. But he was starting to get a feeling that events were beyond his control, that it was not just a hunch that the two would get on, and so it was with increasing confidence that he went with Paul to meet John in a humble place, some say it was a stable, others a simple hut that was used by young men who called themselves 'scouts', a place where they would meet and tie knots. Our Father and his followers, the Quarrymen, were due to play later that night at a church hall dance and it was there in that hall that the magic happened. Present were Saint Pete the First, not to be confused with Saint Peter; this was Pete Shotton, a man associated with our Father from an early age, who had been brave enough to stand up to the God of Fire and so was held in high esteem by John, and thus a man who has become the patron saint of friendship. Also present were Saint Len, Saint Colin and, of course, Saint Ivan and the God of Water, Paul.

"It was here in this hall that it all began. Paul asked John, with no little courage, if He could take up John's most treasured possession, His acoustic guitar and play it. It is said there were frowns and a little laughter when Paul turned the guitar upside down. The frowns were caused by the knowledge that this new, unknown stranger was left-handed, and there was a belief which originated from their ancient and frankly wrong religious beliefs that left-handedness was somehow connected to the devil. Of course, we now know the truth was that this was a further sign of the hand of God the Father who had made Paul, like John, in His own image but with the blessing of left-handedness in order that when, later, the young gods were preaching on stage through the medium of their songs they could stand together and harmonise their message without being hindered by their instruments, could stand together and be seen to be the two halves, fire and water, forming the whole."

This was a surprising statement. It was a given that each order would believe their chosen god was the most significant, although they tried not to make it too obvious, but this gave equal importance to John and Paul. It was also slightly blasphemous in that it seemed to ignore the importance of the other two. The orthodox view was that all four made the whole, not the two halves.

Brother John, caught in the rapture of the telling of this divinely guided moment, a beatific smile on his face, carried on. "There was a silence and more frowns as the stranger fiddled with our Father's guitar, daring to suggest He could make it sound even better. Just as the others were getting restless, ready to move on to some other entertainment, the stranger started to play. He played a song that has been lost to posterity, lost, that is, except the title. It was called 'Twenty Flight Rock' and although we no longer know the words, it has been assumed that it was a clue to John about who Paul really was, that it was a song about the number of flights or steps it took to get to heaven and God on the stairway to heaven. There is some debate as to the number of these steps, as it is argued that the same source as this piece of Scripture asserted that there were actually only three steps to heaven and therefore the flights perhaps referred not to steps but to the meaning of flight as passing above and beyond ordinary bounds, and some believe it hints of the twenty levels of spiritual development that we must go through to reach spiritual enlightenment."

I literally grabbed my right arm in order that it should not go up as I knew there would be trouble if I asked my question. If something could not be explained, the religious hierarchy tended to either ignore it or pretend that it had been lost to history. I had seen the words to "Twenty Flight Rock" and unless I was missing something obvious it seemed to be a story of a young man who had a girlfriend who lived on the twentieth floor of her building, a building with an elevator that had broken down. This meant that the young man had to climb the many stairs to see his young lady and that by the time he reached her apartment he was "too tired to rock". The only debate, it seemed to me, was whether he meant he was too tired to dance or something else. There was little of the sacred in the words, so the church pretended they had gone missing in action.

Brother John continued. "The stranger now had John's attention, the frowns and the laughter of the others present had faded away and had been replaced by nods of appreciation and a growing awareness that they were in the presence of something special. This feeling was cemented when the stranger moved to the piano, another hint that the hand of God was involved as He had been given the divine gift of seemingly being able to play any instrument that was put in front of Him, and started to sing the words of Saint Richard of Macon, patron saint of littleness and uninhibited joyfulness and a particular favourite of John our Father. It was during this recital that Saint Ivan looked on and saw that somehow the light seemed to shine on Paul and that the only other person who shone in that instant was his friend John, who looked on with a knowing and wise look. It was at that moment that Saint Ivan remembered the visit of the angel and he knew that the Holy Spirit had come upon him and that he had fulfilled his most important role. At the time John did not show His true feelings but He knew the stranger had put the members of the Quarrymen in the shade and He immediately made up His mind that Paul, son of Mary, would be in the group. Although He knew, He still mulled it over in his mind simply because He knew Paul was special. He thought to Himself in the words of the Scripture, from the Gospel According to Hunter, that Paul was 'as good as me. I'd been kingpin up to then. Now I thought, if I take him on, what will happen. It went through my head that I'd have to keep him in line, if I let him join. But he was good, so he was worth having.' Although it has been argued that it is a bit disingenuous of John to suggest He had a choice in His union with Paul, at the time, He was the leader of His band and a little older than Paul, so although in hindsight we can see the hand of God in all this, at the time it was very much the hand of John that guided the two together.

"There are many disputed times for the true start of the world, even within our One True Religion, with some in our own order arguing the true start was November the ninth, 1940, the birth of our Father. The followers of the other three have understandably disagreed. The most common date agreed upon is this date, July the sixth, 1957, and is known by many as the Big Bang, the day when two celestial beings crashed into each other and marked the start of a whole new world. From this point on, nothing would ever be the same again."

Brother John had finished the telling of this most famous of stories, some would say the beginning of the Greatest Story Ever Told. To signal he had come to the end of the tale he bowed his head in silent contemplation and I guessed we were supposed to do the same. I looked around at my fellow Johns and Johann and they had all bowed their heads in their own show of devotion. I sighed and kept a firm hold on my twitching arm, which wanted to raise itself to indicate questions I had. But they were questions that would only bring a frown to the face of our esteemed tutor. I wanted to ask the question that if this was seen as the true beginning then surely it meant a corresponding reduction in the significance of the other two, George and Ringo, that logically the true beginning was the first time all four got together. I also wanted to ask about the Saint Richard song that Paul sang on that day. My theory was the song is not mentioned because it is difficult, even for religion, to claim there is anything sacred about it. I had read from a gospel that it was called "Long Tall Sally" and was either about a man who was a cross-dresser or about an acquaintance of the singer who had been having an affair with a woman named Sally who liked her whiskey.

\*\*\*

Later there were fireworks and my fellow novitiates took turns in groups of four to take to a temporary stage and played sacred music on sacred instruments. There was, as was usual on this special day, much scholarly debate on the finer points of the details of the meeting of John and Paul. They included the trivial such as the true purpose and meaning of the tea chest as it was used on this day. In the famous picture of that day, one of the few remaining visual clues, we can see Saint Len, patron saint of architects and tea chests, in charge of the tea chest. Like John, our Father, he is in a checked shirt and has his hand on the top of a piece of wood. Some argue it is a devotional pose, the pose of a man who has walked many miles with his walking stick to meet the young god; perhaps he is even a shepherd, the stick his shepherd's crook. Some have even suggested that he had been visited the previous night by an angel. This version goes that the angel suddenly appeared in the sky and the shepherd, a simple man, was at first terrified of this visitation but the angel reassured him, saying, "Do not be afraid, for see, I bring you good news of great joy which will be to all the people. For there is born this day a union of two that will become four and bring great joy to the world." Suddenly, the whole sky was lit up and a chorus of angels sang the words, "Glory to God in the highest, and on earth, peace and goodwill toward humankind." And just as suddenly, the angel was gone and the night sky was dark again, and the shepherd was left with his thoughts. After some contemplation he decided he must make his way to Woolton to be at the birth of the Beatles.

This was not the official line of the One True Religion. I think even they saw it was difficult to tie this version in with the known facts. Saint Len was not a shepherd, was a friend of John, our Father, and in the Quarrymen. But the church did not discourage those who wished to believe this heavenly version. When one of my more devotional colleagues starts to tell this story I cannot help but interrupt and ask, in this version, where's the tea chest? He mumbles something about how it was probably used by the shepherd as a makeshift seat, something to sit on while he attended his sheep through the long nights. I tell him to go and look closely at the picture and that if he did he would see that the tea chest has a musical note painted on it and is attached to the stick by a piece of string, that the tea chest was called a tea chest because it was a chest, that is, a large box usually made of wood that in this case had been used for storing tea and it was somehow used as an instrument and that, as it was called a tea chest bass, it was probably a bass. There is some nervous laughter at this explanation, that someone should use a tea chest as an instrument, and when I think about it, it does seem a little strange. I am sat at a table of true believers and I sometimes forget what people are capable of believing if they get caught up in a doctrine that is shared by others. The limit is beyond the sky.

I decided, therefore, not to mention my trump card about the fact that even three hundred years ago in 1957, shepherds in the UK had stopped watching their flocks by night, and instead moved on to the next table and left them discussing the probability that tea was a sacred drink, given that it seemed John the Father had a whole chestful rather than the small amounts that were the norm for other mortals. I even heard one devotee start his theory of how it was a gift from a wise man who had come to pay homage that day...

I joined the nearest table. There were four young men all dressed in the traditional garb of Saint Ivan's Day, red checked shirts and jeans with their hair brushed back, deep in conversation. This time the conversation was about Saint Ivan himself and what happened to him after the day he is most remembered for. The young man speaking was a nodding acquaintance of mine. His name was John. He was notable for wearing glasses from John's early days as a god, the bigger, squarer style which some say he copied from Saint Buddy of Lubbock, patron saint of days that will be. I also noticed that he seemed to actually need them, that when he took them off he squinted at you as if trying to focus. When I sat down, he did not stop talking, but he did glance my way and I think he winked at me.

"This is a day which we revere, a day of fate, a day of a fete. What was the fate of Saint Ivan the Much Vaunted?" He stopped and looked at me, a twinkle in his eye. He was a clever young man, a man who was extremely well versed in the Scriptures but I could not help thinking he used his knowledge in ways that undermined the beliefs of his fellow believers without them realising it. Whereas I tried to question their interpretations by using the facts, he examined the orthodox belief in subtle ways that brought the fundamental silliness into the open. So now he looked at me and I fell into his trap.

"Of course," I said, "some people see his saintly vauntedness as simply a mix up with his actual name. That it was a perversion of his surname, Vaughan."

John smiled and nodded. The others looked sceptical, some even angry at this latest heresy.

"I too have heard that. Yet if we look at the meaning of 'much vaunted' perhaps we can see that rather than being extremely praiseworthy, as we tend to assume, it actually means something that is praised more than deserved. Again, what happened to Saint Ivan? I will tell you. He died at the relatively early age of fifty-one, having suffered for many years of an unpleasant disease. It seems a strange fate for one so important in God's design."

"God sometimes moves in mysterious ways," one of the others said.

I looked at John, who was staring at me with a challenge in his eyes which said, "Go on, say it." I did not say it, that when things did not make sense this was what was said. The "Mysterious Ways" get-out clause. Instead, I thought of Ivan, young and full of vitality, a teenager who had two friends and one day decided that it would be interesting for them to meet. Even if that was all it was, it was truly something.

# Chapter Four
## The Other Half of the Sky

---

Saint Ivan's Day neatly dovetailed into the end of the summer term and the beginning of the summer holidays. We were supposed to spend our holidays in deep contemplation and even deeper study of the upcoming topics for the next academic year that would start at the beginning of September. I spent very little time in contemplation; I just was not very good at it.

The religious life puts a deep importance in the act of contemplation. It believes it leads to a deeper sort of knowledge and wisdom and that this happens through meditation and prayer. Frankly, if I had enjoyed meditating and praying, I would have joined the Georgian order down the road in Henley-on-Thames in Friar Park. John, from what I can make out, was not known for his love of meditation, though, like a lot of things, he tried it before moving on to the next thing. I felt an affinity with him because he was a restless thinker, interested in everything and inattentive to detail. When I tried to meditate, my mind would wander, where it would go and rarely in the direction of God, and when I prayed I simply felt silly. So I spent the six or so weeks wandering around the grounds of Tittenhurst carrying the officially sanctioned books in my hand and at least two books in my satchel that would probably get me thrown out of the order. I would find an isolated spot and read the material we were given and then place the forbidden fruit, recently bought from Samizdat, inside these texts and devour their contents.

I went home for a week to visit my parents. They were simple folks who believed almost all the One True Religion told them and seemed happy. They had always shown me and my sister nothing but love and devotion, at the same time passing down their strict moral code. When a woman became pregnant, both parents, whether together or not, had to attend compulsory parenting classes in what was called the Prevention of the Production of Psychopaths and Other Disorders of the Personality Protocol. As far as I could get out of my parents, this seemed to consist of making sure the child was loved and always providing a good example of a healthy relationship between the two parents. This simple but effective indoctrination, along with the political insistence on equality, seemed on the whole to produce children and adults of a healthy psychological disposition. As a result, crime and anti-social behaviour were rare. A murder, so common in the bad old days, would make national headlines.

The education system was also geared towards producing decent human beings. The Beatles made a number of pronouncements on the education system. They derided how it was in their day and suggested ways it should be. In the bad old days school seemed to be about imparting facts and those who could remember the most facts were the most rewarded, no matter how irrelevant or meaningless those facts were to their lives. In the Gospel According to Hunter, John the Father was scathing about His teachers and suggested the best way forward was simple: "They should give you time to develop, encourage what you're interested in." And later on in His sermon on the travails of the working class, he made clear His feelings on the system, telling us of His experience, that they beat you at school, dislike you if you are too clever and dislike you even more if you are a fool. He goes on to tell us education did the opposite of producing decent human beings and that after they had tortured and scared you for many years, they then expected you to pick a career, at a time you could barely function you were so afraid. George, our Lord of the Weeping Guitars, was equally scathing. He stated that "You're quietly growing up and they start trying to force being part of society down your throat. They're all trying to transfigure you from the pure way of thought as a child, forcing their illusions on you." As a result the new education system tried to steer away from just imparting facts and tried to encourage you in whichever subject you were genuinely interested in. Of course, ironically, they were, all the while, trying to indoctrinate you into the basic beliefs of the One True Religion. I liked to wonder if John the Father, even if he had been encouraged in the way he suggested, would have gone along happily with the present system. He was always John the Rebel to me, and a woman close to him had once suggested that institutions "were not made for John".

My parents were a rare couple in that they were still together. The One True Religion revered marriage as a sacred institution but did not expect it to last a lifetime. The example of the Fabulous Four meant the religion expected people to get married at least twice and occasionally three times in their lives, and though it was not exactly frowned upon, if a marriage lasted a lifetime it was seen as a curiosity. It was simply regarded as a self-evident truth that people would sometimes grow apart. I had heard that in ancient wedding ceremonies the wedding vows included the line "Till death do us part", suggesting that it was expected that once married it was a permanent state of affairs. The new vows included the line "Till love dies do us part" as a more realistic statement.

I think I have mentioned my parents were orthodox in their beliefs. They loved each Father equally, went to church every Sunday and said the Lords' Prayer before meals. Their religion was just there, a simple fact, never questioned, and truth be told they never let it get in the way of living their lives. If I mentioned one of my many questions about the doctrines of the religion, they smiled indulgently and gently led the conversation back to less controversial issues such as what a pleasant summer we were having.

My younger sister, Linda, had also come home for the summer. She was studying at university to be a veterinarian, always her dream since she was small. The house was still full of her childhood pets: Martha the dog and the two cats, Peter and

Gordon. We had had a small ceremony in our back garden to mark the passing of Sadie the rabbit, who had passed away at the ripe old age of ten. There were tears and sobbing from my sister as we recited the funeral prayer. My mother said the prayer. "Now it's time to say goodnight to our dear departed one, so good night and sleep tight. Now the sun turns out the light. Good night and sleep tight. Dream sweet dreams for me." My sister pulled herself together enough to give a little speech about how we should be grateful to Paul, our Father, who had taught us that animals were our friends and partners with their own rights and how we should be thankful that we lived in an enlightened age. She recited the "Glass Walls" prayer in which Paul, our Father, stated all those years ago that if slaughterhouses had glass walls then we would all be vegetarians, that if we saw the cruelty, if we saw how we killed animals in those places, no one could stomach eating the flesh of these beautiful creatures.

Later that evening, after too much wine, we reverted to our childhood selves, as people so often do when they return to the old family setting. We got into a fight in which she accused me of being a fish-eating monster, and why could I not see that salmon had feelings too, and that she had a good mind to report me to the fish protection police. I shouted back that there was no such thing, and what about prawns, did they have feelings too? The argument then descended into the familiar old refrain from our younger years along the lines of "my favourite god is better than your favourite god". She screamed that I was just like him, creating chaos everywhere I went, starting fires and generally upsetting people, and I shouted back that at least that was better than her namby-pamby conformism going around showering everything with water and dampening everyone's spirits.

My father, a quiet, wise man who spent a lot of time in his shed absorbed in his latest hobby, had seen the signs and departed for bed some time ago, kissing us both on the top of the head and reminding us that it was the coming together of these two ostensible opposites that had created the new world and that for all their differences it was important to remember that they loved each other. But it was too late for reason to interfere in our madness. We had started along a course that time had set in stone, made more silly by the added fuel of alcohol, and so we continued our unreasoned debate until my sister stormed off to her room muttering dark threats about reporting me to various organisations that existed only in her head.

I sat back in my chair and sighed. I had thoroughly enjoyed myself but even in my drunken state of mind I made a note to apologise in the morning. Dad was right: she was annoying but I loved her. I realised then my mother was still up. She had been sitting in her favourite armchair, listening to her children squabble as she had done for years, sipping her wine and smiling to herself. I gave her an embarrassed look.

"You may well look sheepish, young man."

"At least no one will eat me in this house."

She laughed. "Oh, Johnnie, I do miss my favourite son."

"You only have one son – come on, tell me you miss your favourite child. Your goody-two-shoes daughter has gone to bed and is probably praying to Paul right now that I get attacked by a giant trout as some kind of justifiable revenge."

"Oh, Johnnie, you know we have no favourites when it comes to our gods and our children. We love Ringo, our Starr in Heaven, as much as John, our Father, and we love our children equally."

I did not mind being loved equally with my sister. I expected nothing less from my parents but I could not let the comment about the equal greatness of the two gods go so easily. "Oh, come on, Mum, what did Ringo ever do? He was a god by accident, a lucky so-and-so, a god by association."

I had, of course, blasphemed. My order, the Brotherhood of John, would never say any of this outright, but it was often implied.

My mother shook her head and quoted Scripture at me. "They were four, Johnnie, indivisible. There had been a fourth, he had been there for years but something did not feel right. As our Lord of the Weeping Guitars tells us in His own words, 'When Ringo sat in with us it felt *complete*.' And Paul, our Father, said something even more revealing about the first time He sat in with them. 'That was the moment. That was the beginning really, of the Beatles.'"

"Don't you ever question the official line?"

My mother looked at me blankly. "Why would I do that?"

"Well, aren't you a bit annoyed that this is a religion where all the gods are men? You've God the Father and His four sons. Where's God the Mother and her daughters?"

"Any reading of the Great Story has to accept the elevation of women. There are songs of praise to mothers and motherhood and the example of the relationship between man and woman between John and our Lady Yoko and Paul and the Lovely Linda has served our society well. Especially your fellow, John the Father, expressed His desire for equality between men and women. I can't think of any songs or prayers to fathers and fatherhood, so if anything we women get a better deal. Why would I complain? I have a husband I love, a job I enjoy and two wonderful, if occasionally annoying, children."

She had mentioned three aspects of the "pillars of happiness" so lauded by the church and state, but it sounded like a life sentence to my young ears. I was not drunk enough to say so.

Although it was the last words of a late-night drunken conversation, it also served as a prologue. The first half of the next term in the brotherhood was dedicated to the role of women in the Great Story, and more specifically – we were the Brotherhood of John, after all – the role of women in the life of John.

# Chapter Five
## Mother

I was back at the Lennonary. It was the first day of a new semester. The same eight Johns and one Johann were sat expectantly waiting for the arrival of Brother John. There was a buzz of expectation in the class as it was a different Brother John. He had a reputation for frowning less. Most staid institutions had a few of his types: younger, more progressive, interested in the views of the students rather than just imparting Scripture in a way that brooked no discussion or, God forbid, criticism. He was popular with the novitiates. It was even whispered that his seminars were fun.

We were going to be looking at the women in the life of John but also at the status of women as laid out by the One True Religion. Like a good student I had read extensively around the subject. I was fascinated to read that in the bad old days there was a prevalence of something called domestic abuse, a crime which mainly men would perpetrate against women, although it was not unknown for women to be guilty of it. The causes seemed to be many and varied including the view of some men that women were inferior and therefore they had the right to control them. Another factor was a child witnessing it from an early age and therefore accepting it as a normal part of family life. It had largely been eradicated by the emphasis on equality between the sexes, the emphasis on equality between everybody, and the intense educational reinforcement of the unacceptability of this behaviour from an early age.

It was a part of the story of John because he was said by some to have perpetrated these acts himself. There was some debate over this as one side saw it as sacrilegious to suggest he could possibly ever do anything so outrageous, while the other side saw it as an example of him learning from his mistakes and putting them right later in his life. They argued that through his mistakes we were able to learn the true way to live. I was satisfied with neither side. There definitely seemed to be some evidence that it had occurred. He wrote in one of his sermons that he used to be mean to his woman, that he beat her and kept her apart from the things that she loved. He freely admitted he was mean but that he was changing his scene and doing the best that he could. This seemed to give credence to the argument that it happened and he changed. My problem with this was the question of why he actually needed to beat the woman before knowing it was wrong. If he was the son of God, a god himself, did he not know it was wrong? When I tried to find the cause of John's behaviour I could find no example of it in his childhood, although there were rumours that his mother's long-term lover, John Dykins, could be violent when drunk, so could only conclude it was the result of a rage at life itself. A rage caused by the loss of his mother. He would lash out at women as he would lash out at everybody.

These were my thoughts as Brother John entered the classroom. The Lennonary dress code reflected what was termed the four ages of the Beatles. Last year, our first, we were expected to wear smart suits, collarless if you so wished, with ties and the occasional black polo neck. This year we were in the second age. We could now wear suede or corduroy jackets, ties were less prevalent, jeans were allowed, hair was slightly longer. The third age, our third year, was the psychedelic age. These students stood out with their bright colours, moustaches and smell of incense. The fourth age, for the Johnnists, meant often dressing all in white and having very long hair and beards. I liked this second age, when our souls were said to turn to rubber. This was a progression from the rigidity of the first year when the teachers spoke and the students were expected to listen and not ask too many questions in our smart suits and ties. Now our souls turned to rubber and were thus more flexible and there was even a doctrine that students should "think for yourself", though not too much. When you were a Brother you could choose the look of any age, but Brother John had chosen the look of the second age. He came in, almost scruffy looking in his jeans, calf-length suede boots and chocolate brown corduroy jacket over his black polo neck jumper. He took off his jacket and flung it over the back of his chair and stood looking at us.

"Well, welcome to Year Two at our prestigious establishment. This is where I would normally write my name on the board but I'm guessing you probably already know it. I hope your souls are feeling suitably rubbery. I am hoping to stretch them as much as possible this year. Don't worry if you feel lost at any time. The thing about rubber is that it bounces, so if you fall you'll bounce right back up again. The other property of rubber is that it is elastic, so no matter how far I try to stretch you, you'll go back to being you again afterwards."

Unless we snap, I thought, but I could not believe that any teacher who stretched souls to breaking point would be allowed to stay long in the spiritual home of the Brotherhood of John, so my expectations were limited.

"Hopefully, you've been studious over the summer and read the books and sermons that you were set and"—he paused and looked at me with a smile—"maybe some books that you weren't set. We are going to talk about the women in John's life, so I want to tell you a little parable first that I'm sure you've all either been told or read about. This is the parable of the 'Choice of the Infant John.'"

He picked up a book which had a bookmark in it and opened it at that page.

"'And so the earthly soul who was the father of John, Alfred by birth, though known as Freddie, returned one day to the Holy City of Liverpool and went to see his one begotten son, John, our Father, and asked John's protector if he could take Him to the nearby town of Blackpool for a holiday. They stayed with a friend of Freddie's and there was even talk of taking a long voyage across the seas to start up a new life together.

After some weeks John's mother, Julia, Our Lady with the Seashell Eyes, arrived and asked Freddie to return her beloved only son. So it was that at the tender age of five, John, our Father, was given the heartbreaking task of choosing between His mother and father. And so the little boy, the young god, looked at His father and made as if to go with him, but then, perhaps with the intervening hand of God, His true Father, He turned to His mother. Her windy smile had called Him and He ran to her and went back to the Holy City of Liverpool."

He closed the book and put it on his desk. "Who would like to tell me the traditional interpretation of this tale?"

I kept my hand down. This parable had come from the Gospel According to Hunter, who was said to have got the story from the mouth of Freddie Lennon. The Gospel According to Mark, a gospel not always held in the highest of regards by the church authorities but probably closer to the truth, related this occasion as one of Julia coming to collect her child with Freddie being due to go back to sea to his job rather than having any immediate plans to travel with John to new lands. If there had been talk, that's all it was: talk. But Brother John had referred to it as a parable and a tale so I let it go. There were a number of hands raised. Brother John pointed to a young man behind me.

"Is the lesson we are supposed to learn that He chose His mother over His father? Does it reveal the primacy of motherhood over fatherhood?"

"Not exactly. You are right in that it shows the primacy of motherhood in John's story, but we must be careful not to dismiss the importance of fatherhood. Yes, Johann?"

"It is to downplay the role of the earthly father in the tale because, of course, the real father was God."

"Good, yes, absolutely. In the Great Story we have the example of Saint Jim, the father of Paul, to let us know that fathers are important, but generally the earthly fathers are insignificant, very much in the background to remind us who the true father is."

I wanted to ask how it all worked, biologically speaking, if the earthly fathers were not the real fathers. The church was somewhat vague on the mechanics of the birth of the Beatles. The ultra-orthodox believers proposed that the mothers, all virgins, conceived through the Holy Spirit. Although, at a stretch, this was at least possible for John, Paul and Ringo as they were the firstborn of their mothers, most of the history books tell us that George was the youngest of four siblings, so the insistence on the mother being a virgin was rather difficult to accept. The mainstream church simply dropped the idea of the mothers as virgins and continued to insist the mothers had been visited by the Holy Spirit for the conception of the Beatles. This produced in society a healthier attitude to sex, removing any special status or holiness to the state of virginity, especially for women, and instead promoting the idea that sex was just a natural part of adult life.

John, the God of Fire, was said to be born of fire. He was born during the second of the many world wars that the planet endured until the One True Religion emerged and pointed out that if we stopped killing each other there would be a lot fewer deaths and life would be much nicer. It is one of the tenets of the faith that I have no argument with. John the Father himself describes the circumstances of his arrival as being "on the ninth of October, 1940, when, I believe, the Nasties were still booming us led by Madalf Heatlump (who only had one)."

There is much discussion of this revelation, but most have translated it to mean he was born during a bombing raid by the Nazis under the leadership of Adolf Hitler. There has been much scholarly study put into the exact meaning of what this Hitler had only one of. One scholar has proposed that John was referring to an idea, the idea of racial superiority, but it is generally agreed that he had more than one idea, all of them, in the words of John the Father, nasty. Yet others have suggested it referred to a physical characteristic such as an arm or a leg, but surviving images do not back this up. This being the Great Story there are debates as to whether there was indeed an air raid that day, but according to Scripture John was born amidst the chaos of falling bombs, protected by the hand of his Father but nevertheless born of fire.

Brother John was asking another question. "And so, did the young John go home and live happily ever after with His mother, Our Lady with the Seashell Eyes?"

I raised my hand. "No, the mother chosen by God was a bit fly-by-night, and so when she returned, she handed him over to – I think she was referred to earlier as his protector, but this protector was his aunt, Saint Mimi of Menlove, the patron saint of nurses and naughty boys who may or may not grow into divine beings. She was given the sacred duty of raising John."

This Brother John smiled. Last term's version would have harrumphed at my subtle dig at God at choosing a woman who seemed incapable of properly looking after John to be his mother. Instead he nodded and said, "Yes, Julia faded from the picture, always in the background and to reappear more strongly later in the story but the woman who was to be the rock in John's life was His aunt, now saint, Mimi. He must have suffered to lose His mother not once but several times, but He could never say He was not loved." He picked up his book again and looked through the pages until he found what he was looking for.

"Here, from the Gospel According to Hunter, she says, 'The minute I saw John that was it. I was lost forever.' It is easy to interpret this as a highly spiritual moment for Mimi, who may have felt blessed to be in the presence of John the Father and perhaps knew she would be destined to play an important role in His life."

Or it was the simple longing of a childless woman, smitten by the infant John, I thought but did not say.

Brother John continued. "And so the infant John was the son of His mother Julia, inheriting her nature, wild, free-spirited and fun, but also the child of His Aunt Mimi. She was a woman sometimes painted as the austere, anti-fun guardian who kept John on the straight and narrow. But the truth, as always, was more subtle. Mimi was strict with John and often disapproving of His friends but she herself was a strong, independent woman, well read, with her own sense of fun and importantly, irreverence. So, although we often see John's life as one of pain, a mother flitting in and out of His life, an absent father, it is also one of hope and love. He had, in many ways, a happy childhood, and Aunt Mimi was always there for Him, and her sharpness and wit helped to make Him the man He became. I often wonder if she ever asked herself in later years, after all the effort she put into bringing Him up, why He never wrote a song about her while writing several prayers to His long-lost mother. But perhaps that was the point: she was always there for Him, even as an adult god; sitting in her English garden in Bournemouth, waiting for the sun, she was there for Him; even while He was many miles away in New York, she would speak to Him on the phone, still connected, though thousands of miles apart. He rang her a few days before He was so cruelly taken from us and told her He was homesick and was planning a trip back to England and of course He would have gone to see her. So perhaps He never felt the need to write about her because she was always there for Him; He could quite literally speak to her in a way He could not to His mother. His songs to His mother were therefore either screams of loss, as in the prayer 'Mother' in which He bemoaned the fact that she had Him but He never had her, or His tribute to her, the simply titled 'Julia', which was a song of love and longing for the mother He only briefly had and also the marking of His new life with his new love, Yoko, the Ocean Child of the song and in some ways Julia's replacement, as it is written that in His later years He called Yoko 'Mother'."

A John put his hand up. Brother John nodded in his direction. "Was there then, no father figure in our Father's life?"

"Does anyone want to answer this?"

I put up my hand. "There was a father figure, someone not much talked about and now referred to as the third George or Saint George the second. He was the husband of Mimi, a kind man, a softie compared to Mimi's strictness."

"Yes, George Toogood Smith - note the name Toogood - was a soothing influence on the fiery young god. As John here has just said, he provided an example of a gentle man to the wayward boy, often taking Him to the cinema and, significantly, buying Him a harmonica, His first ever instrument, perhaps setting Him on His way to future greatness. But alas, George proved to be too good for this earthly world and was taken at the relatively young age of fifty-two when John was just fourteen. His father, God in heaven, seemed to be testing Him, directing the man He saw as His real father to disappear from His life and then taking away His surrogate father at an early age. What lessons was John being taught?"

Four or five Johns put their hands up. I was not one of them. This, after all, went to the very heart of the matter. If I told the class that George's death of a liver haemorrhage and the even more random death of his mother in a traffic accident three years later, just as they had re-established a connection, were events that added to my suspicion that the world was a random, absurd place not governed by any supernatural hand and therefore essentially meaningless, I would have been marched out of the Lennonary and told never to darken their enlightened door again. Even our new progressive Brother John could not be relied upon to take this as an interesting opinion, so I kept my arms firmly by side and waited for the orthodox answers.

One of the true believers spoke. "Was not God the Father teaching John that suffering is a fact of life from which we must not retreat, that we must face head on?"

Brother John nodded and turned to another John. "Is it that God was also teaching John to glory in His suffering, that suffering produces perseverance, that perseverance produces character and character produces hope?"

"Good. So, these are both common interpretations of the losses that seemed to permeate John's life."

I noted he did not say he actually believed this, that God had killed John's kind Uncle George and his beloved mother to teach him that life could be about suffering, and I did not ask the question of whether there was perhaps a less traumatic way of conveying this knowledge. Instead he seemed to want to underline the importance of Mimi in the life of John. I later learned this was a subject he had written extensively on as a student, completing a PhD some years earlier on the "Importance of the Influence of Mimi". I was never entirely sure what point he was trying to make, whether there was something subtly subversive in this emphasis on the importance of Mimi to the story or whether he had simply chosen this subject as an interesting angle, knew a lot about it and was stuck as an expert in the field for ever after.

I wanted to ask a question that had intrigued me for a while. Brother John acknowledged my raised hand.

"Can I ask if John, our Father, knew he was a divine being?"

"It's an interesting question and one that we have hints of. When asked about His sermon on humility, 'I'm a loser', He remarked that 'Part of me suspects that I'm a loser and part of me thinks I'm God almighty.' Notice He subtly changes from suspecting He is a loser to *thinking* He is a god. The followers of the Beatles, although it wasn't necessarily explicit at the time, thought of them as divine beings in that they sensed that they knew what was going on, were somehow poised 'above' events and were guiding their many followers through the medium of their music.

"Anyway, I want you to think about the experience of the child. Seemingly rejected by His mother and father, unequivocally loved by His Aunt Mimi, who nevertheless had difficulty showing affection, and loved by His Uncle George who was taken from Him at an early age, and finally the loss of His mother through a traffic accident after He had reconnected with her and was on the cusp of becoming a man. How do you think this left our young man feeling?"

I held my breath. Was he going to articulate what I had just been thinking? That any sane person would fail to see the meaning and purpose in any of this, would conclude there was no higher authority and if there was, he was unusually cruel and heartless and not particularly worth worshipping. I did not risk saying this and waited for one of my classmates to come up with something suitably puerile.

A hand went up. It was a simple one-word answer that managed to be both truthful and uncontroversial. "Confused?"

I looked at the John who had said it and made a mental note to have a conversation with him at some later date. He sounded like a sane person, a rare commodity at Tittenhurst.

"Undoubtedly, but I think the overriding emotion He would have felt was probably anger. We all know, of course, He was born a fire god, but all the painful experiences of His childhood and early adulthood served to act as a slow-burning fuse that would later ignite the fireworks in the years to come that would, in turn, light up the world."

He had cleverly left this open to be interpreted as either destined by the hand of God, an admittedly rather cruel one, or a psychological explanation for the driving force behind the ambition of the man we worshipped. I realised also it could be used to explain some of the less than divine behaviour of John, our Father, in the years following. He was full of rage which only dissipated over time.

I wanted to ask a follow up to my earlier question. If John knew he was divine and the identity of his true father, why did he show his anger to those around him and not aim it instead at his "real" father, God in heaven, who according to Scripture had filled his childhood with loss and pain? Then I remembered a line from one of his later sermons, the rest of which were said to be kept secret deep in the vaults of the Holy See archives for reasons unknown, that stated that God was a concept by which we measured our pain, which seemed to acknowledge that he knew who was responsible for the traumatic events of his childhood and seemed to imply it was simply what God did.

And Brother John was to tell us, later in the week when we were discussing in detail the death of his mother, that when he was told of her fatal accident he uttered the words, "Oh God, oh God," again intimating he knew who was ultimately responsible. Indeed, Scripture suggests that after uttering "Oh God", his father's name, he added the words, "Why have you forsaken me?" at this, the bleakest time of his life.

# Chapter Six
## Half of What Is Said Is Meaningless

---

It was approaching the end of the first week back from the summer recess. We had discussed the role of Saint Mimi quite a lot. It was now we learned that Brother John had spent four years writing about her role for his PhD and were therefore not so surprised when all his conversations, all his classes, eventually returned to her. She was his Rome, all roads eventually lead to her. We had wondered at his seeming obsession with her when she was little talked of elsewhere. Today he was trying to bring it all together. He stood at the front of the class and made the case for Lennonist parenting.

"And so the Lord has given us, through John, two examples of the path to admirable parenting. The first is the example of His childhood and the second is His own role as father. We are concentrating here on His own childhood and what has become known as the holy trinity of parenthood as represented by the three main influences on his young life. They consist of the kindness and indulgences of His Uncle George, the sense of fun and the path to unconventionality of His mother Julia, and the stability and the provision of strict boundaries that a child needs of His Aunt Mimi. So, kindness, fun and boundaries, with of course, lots of love thrown in. These have become the cornerstone of what we aspire to as parents today. They are also used as a blueprint for education. Do you know that once upon a time there was something called 'corporal punishment', when children would be physically punished if they misbehaved? The head of a school would use a stick to thrash the naughty pupil." There were gasps of astonishment from several Johns. "None of the Beatles gained much from their schooldays and they all criticised the education of the day. We now have a system that is based on kindness and fun and, with limits, encourages unconventionality rather than punishing it. It is an exploration of the world around us, not just the repetition of facts and theories. Can anyone think of another part of the education system based on the lessons learned from the life of John?"

The room was silent so I raised my hand. "Is it the proliferation of the institution of the Art School?"

"Yes, very good, John. Where the staid education system failed, the Art School stepped in. It allowed those who could not fit into the traditional academic route to flourish, especially in the field of the creative arts. John, our Father, was one such young man at the time, a veritable fire god, full of ideas and creativity which had no place in the mainstream of academia but which could flourish in the Liverpool Art College, now a holy shrine on the aptly named Hope Street in the Holy City of Liverpool. The Art School has now become a sacred institution, a place where an individual can go based on their potential and talent, not on formal qualifications. In our Father's time it was mainly for the fine arts, painting and sculpture and so on. Now, of course, they are places for the fine arts, music of all kinds, writing, the theatre."

It was true, the One True Religion had found a way to institutionalise rebellion by sending those who wished to pursue their artistic desires to places which allowed them, within certain limits, of course, to spend two or three years "getting it out of their system" or sometimes even producing a work of art worthy of notice. There existed pockets of rebellion in these institutions against the system itself, but these were looked on benevolently by the authorities, much to the disgust of the rebels, and they either soon grew out of it or became outsiders who had no clear idea of what they wanted. The society was designed, after all, to produce equality and was based on love and respect between individuals and nations, and as long as that seemed to work, the rebels could only argue for inequality, hate and suspicion between people, and the argument against that seemed to be *all of history* up to the birth of the One True Religion. Indeed one of the arguments of the art rebels was that they needed something to rebel against to produce meaningful art, that the Beatles themselves were a direct result of the inequalities and societal upheavals of the times they lived in. The mild reply from those in charge suggested that, of course, the Beatles were gods and were therefore above the times they lived in, and that inequality might produce some decent creative works of art but when that was put against the simple fact of all the lives blighted by inequality and the struggle to survive, they thought it better to have a society where all could flourish and that, as the life of John the Father teaches us, there is plenty of scope for tragedy and suffering without adding suffocating poverty, death-dealing war and unreasonable hatred into the mix.

The Art Schools, then, mainly absorbed the rebels and gave them a place to act out their rebellions without causing too much trouble. Because John was a product of an art college they were looked upon kindly and seen as a phase of youth, which often infuriated them. But on the whole it worked, often producing interesting works of creative art and by the end producing model citizens thankful for their chance to shine. Those who continued to rebel were kept in Art School for another year or even longer until they had got their rebellious ways out of their system. The few that continued to rail against the system were eventually thrown out with no means of living and either succumbed to the system, which was, after all, extremely benign, or lived as outcasts, shunned by the majority and propagandised against by the authorities. A select few, not many, seen as overly charismatic and therefore with the potential of gaining a following, were exiled to the territories outside of the lands that were run under the principles of the One True Religion. They were the rebels who when asked what they were rebelling against usually answered with the famous cliché: "What have you got?"

So the exuberant, the creative and the rebellious were sent to Art School, where, given time to flourish – and against the idea that you needed to be up against it, to live in poverty to produce authentic art – they often did just that: produce all kinds of art, actually proving that what you needed was not a terribly hard life but space, time and encouragement. The pious, the ambitious and the lazy were sent to religious orders and the rest of the world just got on with it, initially doing national service, which was a two-year stint at the jobs that no one really wanted to do, before moving to a career of their choice, which they could change at any time if they got bored or just fancied a change. The wage differentials were enough to encourage people to take more responsibility if they so wished, but not enough to create the disharmony of the two worlds of the rich and the poor that we read had existed in the past. It was plain even at the time that those societies that were more equal were more healthy in every respect, from life expectancy to mental illness. From violence to low education, inequality had produced societies that were bad for everybody, even the rich. The One True Religion constantly reminded us that material things were not as important as our spiritual journey, so after an individual had gained all the things they needed, it was frowned upon to want more and more, and this was enshrined in the prayer by George, our Lord of the Weeping Guitars, "'Living in the Material World".

Brother John was speaking again. "So we have a whole network of Art Schools that are cherished institutions based on the experience of John, our Father. There is some irony here as history suggests that it was not His idea to go, that His enthusiasm was limited. The Gospel According to Hunter has Him saying that He agreed to go 'because it was better than working'. Behind this decision was the hand of Mimi, who had been to see His headmaster to demand he come up with a suitable future for John. Then, like now, to enable everyone who wishes to go, the tuition was free, but it was Mimi who would provide His materials and pocket money and provide for Him at home, a saint worthy of the name. Indeed, it is said He treated His time at art school with a typical unseriousness, but the point is, as is now acknowledged, it gave Him time and space to think and develop, opened His eyes to new ideas and, just by the people He met, He was given an enlightening education. From His new best friend Saint Stuart to His first long-term love Saint Cynthia to the influence of Saint Jeff. Although He would not finish the course, would eventually be asked to leave, those two to three years were crucial in making the man."

He paused and looked around the class. "So, we have our young god, at art school, dipping in and out, looked upon with awe by His fellow art students because of His rebellious, devil-may-care attitude. The art school was also next door to the Liverpool Institute, where a couple of young gods happened to be in attendance, a certain Paul McCartney and George Harrison, by then members of the Quarrymen, the first incarnation of the Beatles. Despite their youth they would visit their older friend at lunchtimes and hang out with the arty types. At this time John, our Father, was also seeing much more of His mother, Julia, with the seashell eyes, dividing His time between His strict Aunt Mimi and His fun-loving mother. We can perhaps imagine that life seemed pretty good. But we are heading, with increasing speed, rather like a runaway train, straight into an unnatural disaster that was to darken and hang like a shadow over the life of the young god for years to come. I am, of course, referring to the death of Julia. Who knows the details?"

Several hands went up. Brother John waved his hand in their direction, a conductor of the sad tale, missing only a baton.

"It was July, the summer holidays for our Father, after His first year at art school."

"Julia was leaving His Aunt Mimi's after a visit."

"John, our Father, wasn't there. It was just Mimi who walked her to the gate."

"She was crossing Menlove Avenue, accompanied by a friend of John's, Saint Nigel, patron saint of accidents."

Brother John's head was nodding, his hand moving from student to student as they delivered their lines. Now he stopped as we reached the climax of the story, his eyes closed as if he was picturing in his head that climactic moment. All hands were now down as if no one wanted to deliver that final description, perhaps not wanting to once again upset their beloved Lord by saying the words. Brother John opened his eyes and completed the story himself.

"And Saint Nigel heard a sickening thump and turned to see Julia as she flew through the air, her red hair fluttering against the bright blue sky, on her final journey, landing in the road. Her red blood mingling with her red hair, she was killed instantly, and despite the horror of the situation, is said to have looked peaceful in her repose."

He bowed his head as if in prayer and the rest of the class followed suit. I bowed my head in pale imitation while wondering what I was praying for. Thanking our omnipotent Father for allowing our Lord's mother to be run over by a car? I knew the inevitable interpretations of the event would come next and looked forward with some glee to their attempts to explain this seemingly random, awful accident. One of the consequences of this story is that modern cars, which look a lot like the cars of the sacred period known as the Sixties, except nowadays run on solar energy and not the pollutants of the time, are driven, especially by the close followers of John the Father, at speeds too slow to cause death. In Johnnist communities this so drastically reduced the fatalities of road traffic accidents that it was, sometimes reluctantly, especially by the Georgists, taken up by the rest of society. If you were late for an appointment you had to hope you were not getting a lift from a strict Johnnist, who saw it as their sacred duty to not go faster than twenty miles an hour.

Brother John had sat down in his brown faux leather swivel chair and was sitting back in his now familiar pose that signalled we were going to discuss something of importance in a relaxed manner. He would guide us in the right direction but he wanted us to speak. He leant back and closed his eyes.

"Who wants to explain this traumatic day in the life of our Father?" he asked.

As usual a number of hands went up. Not mine, as this was dangerous territory. The answers tended to reflect the extent of the piety of the student. The first couple of answers reflected the orthodox view that it was all part of God the Father's intricate plan for His favourite son. It was designed to bring John into alignment with his fellow god, Paul, who had lost his mother at an even younger age to breast cancer. There was now, so the theory went, an unbreakable bond between the two. God had initially brought them together on that July day in 1957 in the nativity of the Beatles and was now seeking to cement that relationship more solidly with the fact of this common experience. A particularly pious John was spouting this nonsense and quoting Scripture.

"And Paul said 'We had a bond there that we never talked about but each of us knew that had happened to the other,' and before Julia's death John had said to Paul on hearing of His mother's death about how awful that was and how could He cope and of course after the death of Julia, He knew, God had shown Him."

I wanted to scream. I wanted to ask if perhaps God could not find a nicer way to bring them together, to ask if they did not find it a cruel and unusual way to get them to form a bond and that actually, although the church, for obvious reasons, liked to gloss over the end of the Beatles' time together, the bond between the two was clearly, if not irrevocably, broken. But I held my tongue and Brother John, who was nodding but saying little, pointed to another John.

"I have read that there is a suggestion that there were dark forces at play. That Julia had brought a man into her life who was an agent of the dark side, perhaps an agent of the anti-John, that he was responsible for setting in motion the chain of events that lead to the death of Julia."

Brother John opened his eyes and leant forward. He had seemed bored with the orthodox explanations and now there seemed a spark of interest in his eyes. "Go on."

"Well, as we know, most of those who came into contact with all of our blessed Lords have been proclaimed saints, but the man in Julia's life, the father of John's two half-sisters, was never proclaimed to be a saint. Some have taken this to mean he was in fact a demon sent to sow discord into our Father's world. It is said in some texts that he was cursed with a predilection for the demon drink and was caught drink-driving by the police, which in turn led him to lose his job, which left the household short of money. In these straitened circumstances he had asked Julia to go round to Mimi's to ask her to take on the brunt of providing for John, as at this time He was dividing His time between the two households. It was when Julia was returning from this visit that the fatal accident occurred, and the demon known as Twitchy had served his purpose. The Lord, who is said to have been distracted on this day, later got His revenge on the demon Twitchy, who was later killed in a car crash on the sacred way that was called Penny Lane."

I tried hard not to scream and bang my head on the table. I looked to Brother John for sanity. I wanted him to point out that these were two opposite explanations. The first was that it was a bizarre and unnecessarily cruel plan from our Lord on high to bring our two young gods closer together, and the second that it was the result of a demon doing the devil's work while our omnipotent God the Father was distracted. I wanted him to get the dictionary out and explain the meaning of omnipotence. But I knew I would wait in vain for any of this to happen. The church, after all, was not stupid and therefore the Scripture was suitably vague on the meaning of the death of Julia. This meant that the human mind, not liking vagueness, and with a tendency of seeing patterns in random events, invented its own meaning depending on its point of view – or as I have said, in this case their extremes of piousness. If gaps existed then they were filled in with nonsense. Brother John neither agreed or disagreed with these theories, just smiled and nodded. What else could he do?

There was antipathy towards John Dykins, Julia's partner, especially from Johnnists because of the words of John himself, who stated that Twitchy, a cruel name that John had given him because of a physical tic, after finding out about Julia's death said the words "Who will look after the kids?", which our Father thought incredibly selfish. There is also evidence that he was an alcoholic and was occasionally violent and that Julia with the seashell eyes sometimes became Julia with the black eyes. But John also stated that he "took it worse than me", which makes me think that despite his faults perhaps he truly loved

Julia. After her death, he fades from the story, whether because he had fulfilled his demon destiny or simply as an inevitable drifting apart now that the woman who linked them together was gone, I will leave for you to decide. The Greatest Story Ever Told, the story of the Beatles, is interspersed with cameos of malevolent individuals, from mischievous sprites to violent demons, from the impish Magic Alex to the evil spirit Charlie, the patron demon of violent misinterpretation, who took the words of our Lords and gave them murderous meaning, and of course the demon who shall not be named, a former follower of John who ended his life in this world. But more of these dark forces later.

Meanwhile, Brother John, while not explicitly commenting on the meaning of the event, was bringing it back to his favourite subject, Saint Mimi.

"And so our young god was devastated, and the next few years would be spent in a state of pent up anger. He would be saved by the love of His friends, the love of a girl and the solace of music. And always with Him through the good and the bad was the woman who had always been there for Him with her undying, if unquestionably English, love. Undemonstrative and a little strict but always wanting the best and always being there when needed, His Aunt Mimi, the woman strong enough to stand up to His fiery nature and loving enough to put up with it. For me, the grandest of all the saints. She even had a little saying that acted as a spur to her rebellious nephew: 'The guitar's all right, John, but you'll never make a living out of it.'"

The conversation carried on around me while I sank into deep thought. Our Father was just seventeen, his mother was dead, cruelly taken either by his stony-hearted Father or by uncaring chance. Or, most outlandishly to my mind, taken by dark forces in the world determined to undermine the adolescent god. However ridiculous I found this, I could not help but remember the words of John later in his life which seemed to imply some of that darkness had seeped into his soul: "Songwriting is about getting the demon out of me. It's like being possessed. You try to go to sleep, but the song won't let you. So you have to get up and make it into something and then you're allowed to sleep." There, in his own words he talks of demons and possession. Perhaps his songs, prayers, sermons, call them what you will, were incantations against the darkness within him and without. Perhaps I had spent too long at the Lennonary and was beginning to sound like the worst of my pious colleagues, whose relationship to reality was at best a distant one.

# Chapter Seven
## Saint Stuart

---

We had discussed Julia to death. Thankfully it was Friday and we had the weekend to escape the pain and anger of our Father if we so wished. In order to break free from the intensity of the past week in class I had arranged to meet a friend from another part of the Lennonary. He was a Stuartite, a member of the order of monks who lived in their own community in the grounds of Tittenhurst. They could easily be recognised by their brushed-back quiffs and dark, square sunglasses that they wore rain or shine, inside and out. They were followers of Saint Stuart, who they whispered was perhaps an angel sent to help guide John through his years at art school. It was also said he was sent in recompense by a guilty God to make up for the loss of his mother. On the surface they seemed an eccentric, if not insane, bunch of individuals, a sect within a sect, but when I got to know one, John Stuart, I realised the group mainly consisted of those with a religious bent but whose main love in life was painting.

There were tales and rumours of art descending into chaos during and after the time of our Lords, with rumours of exploding sheds, used tampons and mutilated animals being put forward as works of art while paintings were relegated to the garbage heap of art history. The Stuartites were dedicated to putting paintings back to the centre of fine art. This sometimes clashed with other Lennonist sects who saw conceptual art, as practised by Yoko, Ocean Child, as the way forward. The Stuartites dismissed this as a time-bound fad, some suggesting it was merely a bridge for John the Father to cross in order to meet his new love or, as actually happened, a ladder.

It was a pleasant early autumn English evening as I made my way across the grounds to the Stuartite community. It consisted of nine rural cottages and in the centre a studio that had three sides mainly made of glass, allowing maximum light to enter into its large interior workspace. Unsurprisingly, for the Stuartites, Saint Stuart was central to the Great Story, as John the Father was central to the rest of us in the Lennonary. Like the fine art he produced, it was a matter of perspective. John Stuart and I had spent many hours discussing the merits of our chosen saviours. The talk was not always serious, but nevertheless carried on behind closed doors due to being often heretical to an orthodox ear, especially if too much red wine had been drunk. The One True Religion saw Saint Stuart as a minor player and John the Father as One of Four, and our often drunken claims of their centrality sometimes veered into the heretical. Although they were usually meant in a light-hearted way, like all religions, the One True Religion, despite the importance of laughter to the gods, seemed to lack a sense of humour when discussing itself.

Although it was eight in the evening when I arrived, I could see through one of the large side windows that John Stuart was still in the studio, standing in front of a large canvas and talking to his religious art mentor, Brother Stuart. The older man, tall and lean but with the trademark swept-back hair and dark glasses, was nodding his head and offering quiet advice while his younger, smaller student nodded his head and spoke animatedly, making quick Italian gestures with his hands, arms and shoulders. I remembered the last time we had met we had had a drunken discussion about the hair. We had drunk quite a lot of wine at this point.

"So what's with the hair?" I asked.

"It's how our saviour styled his hair."

"But surely, at the end, he had brushed his hair forward in the famous style of John, our Father. In fact wasn't he…" I stopped mid-sentence.

"Wasn't he what?" he asked, knowing the answer.

"Nothing."

"You were going to say, wasn't he the *first* of the Beatles to change their hair into their famous style?"

"Maybe."

"Thereby proving the centrality of Saint Stuart to the Great Story."

"I think there was more to the Beatles than their hair. Their music was quite good apparently, though a follower of the patron saint of blokes who are rubbish at playing the bass would probably lack insight into that."

"Are you telling me that they would have been as successful if they were all bald?"

Neither of us could keep a straight face. "Are you saying, no hair, no Beatles?"

"As you know I could be burnt at the stake for suggesting such heresies, so yes, it was definitely all about the hair and Saint Stuart, patron saint of art and haircuts, was the first to brush his forward in the divine style. It's all there in the Scripture if you look hard enough."

"That's the thing with Scripture, you can find whatever you want if you look hard enough. Even if it's not there you can interpret it to suit your perspective."

"But it's there in the Scripture from the Gospel According to Hunter. I quote 'And our Lady Astrid said unto Stuart, "Tonight you will wear your hair forward and although your friends will laugh, they too, in the not too distant future, will see that you have shown them the way, that their hair will be a part of them that will show the masses that they are different and be one more piece in the puzzle in their forward march to global domination." And so Stuart did as Astrid wished and went to meet the three young gods and they mightily laughed at his new hairstyle, especially John and Paul, while the younger but equally wise George secretly thought it looked quite good. And sometime later in a secret ceremony in the city of Paris, John and Paul had their hair brushed forward and they were born anew."

He had stopped and looked at me with a victorious smile.

"Hang on," I said. "Surely that implies that Saint Astrid was responsible. You should be a follower of her, should dye your hair blonde and wear dresses."

He peered at me over the top of his sunglasses, his face bent forward to do so. It was a familiar pose of the Stuartites. When they first started as a community, they had been accused of painting the world as though through a glass darkly, their paintings having a seemingly sinister shade of darkness. It was soon realised that it was the constant wearing of sunglasses that accounted for this dark shade. Rather than give up their trademark shades, they had taken up peering over them when they wanted to see the world in its full unshaded glory.

"We do have a few Astridians as a matter of fact. They follow our Lady Astrid by being fascinated in the art of photography. And no, most of them don't wear dresses unless they are women."

"There are women here?" I asked with interest. My religious order was male only; there was a female order but they operated separately at the similarly sacred site of Kenwood. I never understood why. The Beatles never preached separation of the sexes; it simply seemed a religious thing to do. We were not asked to be celibate, but it was rather seen as a distraction from the more important activity of studying all aspects of the religion pertaining to John the Father.

"No, I'm afraid not. We have a few male Astridians. You should be able to tell who they are; they look incredibly pale from spending too much time in the dark room."

"Well, you've neatly avoided answering the question over who was responsible for the haircut and why you wear yours pre-Beatle style."

"I know this may come as a surprise to you but we don't revere Saint Stuart for his hair – it's all about the art. As for our hair…"

He had no answer but I guessed it was that thing that humans did to be seen as different but at the same time be part of their own tribe. The fact was hair had an absurdly important role and place in the One True Religion. Luckily, throughout their career the Beatles had gone through all sorts of style changes, so you could pretty much choose what you wanted without offending anyone.

John Stuart had finished his discussion with Brother Stuart and came outside to greet me. He held up a bottle of red wine and I did the same. I followed as he led me towards his cottage.

"Are we not going to the Art Room?"

The Art Room was their common room, a simple wooden structure that had a few tables and chairs where they went to drink tea and coffee in the day and wine and beer in the evening.

John Stuart turned and smiled. "No, it's band night tonight."

"Dear God, let's get away, quick."

The Stuartites, as part of their homage to their chosen saint, all chose an instrument to play that they did not know how to play, even if they were proficient in another instrument. They would form bands, usually of four to five members, and occasionally perform to the other students. I was never quite sure of the point but it seemed tremendous fun for the performers although frankly horrific for the listeners. If they played an instrument too long they would sometimes accidentally grow quite good at it and would then have to move on to another instrument. Every fortnight or so the community would hold band nights when these groups would perform on a rudimentary stage in the Art Room, often, like their hero, with their backs to the audience, thrashing away on their chosen instruments, producing sounds that could best be described as cacophonous. When I asked John Stuart about these events, he told me it was part of a sacred Stuartite ritual in which they, like their hero, took time out from their true calling – that is, painting – and the awfulness of the sound they produced reminded them that their purpose was to paint and not to play music, and that they could go back to their painting with a sense of renewal. John Stuart himself played the holy bass for years and was proudly terrible at it until one evening, to his horror, he found himself playing what sounded like a semi-groovy bass line over and over again. It was roundly booed by the audience, which showed how good it was. He reluctantly moved on from the instrument of his hero to the piano, which he still cannot play to this day.

Of course, because human nature was, well, human nature, sometimes the band would discover that they were quite good all at the same time and so enjoy the music they made. They would then have to continue in secret with their newfound musical expression while in public they would exchange instruments and be suitably terrible. Thus there were a few rather good not-very-secret Stuartite bands who were seen as sacrilegious by some of their more devout colleagues but who had no one to complain to because they would have got short shrift from the One True Religion, who regarded anyone with musical talent as touched by the gods.

As we entered John Stuart's cottage a terrible sound was heard emanating from the Art Room as the first of the bands took to the stage. I could just hear the enthusiastic applause, so they must have been really bad. John Stuart closed the door and the sound was mercifully muffled. The cottage was a simple affair, three bedrooms to house the three students, one from each year. The idea was that the student in the third year acted as mentor to the second year student and the second year student acted as mentor to the new first year man. We had the place to ourselves as his two younger colleagues were at the Art Room either listening to or committing aural torture.

A bottle of wine stood open on the table. My glass was full and a feeling of wellbeing was creeping over me. John Stuart was sitting in a chair clutching his beloved bass guitar which, because of his newfound proficiency, he could only now play either in secret or in front of people like me who preferred listening to people who could actually play their instruments – or as I liked to call them, sane people. It was a reproduction of Saint Stuart's Hofner President bass guitar, which the saint had bought after exhibiting a painting called "Summer Painting" at the John Moores Liverpool Art Exhibition in 1960. His painting was bought by John Moores himself for what seemed a fortune at the time. Scripture has it that the three gods, John, Paul and George, saw this as a sign from God. They needed a bass player and the Lord had provided this opportunity for him to do just that. They argued that the wisest decision that he could make was to buy a bass guitar and join them in their journey. Stuart, a wise man, initially refused, firstly because he could not play the bass guitar and secondly because the most likely meaning of the sign of selling his painting was that he was probably quite good at art and he should therefore stick to that. But the three gods, especially John the Father, were quite persuasive, being gods and all, and so he ended up buying the bass guitar.

The two young men, the god and the saint, were at this time inseparable and even moved into the same flat, a now sacred place, Flat 3, Hillary Mansions, Gambier Terrace, in the Holy City of Liverpool. In the Scriptures it was a holy place where John helped his good friend and new band member to learn the bass. At the time most who visited it probably would have used the word shithole rather than sacred. Dirty, full of art equipment and occupied by three young men who, despite one of them being divine, were strangers to the art of cleaning – it appeared that cleanliness was not next to godliness.

The cottage was full of art materials but thankfully they did not see it as a sacred duty to never clean the place, and it was a pleasant living room with a large fireplace to provide heat when the nights and days got colder. There was a fireplace in the sacred flat, but it was said to be full of cigarette butts and fish and chip papers.

"Can you explain the wisdom of God in providing a sum of money to Saint Stuart to buy a bass when he could not play?" I asked.

"As you well know, God is known to move in mysterious ways, sometimes so mysterious as to cause confusion and to lead you to believe He has either taken up napping in His old age and is continually waking up to find the world has moved on without telling Him and in ways that make no sense to Him or anyone else, or that when His followers first described Him as omnipotent what they really meant to say was 'incompetent and given to random acts of cruelty or absurdity that might lead a rational person to wonder if He might not benefit from a few sessions of intense therapy.'"

"I'll tell Brother Stuart about your profanities."

"What you don't understand, what you *should* understand given what happened to your saviour, is that it is expected of us Stuartites to be a little angry at God. The story of Saint Stuart does not end well. But we also believe that God had other purposes for Saint Stuart other than completing the line-up of the Beatles. That, after all, was always written in the stars."

"Oh, that's good, that's clever that is. You can criticise God because you're angry at Him for taking your man at an early age. Your anger is proof of your belief. So you can get away with saying stuff I'd be booted out for, very neat. So tell me, what was God's purpose for Saint Stuart?"

"Your Father was a fiery God drawing many into His orbit by the force of His divine personality, and Saint Stuart was one of these, but we believe this was a two-way process. John admired Stuart, He admired his talent as an artist and realised that he knew a lot of things that He could learn from him. They were two different personalities, opposites in many ways. John, the brash, loud, aggressive young god. Stuart, the quiet, cool and generally nice guy. George, our Lord of the Weeping Guitars, thought him very gentle. And if you remember your Scripture, this was the time when God, in His infinite wisdom, chose to take John's mother from Him."

"Funny you should mention that," I said, thinking of the last week in class, of Brother John, Saint Julia and, of course, Saint Mimi.

"And so John, all rage and anger on the outside, needed a sensitive soul, and Saint Stuart was the perfect embodiment of that sensitive soul able to see beneath John's hard exterior. When he left the Beatles to return to his true love of painting, he and John wrote long letters to each other in which John revealed the pain in the centre of his very being, writing once, 'I can't remember anything without a sadness so deep that it hardly becomes known to me, so deep that its tears leave me a spectator.' He could reveal his true heart to Stuart, which meant revealing the pain and the sadness since losing Julia and her seashell eyes."

"So, the Lord introduced him into John's life to teach him about art and culture and to be a shoulder to cry on to help him get over the loss of his mother and then, what, took him away when he'd fulfilled his role? No wonder you're pissed off with God."

"We are, like Stuart, gentle in our anger and, at the same time, thankful that he was brought into the world so that we may follow his example."

"When you talk like that I never know if you're serious or not."

"Ah, John, ye of little faith, you would like for me to state my case in terms of black and white. Surely you must accept that that would be a perilous way of thinking for a man who spent his days painting, that it was the very shades of every colour that defined life itself. You would have me bite the hand that feeds me?"

"I always hold in the back of my mind John, our Father's declaration that the one thing he could tell us is we've got to be free."

"But free from what? I am an artist who loves to paint. I live in a world in which not only is art enshrined as centrally important in our system of Art Schools but allows me to come here and paint, for three uninterrupted years, pretty much whatever I like."

"No one tells you what you should paint?"

"No. We each do an occasional religious painting, one of the four gods, the meeting of John and Paul, the assassination of John, that kind of thing, but that's always been a part of the history of art. Saint Stuart himself did a painting entitled 'Crucifixion', which some have interpreted as a forewarning of the fate of John, while others say it is a traditional rendering of a messiah from the past. Before he died, Saint Stuart seemed to have settled on abstract art as his preferred choice but he had painted all kinds before that: portraits, self-portraits, figurative paintings that told stories, and other religious studies such as his painting of Elvis the Baptist."

I finished the wine in my glass and refilled both our glasses. "It's my understanding that art, in the days before the One True Religion, was a forward progression, moving from one style to the next. How does that work now? Don't you get stuck in a rut?"

"No, art goes on in other forms, in other mediums outside these walls. We just like to paint and we are encouraged to paint what we want."

"So what's in at the moment, what's the flavour of the day?"

"Well, if you weren't such a philistine and actually looked at our paintings occasionally, you might know. We are chosen to attend because we represent the best of the different strands of art. We have a romantic, an impressionist, an expressionist, a symbolist, an orientalist, several abstract expressionists as this was the style favoured by Saint Stuart, a surrealist and a pop artist."

"So, you're like a potpourri of art."

"I don't think you should drink any more wine, you're starting to sound like an idiot. I seriously wonder what would happen to you in the Norwegian Wood ritual."

He was referring to the official One True Religion courting ritual. If you met someone you liked, you would invite them back to your place and invite them to sit on your rug and offer them wine, thus signalling your desire to sleep with them. You would then talk until two in order to establish a rapport, and sip wine to relax before retiring to the bedroom. It was considered best to make sure that the object of your desire was fully aware of the situation by not just inviting them back to your place but specifying there would be a rug and some wine involved. Otherwise you would sometimes get awkward situations when someone would go back to a person's place in order, for example, to look at their collection of rare books and find themselves being invited into a room with one chair, one rug and a bottle of wine, and putting two and two together and making sex when all they'd wanted was to see the books. This happened so often that in the end a phrase was invented to politely suggest wires had been crossed. The person invited would remain standing, away from the rug, and state, 'I've looked around and I've noticed that there aren't any chairs and I'm not so keen on the rug.' Other times the reverse would occur, when the person invited would be safely ensconced on the rug, sipping their wine, talking away, fully expecting sex to follow, when the person who had invited them would change their mind due to the drivel being spoken by the person on the rug. It was this that John Stuart was accusing me of. That I had the gift, after a few glasses of wine, of talking myself out of certain sex. I hoped he was wrong. I had never put myself to the test, although it was never far from my mind. I mildly cursed him.

"May Paul the Father visit you in the night."

He grimaced. It was another open secret that Paul was the least favourite god of the Stuartites. It was, of course, not discussed openly, but whispered surreptitiously and hinted at by the icons dotted about their cottages. There were plenty of John and quite a few of George but never any of Paul. Scripture could not say detrimental words about the Fabulous Four but there were clues in the text, with the Gospel According to Hunter admitting they were all a bit horrible to Stuart and that they felt guilty how they had treated Stu. But Paul was known to have picked on him the most. His antagonism was justified to himself by Stuart's inability to play the bass but was probably due to his jealousy of his friendship with John. Brushed over by Scripture but mentioned in all the unofficial texts was the culmination of this dislike in a full-on fight on stage while they were in the Holy City of Hamburg. The diminutive Stuart, possibly fed up with the preceding months and months of sniping from the others, mainly Paul, and fuelled by his love for Astrid, who Paul had besmirched, surprised everybody by giving a good account of himself in the hand-to-hand combat that went on for some time. In Scripture it is written that this was a ceremonial combat signalling the time had come for Stuart to hand over the sacred role of the playing of the bass guitar over to Paul, the true god, while Stuart went back to his true path, the path his acolytes now revered him for, his painting.

"Let him come, I will knock his divine block off, just like Saint Stuart did that fateful night in Hamburg."

"But surely, according to Scripture, Paul was victorious that night for he ended up playing the bass and Saint Stuart left."

"Oh Scripture," he said with some disdain, his orthodox faith slipping and pride in his tribe taking over. "There was no winner, no loser, just a good old punch-up. When you think about it, it seems a strange way to decide something in a religion that prizes peace and non-violence over just about everything. Saint Stuart gave as good as he got, and as for winning the prize of playing the bass, according to your favourite gospel, due to its, for the church, annoying habit of providing truthful accounts, the Gospel According to Mark suggests this prize was something of a wooden spoon. George of the Weeping Guitars, after Stuart had left, said unto the others, John and Paul, 'One of us three is going to be the bass player and it's not going to be me.' I know the church tries to explain this as a vision, a premonition, but it was just George putting His foot down and saying He was the lead guitarist and would not be relegated to bass player. That left John and Paul, and John said, in one of His less inspirational quotes, 'I'm not doing it either.' Paul was essentially left with no choice. It was our saviour's recompense, His mild revenge for the years of niggling from Paul. He was essentially cursed to play the bass!"

"Well, that's slightly nuts. I would accept 'lumbered' but if you want 'cursed' I suppose we are in a religious community so anything goes. What do you take to be the meaning of the death of Stuart?"

It was a loaded question. What meaning could you give to the death of a twenty-one-year-old who had been in the orbit of the Beatles and then decided to take up his true vocation of painting, which he was clearly very good at, and at the same time had found the love of his life in Astrid Kirchherr? He died in April 1962 of a brain haemorrhage. Twenty-one, the world at his feet, in love, dead. And what of John the Father? His Uncle George, his beloved mother and now his best friend, all dead. How could you possibly give a reason for this? If John, as we in the Lennonary liked to believe, was his father's favourite son, he was bloody horrible to him, a veritable Mean Mister. It was suggested by some that God so loved his favourite son that he became jealous with rage when he saw anyone on the mortal plane become too close to John, that the only ones to survive were the other Beatles, which therefore proved their divinity, that he would not kill his own children. This, of course, tended to ignore those who also survived. His Aunt Mimi, our Lady Yoko for instance. To counter this, it is sometimes whispered that he finally could stand it no longer, this closeness between John and Yoko, and decided it was time for John to return to his side for all eternity and so sent an avenging angel to carry out the Assassination.

This was all heretical and so only whispered in the Order of John. Officially God had no favourites and loved Ringo, our Starr in Heaven, equally to John the Father, which made no sense to anyone except the devout followers of the Drumming God. The same logic might suggest that he loved Stuart even more and took him early for that reason. It could drive a person insane to think about these things, and I had a suspicion that was exactly what happened to the devout. The taking of an event in history and trying to explain it in religious terms, often going against nature itself to explain something.

John Stuart paused for a long time before giving his reply.

"It is not a question that is given much attention in our little community. It is an event that speaks of a cruel or absent God, so it is best not to look too close. Instead we are taught to celebrate his life, his searching for answers in philosophy and literature and his proclamation that 'We need to give our souls to our work'. It was Stuart who nurtured the lazy young god, who educated Him, who encouraged His search for the answers to the mysteries of life. I cannot give meaning to his early death. I could give you platitudes such as 'they are taken to protect them from future torment or as an instrument for good'. I have a colleague who says to me that it is written that the righteous pass away, the godly often die before their time. He says that no one seems to understand that God is protecting them from evil to come. It is comforting but I know you will say it is meaningless. The first part states the obvious because it happens and the second gives a reason which is perfect as it can never be proved. It is saying that although the person taken may have lived a good life in the last few years, they will be saved from being touched by evil in the years to come. Therefore God, appearing cruel, is being kind. And so I have no line to give you on the meaning of his death. I prefer to concentrate on what he gave us in the brief, dazzling example of his life."

I left at midnight, not a little drunk. The wine was finished and much nonsense had been spoken. The company was most enjoyable, intellectually stimulating after the confines of the mostly conformist Johnnists. I felt a little as John must have felt when Stuart opened his eyes to the wider world of art and literature and philosophy as we gently teased each other about the respective worth of our chosen saviours and the points where they perfectly intersected, such as their admiration for Elvis the Baptist, a preacher singer from across the waters who had awakened in John his love of a new kind of music. It was a music he would play with his three divine friends, initially in homage to this preacher singer, at first just walking and strumming, filled with the pure joy of the music like humble minstrels of old, but then picking up pace and eventually sprinting so fast with it and creating their own inimitable style that they eventually transcended the man, the Baptist, who had first lit the spark in the God of Fire.

And so as I left John Stuart, Saint Stuart left the story of John. John, who had looked up to him, had depended on him to tell him the truth and had believed that truth. When Stuart left the Beatles and stayed with Astrid in Hamburg they had written to each other, John pouring out his feelings of grief and loneliness that gave a lie to the hard and brash exterior that everyone else saw. There was nothing that John could not tell Stuart, and now Stuart was gone too. It must have seemed to him that everyone he really loved was cursed to die. He must have felt a long way from being godlike.

# Chapter Eight
## Elvis the Baptist

Scripture tells us that there was a preacher of enormous importance that came before the Beatles. Some even blasphemously suggest that without him there would have been no Beatles. Of course, Scripture tells us instead that he was sent by God to pave the way for the coming of the Lords. He was a beacon for a new religion that would become the One True Religion that we know today. Ironically he was steeped in the old religion of the time but it was not this aspect of him that attracted the Beatles; it was the music, the new sound of rock and roll, that was the new religion.

John the Father was also subject to the same teachings of the same religion as Elvis, but it was the watered-down English version that seemed slightly embarrassed and a little incredulous at what it taught. So much so that it was to die a death and become a gathering place for the old to drink tea and hopelessly hope that at the end there was something more than soil falling over them or the furnace to look forward to. Years and years of dreary English church Sunday school never touched John the way that this new music did. Whereas the old religion literally bored itself out of existence in England, the new religion, personified by Elvis, excited the young John like nothing else. He even said that at church "nothing touched us" but it took just a few listens to rock and roll and he was changed forever. And of the rock and rollers, it was Elvis that 'touched' him the most. "Elvis was bigger than religion in my life," he said. What he did not seem to realise was that Elvis represented the *new* religion that he was to lead in the years to come. He once admitted, "I worshipped Elvis like people worship the Beatles." His use of the word "worship" has led his followers to believe that he was aware of the divine path he was on. He was, in every sense of the word, baptised in the music of Elvis.

I had been thinking of this because of my meeting with John Stuart. Saint Stuart was also a follower of Elvis. He had presciently painted a picture entitled "Elvis Presley" in the style of a stained glass window, which the devout Stuartites believed showed his early understanding of the importance of Elvis to the new religion and the secret insight of Saint Stuart which showed his inner divinity. Other, less devout followers suggested that it, of course, showed that Elvis was important to Stuart but that rather than stained glass it was simply derivative of the artists Mondrian and Picasso. It seemed that everything in life was interpreted not by what you saw but by the lens you saw it through.

And so, Scripture tells us, Elvis was sent to the Beatles as a prophet to inspire them to become what they did indeed become, to pick up their guitars and play. We were told this in reverential tones by Brother John last year. He also told us that Elvis fulfilled a prophecy of a messenger being sent ahead to prepare the world for the true messiahs to come.

Elvis came from a land far away across the oceans, and to reach the Beatles and the rest of the world he made a record which would spark the interest of the four gods. Whilst lying in his bed, late in the evenings in Saint Mimi's house, the young John the Father listened to Radio Luxembourg, a pirate radio station. Listening to the radio station was an ordeal in itself as the signal was so weak it faded in and out, which meant a continual fiddling with the dial to achieve a better sound. It was on his radio and it was through this medium that Elvis sent his message in a song called "Heartbreak Hotel", which transformed John's life. The night he first heard the song it seemed that all the annoying static disappeared, the continual fading in and out stopped and the sound was crystal clear in his ears. He immediately decided that he wanted to be like

Elvis, not realising that the message, listened to by millions, was meant for him and his three future friends alone, sent by his father, God in heaven. It seemed a long-winded way of showing John the future to me. Could he not have sent him a note? Also no matter how hard I looked at the lyrics to "Heartbreak Hotel", I could find no obvious message to the Beatles. Scripture also struggled, so it is written that it was the feel and emotion of the song that revealed to them the path they should take, which is probably close to the truth.

John the Father clearly heard the message as he decided to buy himself a guitar and from that moment on was on his way to becoming what he would become. As usual he was initially thwarted by his Aunt Mimi, who saw nothing good in the new music, but at the same time he was encouraged by his then still alive mother who, like John, loved the new religion. Mimi's disapproval and Julia's approval would have sealed the deal for him. Mimi's disapproval would have made the music just that bit more enticing. Though it was, of course, his ever-present aunt who bought him his first proper guitar – making her a worthy saint, if for no other reason – saying that she hoped it would keep him quiet. It seemed a strange reason to buy a teenager a guitar, to keep him quiet.

All four Beatles had their Elvis epiphany. Whether seeing a picture of him or hearing his songs or both, from that point on he was the message, he was *it*. But the authorities of the time were not pleased. That this young man sang the way he did and *moved* the way he did was a threat to everything the old order believed in. He could not be allowed to carry on in the same way; he had to be destroyed. Scripture tells us that the authorities of the time called for the head of Elvis the Baptist. As beheading was one of the few things not allowed in the country he lived in, the old United States, he was, instead, exiled to Germany for two years, sent away to live in contemplation of his mistakes, made to wear a uniform and perform menial duties as punishment for his crimes.

Scripture tells us that in the womb Elvis was filled with the Holy Spirit. He was born in the wilderness in a place called Tupelo and was, from an early age, different. He reached out and touched young people with his music and they came in droves to be baptised in the thrill and excitement of this new sound. They screamed in religious fervour and rapture, scaring the authorities of the old order, who mistakenly took his message to be from the devil. And so he was exiled to Germany, neutralised in the army of the old United States of America. The divine connection has been made by many that Elvis was sent to Germany for two years in exile and while he left in March 1960, the Beatles arrived there a few months later as if drawn by a celestial spirit and spent their time also in a kind of exile. But whereas Elvis had lost his early spark, some say because he had fulfilled his role to ignite the fire beneath the Beatles, they used their time in exile from the Holy City of Liverpool to hone their skills and the delivery of their message so that they would come back as if renewed.

Scripture tells us that Elvis carried on preaching when he returned from Germany but that he was no longer the force that he once was. John the Father forever after told the world that Elvis had died in 1958, that "Elvis died the day he went in the army, that's when they killed him and the rest was a living death." It is said that Elvis continually foretold the coming of the Lords from England, that he was just a messenger sent from God, although there is no actual evidence of this.

The four gods maintained their reverence for Elvis, and to show this they went on a pilgrimage to visit him in August 1965. It is said that Elvis had sent the message but was just a prophet; he did not even write the words to his songs. This is what distinguished him from the Beatles, who actually performed the miracle of writing and performing their songs and sermons. God had simply given Elvis his voice; he gave the Beatles everything they needed. Elvis knew he was sent by God. He told his spiritual guide, who happened to be his hairdresser, "I've always known that there had to be a purpose for my life. I've always felt an unseen hand behind me, guiding my life. I mean, there *has* to be a purpose... there's got to be a reason... why I was chosen to be Elvis Presley." We now know that reason, and Scripture hints that Elvis came to know the reason too.

Scripture tells the meeting happened as follows. "The Beatles were in America and had been wondering amongst themselves whether to visit the man who had inspired them when John, at noon, put down his guitar and said to the other three, 'The hour has come, let us go to meet Elvis.' The others nodded in assent and they made their way to the home of Elvis, arriving late at night. It was no surprise to Elvis that they would visit, because he had heard the Beatles eulogise about his preaching and music and he was expecting them to appear at some point. But as it happened, he was baptising men and women that day and did not, of course, expect the sons of god to stand in line and be baptised like all the others. He was therefore completely engrossed in his work of baptising those in line and was taken by surprise when he looked up to see the smiling faces of the four young gods. Elvis, for a while speechless, stared at the young men to whom he had sent his message so many years ago.

"'Why have you come to see me here?' he asked.

"'We have been blessed by your music, now we have come to be baptised by you in the flesh,' they all said.

"Elvis was impressed by their modesty and replied, equally modest, 'But it is I that should be blessed by you.'

"And John whispered to Elvis. 'Please bear with us, we have come here to be blessed by you as an example to the world and to show the world that our time has come.'

"And Elvis, trembling in the presence of the Beatles, blessed them with a song and called for everyone to leave and to come back tomorrow for he wished to spend time with the Beatles alone. When everyone had left there appeared an apparition above the heads of the Beatles, and Elvis heard a voice saying, 'These are my beloved sons and I am well pleased.'

"Elvis then knew he was in the presence of God and said to them, 'Now I know for certain you are the Deliverers,' and the Beatles all smiled but said nothing."

Thus we are told about the one and only meeting between the prophet and the messiahs. It is an account written over a hundred years after the event occurred by an early scholar of the One True Religion, a man now revered as a saint but at the time dismissed as a man without close ties to reality and with a much closer relation to psychedelic drugs. Much of the spiritual revelations that we now take as gospel come from him. He was said to be a follower of a contemporary preacher of the time of the Beatles, Saint Timothy, the patron saint of turning on, tuning in and dropping out, who had written in an essay a clear message telling the world that the Beatles were sent from God.

"How clever and unexpected," he wrote, "and yet typical of God to send his message this time through the instruments of four men from Liverpool."

Although this has become the official version of the sacred truth, that Elvis had baptised the Beatles in August 1965 and had thus shown the world the coming of the Lords, all the contemporary accounts seemed to have missed this act of baptism. Although this episode was central to the Great Story there have, like all episodes in the life of the Beatles, been different interpretations.

There are some who believe that Elvis was much more than a prophet, that he was a god himself and saw the Beatles as rivals to his own vision of heaven on earth. Scripture tells us that before they left, Elvis begged them to tell him of his own preaching and mission and that they had told him, "Our Father will guide you now as in the future as he has in the past," and then these great men separated, never again to meet in the flesh.

To my ears it all sounded too good to be true so I searched for historical accounts of the meeting and found a darker, starker truth. That Elvis had ignited a spark in the Beatles either through the message of God or the raw talent of the early Elvis records was undoubtedly true. That their meeting was a sacred blessing conferred by Elvis on the Beatles seemed to be a stretching of the truth to breaking point. He admired them and probably saw they were the future and he was the past, but this led to simmering envy rather than a welcoming with open arms and a proclamation to the world of the coming of the Lords and the kingdom of heaven on earth. Elvis was not bothered about meeting them, and if it was the only meeting between them that was his choice. After their visit to him, they had invited him to visit them, had sent a message through his disciples that they would love to see him again, with John the Father telling one of Elvis' disciples how much Elvis meant to him and to pass the message that "If it hadn't been for him, I would have been nothing."

The message was duly passed back to Elvis but he apparently smiled and said nothing. This has led Johnnists to have a strange relationship to Elvis, as they cannot dismiss him because of John's proclamation of his importance while at the same time there is some anger at his perceived snubbing of our Lord. There is even one account that sees him in later years making a pact with an emissary of the devil, a man who had come to earth in the human form of a man called Richard Nixon who had taken control of the old United States of America. It is written that Elvis even suggested that the Beatles were a force of darkness in the country with their suggestive music and unkempt appearance leading the youth astray. Of course, officially he will always be the Baptist, the man who sent his message to the Beatles to light their way and to prepare the world for their coming, and who blessed them on their one and only meeting before fading into fatness.

It is written that George, Lord of the Weeping Guitars, did meet Elvis once more before he passed on, and it is a parable on the importance of others, the primacy of the group over the individual, gleaned from the words of George that I like to take from their meeting. He saw that Elvis was surrounded constantly by his disciples but they were just that, followers (or "sycophants" in the words of Ringo) and George felt that though Elvis was always surrounded by this entourage he was essentially alone, that the fact that there were four Beatles meant there were four of them to make sense of the world together. They all experienced what it felt like to be a Beatle whereas there was only one Elvis and no one else could know what it felt like to be Elvis.

Of course, this being the One True Religion, there is another story, another interpretation, another *baptist*. This story is mainly believed by the Paulists, so it pains me to say but it makes more sense, is more believable. In this version Elvis is just one prophet, but the facts seem to suggest he was a jealous prophet, no friend of the Beatles. The true Baptist was a man we have already briefly met, acknowledged as a saint, but there are some who argue he was more than that, that it was him that was sent by God to baptise and bless the Beatles and send them on their sacred way.

And so there are some who speak of Richard the Baptist, another American from the old United States of America. He also spoke to the individual gods through his records and from the silver screen. Even John the Father, who certainly worshipped at the altar of Elvis as a young man, was torn. He was speechless upon first hearing Saint Richard on a record at a friend's house. He was torn between his love for Elvis and this new sound coming from the record player. At issue at the time was an important distinction which makes little sense in these modern times. Elvis was white and Richard was black. Incredibly, and completely impossible to comprehend now, at the time this was a significant fact. *People were treated differently because of the colour of their skin.* This was particularly prevalent in the old United States of the two rival baptists, but was also an issue in the contemporary world of the Beatles' England. This all seems a distant, fuzzy nightmare in our world where equality trumps all. The seeds of this change came from the attitude of the Beatles, who were outraged to find that some of their concerts were to be performed in front of segregated audiences. This, they refused to do.

Thus, the equality of worth of humans is the underlying principle of the One True Religion. This is particularly hammered into the English from an early age, who had a reputation for thinking themselves better than others and from an early period of time had had a sneaking suspicion that God was an Englishman. It turns out they were right, the gods *were* Englishmen. To be precise, the Gods were Scousers. The church therefore teaches, using the words of a slain president, that place is important but that essentially we all lived on the same planet, we all breathed the same air, we all loved our children and bled the same blood. In order to prove this to us, the gods themselves made sure they chose life partners who were from all over the planet, from Japan and America with Jewish and Mexican flavours thrown in for good measure.

And so the Beatles embraced the music of Saint Richard, and it is written that Saint Brian, the man who introduced the Beatles to the world, brought Saint Richard across the ocean to meet the Beatles in the Holy City of Liverpool. The fateful night was Friday 12 October 1962 at the New Brighton Tower Ballroom. The date is important because it gives credence to the story that Saint Richard was *the* Baptist. It was a time that was essentially the eve of their taking over the world. Their comet was just starting its journey across the universe; their words were just about to fly out like endless rain. And so it makes more sense that they be baptised and blessed at this time rather than by Elvis in 1965, when they were in the middle of their glory, when their undying love was shining around them like a million suns. In the words of John the Father, they "were almost paralysed by their adoration" of Saint Richard. It is instructive that he used the term "adoration", a religious form of reverence. There is a famous photograph of the Beatles huddled around Saint Richard, who is sitting in a chair beaming at the camera, looking, as ever, larger than life and dwarfing the four gods, who are each grasping a hand of the saint. There are no pictures of the meeting with Elvis and it was a one off, history suggesting he admired them but was envious. The Beatles met Saint Richard more than once, touring with him in Hamburg and spending time with him backstage. He was his flamboyant self and generously gave them his time and experience. Saint Richard himself tells of their adoration in his own words. He related in later life how Saint Brian had invited him to Liverpool, where he said Saint Brian "had these four little boys, looking very strange to me" and he told how Saint Brian had said "they just love you" and he tells of them taking his hands and pulling his fingers in their obeisance and reverence.

His role as baptiser of the Beatles seems assured to me, but Johnnists are generally not convinced because they see it as an essentially Paulist tale. Saint Richard himself said of the

Beatles when they first met, Paul was the one that pulled his fingers the hardest, harder than John and that John, although he loved him, lived up to his mischievous fire-godliness, and as Saint Richard tells it: "Paul was so nice, but John liked to mess with me in my dressing room quite a bit. I can't say what he did, he was something else, in fact I never met nobody like him." It was nothing bad, just John the Father being his usual irreverent self, locking the saint in his dressing room until he screamed to be let out. But Saint Richard's greater praise for Paul has led, in the world of the religious orders and their jealous love of their particular Father, to some plumping for Elvis as the Baptist.

# A Brief Interlude
## On Suffering

emerged from Brother John's room and made my way to our classroom with an excited expectation in my heart. My visit to John was my monthly religious supervision where we discussed any questions I had and he was supposed to guide me in the "correct" way forward. After our discussion of the loss of John's mother and my own talks with John Stuart about his good friend Saint Stuart and his early death, the supervision inevitably turned to the role of suffering in the life of John, and more generally in the world. After all, it was a central question for religion to answer. If God was omniscient, omnipotent and benevolent, why did He let people suffer?

"Ah, suffering," Brother John said, as if it was much on his mind.

Behind him, on the wall of his office, was a rare portrait of John the Father – rare in that it was painted in the time of his life. It was painted while he was at Liverpool Art School by a fellow student, Ann Mason. Brother John briefly glanced at it now. The portrait seemed to have caught John off guard, slumped in a chair, sat astride it the wrong way round, all in black, wearing his thick National Health glasses, looking thoughtful, mournful even. Or was that my own perception, knowing that he was seventeen and angry and had just lost his mother? Or had he? The date of the painting is 1958 but we do not know when exactly. Before or after, it seems to me the weight of the world is on his shoulders, his eyes hidden behind the thick lenses of his glasses.

"You know there is a secret sermon from John the Father kept in the holy vaults. It is said to be called 'God', in which He acknowledges His own suffering and hints that He sees it as a gift from God. The only line that has escaped the vaults is the statement that 'God is a concept by which we measure our pain.' The church believes that God, in His generosity, has given us all the gift of choice. Would you prefer that we lived a predetermined life, automatons living every moment that has already been decided? The Beatles, and especially John the Father, wanted us to know that the important thing was to be free, to free our minds. The one thing He said He could tell us was that we had to be free.

"How can we reconcile that with a God who controls our every move? Of course, with that freedom comes the possibility of making the wrong choices, of causing suffering or experiencing suffering ourselves. We can see that when John spoke out, started seriously putting forward His idea of heaven on earth, He was made to suffer by the world around Him. When He proclaimed that we should give peace a chance, that war solved nothing, He was not welcomed as our saviour but met with anger, insults and disbelief. So the suffering of John was a way of preparing His followers for the same treatment when they too saw the light and followed His example."

"But that is suffering to some higher purpose. I am talking about the loss of his mother through a random road traffic accident, the loss of a close friend with a brain haemorrhage. This seems to me to be suffering for no purpose."

Brother John sighed and rubbed his eyes as if the question had brought upon him a great weariness. "I don't know, John. Suffering can be a great teacher. The experience of pain or great loss gives us the opportunity to have an insight into the human condition. Perhaps it was a gift from God to allow his favoured son the knowledge of suffering so he could have compassion for the sufferings of others."

He now sounded like he was trying to convince himself more than me, and he did not look like he had succeeded.

"Perhaps it has a purpose or meaning that is beyond our comprehension," he said in a dubious voice. He may just as well have used the religious get-out clause about God moving in mysterious ways, and he looked like he knew. He seemed to realise that not only was he not convincing me, but the longer he went on he seemed to be actually increasing his own doubts, so he changed the subject.

"There is suffering in the world, John, and it's sometimes difficult to find meaning in it," he said, which seemed to admit that he could not really explain it. "But there is joy and lightness too. This last week has been heavy-going and I can tell that you feel the pain of John, his suffering. But he and the other Beatles gave us the gift of lightheartedness, the gift of laughter; even when he was putting across his serious message of peace it was done as a cosmic joke. He sent out the message via a bed-in as part of His policy not to be taken too seriously. Indeed, it was partly a fight against seriousness, because their enemies, the warmongers, the people in power did not know how to handle humour. I know you love this aspect of the man, his humour and irreverence, and this week as a surprise and as a counterweight to the suffering he endured we have some guests. So go to class and enjoy yourself today."

# Chapter Nine
## Saint Spike and the Importance of Laughter

---

entered the classroom, breathless, as I was late, my supervision having run over a little, and was surprised to find three men in their late twenties who were grinning at the seven Johns and Johann, who were already sitting in their seats and staring at them as if they were escaped lunatics. One of the men was speaking to them in an extraordinary voice that I could not place as belonging to any region of the world. He stopped talking when I came in, and they looked at each other and winked and then looked towards me.

"I'm sorry I'm late," I said.

"No need to be sorry, although it is a strange name, Mr Late," one of them said in an equally silly voice.

"No, he means he's late, you fool," another one said in an old-fashioned posh accent.

"What time is it then?"

"Hang on, I've got it writted down on this piece of paper – a nice man wrote it down for me this morning. Look, it says eight o'clock."

One of the other men grabbed it off him and put it to his ear. "'Ere, this piece of paper has stopped."

"What! I must have been sold a forgery."

Although some of the class continued to stare at the three men in bemusement, some were starting to laugh. I was smiling myself as I had now guessed who they were. They belonged to the Order of the Milligoons, a small religious sect who were based in Rye, East Sussex. They devoted their lives to the study of the Goon sermons of the 1950s written by Saint Spike and read by him and Saint Peter and Saint Harry. Despite their apparent lunacy they were afforded much respect by the religious establishment because of the debt of gratitude expressed by the Beatles. They were particularly important to John the Father, who wrote that "Spike Milligan is a cherished memory for me" and that the humour of the Goons "was the only proof that the world was insane". For the four Beatles, yet to meet, they provided a hilarious escape from the dreary times they lived in in 1950s England. They are also seen by the One True Religion as sent by God as a bridge between his young sons and the man who was destined to shape their sound in the studio.

Saint George, patron saint of making people sound good, had worked with the Goons and this simple fact was enough to impress the young Beatles and convince them they could trust and work with him.

The elevation of Saint Spike has meant that humour has largely replaced fighting in the modern world. One of the attributes a politician has to have, along with a grounding in the One True Religion, is the ability to be funny, to reduce difficult situations to the absurd reality they represent and therefore be able to move forward in a constructive way. Humorous self-deprecation and not taking oneself too seriously are considered useful assets, and hints of narcissism and self-aggrandisement have luckily led to those exhibiting those traits being blocked from power.

Remarkably, in the time the Beatles walked this earth, there existed leaders in the world that rose to prominence despite their bad character, that were popular even despite their message of hate. Narcissism, grandiosity and being generally disagreeable did not seem to hinder a person's rise to power. Thankfully, we live in an age in which the Beatle philosophy means that to rise to power you must have a certificate of agreeableness, showing that you can be caring, loving, affectionate and kind, with an emphasis on loving, and it must extend to everybody not just people close to you.

Therefore, a sense of humour was given great importance in many important roles in society, leading some to suggest we live in a witocracy. Officially, of course, it is the principals of peace and love that are most prized in the One True Religion, so a person's capacity to love as many people as possible is said to be the most important character trait in a leader. Officially, we lived in a loveocracy.

But humour was important. John the Father, in his own words, as Brother John had told me, when fighting the violence of his times told us that the only things the enemies of peace "don't know how to handle is non-violence and humour". He told us that his policy was not to be taken seriously, that he was proud to be a clown in a world where the serious people were killing themselves and each other and destroying the world. He also thought it would serve as a shield to put his message of peace across in the guise of a clown "because all the serious people like Martin Luther King and Kennedy and Gandhi got shot". Unfortunately, his own father, it seems, had other plans.

I liked this aspect of the Order of John, though it was important to remember that humour could be used in a negative way, picking on certain groups in society and reinforcing negative stereotypes. It is whispered that John himself in his young days of anger at the world used humour in a way that could only be described as cruel. Like any example of less than exemplary behaviour by the four gods this was ignored, denied or said to have happened as an example to future generations of how not to behave. There was also, for me, the central paradox that any religion that elevated the importance of humour would lay itself open to the sort of scrutiny that could be damaging, especially a Lennonist-Goonist surreal sense of humour that tended to highlight the absurdity of the world.

One of the men was looking at me with comic mischief. "Please sit down and we will think of a suitable punishment for your lateness later."

"Punishment," one of his colleagues said. "I'm not sure we're allowed to punish them, haven't you read the Geneva Convention?"

"I have not read the book of the Geneva Convention, nor seen the film, and this is no time to be making small talk about my reading habits."

They introduced themselves as Brother Neddie, Brother Eccles and Brother Bluebottle.

"My name is Brother Neddie," one of them said, a small round man with unruly brown wavy hair.

"What a memory you have," one of his colleagues said. "I'm Brother Eccles and I'm feeling very tired today." He was a tall, thin man with equally unruly hair that stood on end, making him seem even taller.

"Why don't you pull up a chair?" the third man, smartly suited and wearing glasses, said to him.

"I'd rather stand if you don't mind."

"Well, pull up a floor then. My name is Brother Bluebottle, by the way."

Apropos of nothing, Brother Neddie blew a loud raspberry.

Brother Bluebottle continued. "This desk is in the way, Neddie, if you wouldn't mind moving it I'll pay you a thousand pounds."

Another loud raspberry was blown. "A thousand pounds for moving the desk, that's money for old rope."

"I'd've thought you would find something more useful to buy."

"No, I'm a man of simple tastes."

Brother Eccles had disappeared behind a screen that had been erected in the corner of the classroom. The original Goon Show was broadcast on radio, enabling them to create situations of huge flights of fancy that were not seen by the listeners but painted inside their minds. It became renowned for a bizarre array of sound effects. Now from behind the screen came the sound of singing in yet another silly voice.

"I talk to the trees, that's why they put me away..." I could hear the sound of a button being pressed and an announcer's voice from a tape recorder told us, "Neddie was stowed away on a boat on his way to France..."

Brother Eccles wandered out from behind the screen. "Oh, hello, shipmate of mine. Where are you going?"

"Nowhere, I think it's safer to stay on the ship until we reach France."

"Hey, are you going to France? What a coincidence, that's where the ship's going."

This time Brother Bluebottle had disappeared behind the screen and was saying, "A group of British scientists had come up with the idea of an atomic dustbin and were, at this moment, presenting the idea to a group of high-ranking idiots."

Brother Eccles put on the voice of a posh old man. "This idea, this atomic dustbin, has great potential."

"Can it go to the moon?"

"No, but from small beginnings…"

"Is that the prototype?"

A crashing metallic sound came from behind the screen. "No, that's the dustbin."

"Hmm, it sounds like a dustbin." More metallic crashing sounds followed by demented laughter.

And so the next thirty minutes went, with silly voices, a variety of sound effects and an excess of puns. Brother John had joined us, and when they appeared to have finished their chaotic lunacy he led the class in appreciative applause, although some still looked slightly bemused.

Brother Eccles looked around at us and spoke in what I presumed was his own voice. There was still a twinkle in his eye.

"We'd like to thank you for listening to us this morning, and just to finish off we'd like to say our Order's Prayer. If you would bow your heads."

We did as he asked.

"There's a prayer that I recall, my mother said to me, she said it as she tucked me in, when I was ninety-three."

There was a brief pause and then all three Brothers took it in turn to say:

"Ying tong, ying tong, ying tong, ying tong, ying tong iddle I po."

They would stop for about ten seconds and just as we were raising our heads and opening our eyes they would start again, at one point leaving the room and reciting the prayer outside before coming back and saying it one more time. Instead of saying "let it be so", as was customarily the way to end prayers in the One True Religion, they each blew a loud raspberry. We looked up and opened our eyes again to see them looking at us, all innocence. This actually seemed, despite its apparent lunacy, to be performed in all seriousness.

Brother John joined them at the front of the class, shook their hands and thanked them. He turned to us. "Have any of you got any questions?"

A John, not known for his sense of humour and rather orthodox in his beliefs, something I had come to realise were connected phenomena, raised his hand. We had had several arguments along the lines of him telling me he was a true follower of John, that he took the religion deadly seriously, while I would reply that I was the true follower of John because I did not take it seriously, that he was precisely missing the point. The three Brothers from the Order of Milligoons seemed to suggest they agreed with me. Unsurprisingly his question revealed his confusion as to their purpose.

"What exactly is the connection between Saint Spike and the Beatles, and particularly John the Father?"

"I'm glad you asked that," said Brother Eccles. "We are going to read you excerpts from Scripture."

He nodded at Brother Bluebottle, who put on a posh English accent.

"Have you heard there is a Detroit University movement to stamp out the Beatles?"

"Well, we're starting a movement to stamp out Detroit."

"They think your haircuts are un-American."

"Well, that's very observant of them. We're not American!"

"How do you normally approach songwriting?"

"We normally approach it by the M1."

Brother Neddie put on an American accent and asked, "What is the secret to your success?"

"We don't know. If we did, we'd form another group and be managers."

"What do you do when you're cooped up in your hotel rooms?"

"We ice skate."

Brother Eccles turned to the John who had asked the question. "These came from early press conferences, when they usually answered the questions with humour. Early on a lot of the questions were simply moronic. For example, they were obsessed with their hair. One reporter asked if they believed their hair helped them with their music and followed it up with the question that, like Samson, if they had their hair cut off would their output suffer. Imagine knowing you were a god, waiting to be asked any question so you could impart your wisdom and all you were getting were questions about your hair. The Beatles therefore used humour to gently rebuke these questions until their later years, when they were able to get their message of love and peace across."

Brother Bluebottle stood forward and held in his hand a small book that looked vaguely familiar. He read, "Azue orl gnome, Harassed Wilsod won the General Erection, with a very small marjorie over the torchies…"

He continued to read the short story, and I recognised it as coming from one of John the Father's two books that he gifted to us in his time on earth.

Brother Bluebottle finished the story and looked around at us. "This is from 'A Spaniard in the Works', the second of two books that were written by John, one of our Fathers. As well as reading and researching every Goon script, we also have made it our life's work to read and understand the writings in these two small books. Now this of course has been undertaken by many scholars of the One True Religion, the study of any words of the Fabulous Four have, of course, been closely scrutinised, but we have studied them with the viewpoint that they have been significantly influenced by the writings of Saint Spike."

The John who had asked the original question had raised his hand again. "I too have studied these writings and believe they were a kind of code, the Lennon code, to secretly tell us of his times and of his feelings. The General Erection actually referred to a general election and Harassed Wilsod was in fact Harold Wilson, a Labour prime minister of the time, a leader of a democratic socialist party that had defeated the 'Torchies', which actually referred to the Tories, a reactionary party led by Edward Heath, who had said bad things of the Beatles and their accents. This has therefore been seen as another parable, telling us that political parties should have as their main priority achieving maximum equality but with an added warning of the perils of war added on to the end. John the Father, as you have just read, ends the story: 'Lastly, but not priest, we must not forget to put the clocks back when we all get bombed. Harold.' This has been translated as a dismissal of the false religion of the time ('but not priest') and a pointed reminder to the leader (Harold) to avoid situations in which we would get bombed."

He sat back, a self-satisfied look on his smug face. It looked ripe for a slap. I banished this slightly violent and therefore blasphemous thought from my head. He was, in fact, half right. John the Father, had once been asked a question about Edward Heath, the leader of the Conservative Party, suggesting the Beatles seemed nice enough fellows but did not speak the Queen's English and made a jokey reply but then added with some feeling, 'We're not gonna vote for Ted,' thus ruling out the possibility of the existence of reactionary parties in a Beatle religion based society. Although there was some debate around who they *would* vote for, their seemingly closer association to Harold Wilson of the Labour Party came to be the accepted wisdom of the One True Religion. All parties in this society had to be based on promoting the two main tenets of the Beatles, peace and love, and also the central tenet of democratic socialist parties, that of greater equality. It came to be seen that despite achieving levels of wealth and comfort never before seen in the history of mankind, instead of bringing happiness, societies seemed to be suffering from epidemics of anxiety, depression and numerous other social problems. Wealth itself seemed to cause more problems than it solved. It had been shown, for example, that the greater the disparity of wealth within a country the more murders there were, that in more equal countries there were a lot less homicides and generally less violence. With the Beatle emphasis on peace and love, equality became an essential part of the fabric of Beatle-based societies. At first, there were some who proclaimed this could not work because the constant influx of immigration from the poorer to the richer countries would constantly upset the balance. So someone suggested the revolutionary idea that if we made sure that all those countries had the same levels of wealth then there would be no need for the mass emigration from poor to richer countries. People would move between countries as lifestyle choices rather than economic necessity.

In the regions where the One True Religion was not practised there were rumoured to be vastly wealthy individuals who lived in gated communities, counting their money and too scared to venture out in fear of being murdered by the unruly hordes who looked on enviously. These hordes, not being able to reach the protected wealthy, murdered each other instead. They lived in abject poverty, which they accepted because of the Dream ideology which pervaded their society and stated that as long as you worked hard, there were no real barriers to upward mobility and everyone could prosper and be successful. This seemed to completely ignore the fact that once wealthy individuals and businesses achieved this success they aggressively protected their own interests and made the success of others that much more difficult. We in the Beatleverse believed it was rightly called a dream because the definitions of a dream tended to suggest the reality of the situation. A dream was either something that happened in your mind when you were asleep but disappeared when you awoke, or something that you wanted to happen very much but was not very likely.

Thus we lived in egalitarian nations and tended not to kill each other or even beat the shit out of each other, while those who came to us from the Dream regions had to be put through a processing centre to be taught our ways of peace and love and equality. Sometimes, especially the older immigrants, their attachment to the "dream" was such that they had to return to the processing centres to be "reprocessed". Occasionally it just did not work out and they were asked to leave, to return to their place of origin, the Dream regions. Some could not handle the excessive peace, tranquillity and equality and voluntarily returned to their lands, forgetting why they had escaped in the first place. The biggest problems occurred when the immigrants had a strong attachment to their own religion. The "contract" that governed society was that there was only One True Religion, even if you only paid lip service to it. The Lords' Prayer implored us, after all, to imagine one religion. The introduction of a rival religion was seen as dangerous, as history had shown that rival religions led to wars and therefore could not be tolerated. History had even shown us that, difficult to believe though it was, some of the bloodiest wars were between rival factions of the *same religion*. Most newcomers were relieved to arrive in a society where their basic needs were taken care of and they were treated with respect. In the Dream regions the young men at the bottom of the heap were deprived of status and this often resulted in them resorting to violence in order to achieve status, something they eventually realised was not necessary in the egalitarian world into which they had arrived. In the Dream regions it had been simply assumed that men were naturally violent, but the peace that reigned in our world showed that to be false, that it was the unequal conditions that led young men to express their desire for respect through explosions of violence.

The words of John the Father were therefore pored over to justify the emphasis on equality, and the fact of his own fabulous wealth was largely ignored. Some whispered, of course, that he was a tremendously rich and successful man, despite his espousal of the importance of equality, and was gunned down by a poor loser and this was itself partly a demonstration by God of the dangers of huge inequality. Thus, in this school of thought, God sacrificed his favourite son to show us the way.

"The General Erection" was seen to be one of his writings that demonstrated, if a little vaguely, his belief in social democracy, which as a way of thinking was open to a vast amount of different interpretations, but at its core was the importance of equality. Brother Eccles was nodding his head at my pious colleague's comments about the meaning of the text and then, with a nervous glance at his colleagues and a clearing of the throat, he replied:

"That is, of course, a distinct possibility, that John was telling us, in a sort of code, important messages about how to live our lives. We believe, instead, that if there is a message it is the importance of humour in life. That if the stories seemed nonsensical it is because they were intended that way, that it was a demonstration of his love of puns and wordplay and also creative misspellings."

Pious John looked nonplussed. He could not understand that a god could put words on paper that had no meaning, that were simply there to entertain and make you smile. For him everything that came from the pen or the mouth of John the Father was pregnant with meaning and to suggest otherwise was on the verge of blasphemous. I thought about that for a moment. To live a life in which every word, every poem, every lyric, everything ever said and recorded was pored over and examined in the minutest detail. I thought of my own propensity to talk absolute shit, to change my mind from week to week, to say things I did not mean just to get a reaction, to take the opposite side in an argument because I liked arguing or disliked the person who was putting the idea forward.

If you were born a God and knew it then you would always know the right thing to say, would measure each word with care, would make sure each statement you made was immaculate. The One True Religion accepted the mistakes of John the Father and explained them as providing examples from him to us that we could learn from. In the back of my mind was an old adage that to err is human. Although this was a weakness at the very centre of the claim to the divinity of the Beatles, it was also a strength. The past leaders of religious movements had tended to be, at least in the mythology of their stories, perfect human beings who never made a mistake and never had sex, which seemed to be unrealistic goals for human beings to live up to, if not downright undesirable.

People had different views on how they wanted their gods to behave. Pious John would have been much happier for John the Father to have lived a life of simple contemplation, preaching his gospel and only speaking words of wisdom. But part of the acceptance and lasting popularity of the Beatle gospel was the fact that they were not perfect, that they made mistakes, and the Order of the Milligoons emphasised an element that was missing from most religions: the importance of a sense of humour. Here they were, standing in front of us, telling us that not everything they said was profound but was said to provide that most human of responses, a smile. Maybe even a laugh.

Other religions had invented hell in order to scare their flocks into continued obeisance and belief. Often people were exiled to hell not through bad behaviour but simply through a lack of belief in that particular god. Those that wanted to believe in a Beatle hell – and there were a few, despite the official line that there was no such thing – argued it was a place not of eternal fire and physical pain but a place of eternal frowns, a place where smiles and laughter were banished and of course no music was ever heard. We were told the Beatles did not believe in hell; it was a religion that wanted to entice you in by its unwavering reasonableness and promise of a version of heaven on earth rather than scare you into believing in it by threats. There was a heaven; it was a part of the "contract". After all, one of the main attractions of religion was that it promised us that we did not die and simply crumble to dust to be embraced by an eternal darkness, but instead offered us the prospect of everlasting life in a fabulous place where we would be unable to stop smiling and be brought joy by the music of the Beatles, who would play a concert every day (which is rumoured to have upset George, Lord of the Weeping Guitars, upon his arrival, as he had come to dislike live gigs). This is, of course, just one version of heaven; the emphasis tended to change depending on the desires of the person describing it. The important thing was not knowing exactly what heaven was like but that it existed, so we could forget the main cause of human anxiety and misery: that we lived and we died and, unlike other animals, we were aware of this fact. Many studies showed that those that believed in God and an afterlife lived longer than those that did not.

We were told it was a gift from God for believing. Some whispered that surely those that went to heaven earlier were the true winners. The One True Religion stayed silent, and I imagined a pained expression on their collection of beatific faces. They also had to come up with an explanation that if there was no hell and heaven was such a fun place to be, why should people refrain from committing suicide? The somewhat mumbled answer is that the religion is essentially a religion for peace and against violence and this includes violence towards oneself.

To my question of why we need to spend time on earth in the first place before being transported to paradise, I have only received blank stares.

Brother Eccles was speaking again. "We, as an order, see our role as reminding people of the message of the importance of laughter. The Beatles conquered the most powerful country on earth, the old United States of America, by their music but also by their humour. The gospel tells us that this country was in mourning, had been set back by another example of their then favourite hobby of shooting each other, a hobby that was set to continue unabated for some time and was even to claim our very own Lord and Beatle, John the Father. The man murdered, another John, was their leader, known by all and loved by many. The Beatles landed in a country desperate to laugh again. In the past, and I know this is difficult to understand now, people from one nation used to conquer other people from other nations by use of violence and power. The Beatles conquered the world through their music and their sense of humour and once they had conquered the world they were able to spread their gospel of peace and love."

Brother Bluebottle put on his silly voice and uttered, as if reading stage directions, "After the serious bit, the three idiots shuffle off amidst thunderous applause." He paused. "Typical, not a sausage."

The three Brothers made their way to the door, Brother Neddie asking, "Did someone mention a sausage? I'm starving." As they exited the door, he blew a loud raspberry.

Brother John moved to the front of the class. "I hope you all enjoyed that little diversion. I know sometimes it seems there is a lot of darkness in the life of John the Father, especially in the times we are talking about, so I thought it important that you were aware that there was also some light."

He then talked briefly of his favourite subject, Saint Mimi. "Saint Mimi recalled the young John coming down to see her after He had listened to a Goon Show and He proceeded to reenact the entire show for her, complete with silly accents. Uncle George, hearing the laughter of Saint Mimi, was curious to discover the source. Upon entering the kitchen he was told by his wife that John was performing the Goon Show for her. So Saint George sat down next to his wife and watched John the Father perform the rest of the show."

I waited for Brother John to tell us the moral of the tale, but nothing was forthcoming. It seemed for him, the veracity of the message of the Milligoons was set in stone simply because there was a story connecting Mimi, John and the Goons. I wanted to blow a loud raspberry, but the truth was I liked this emphasis on the importance of humour, this implication that the world was a trifle absurd. A famous French writer once wrote that it was an English trait to look at everything with a sense of irony, but he believed they were stupid to do so, that no matter how long you went through life seeing the funny side, "in the end, there's just the cold, the silence and the loneliness. In the end, there's only death." It seemed to me that was a pretty good reason to see the funny side of things, or you would spend the rest of your life running around waving your hands in the air, screaming "We're all going to die!"

This is also where Beatle Heaven came in. If you could just convince yourself that when you died you went to heaven and met the Fab Four, who would entertain us with a witty press conference and a live performance every day, then you had nothing to worry about. Unfortunately, in my mind you had to be a deluded lunatic to believe such nonsense, so although I kept this heresy to myself, it meant I still worried about my death.

I was constantly surprised by the number of people who did believe in Beatle Heaven. As I have said, each person's version of heaven tended to depend on their own individual tastes. They were essentially bespoke heavens. Johnnists tended to believe that they would be spending a lot of time hanging out with John the Father, and that although there was no such thing as hell, if you had been a bad person you would spend some time in purgatory, which, it was whispered, involved listening to a lot of Ringo's solo records before being finally let in the gates of Beatle Heaven by Saint Pete. He had been given the job by John as in his earthly life he had been Pete Shotton, the lifelong friend of John the Father, from the time they met at Dovedale Infants School. In this version of Beatle Heaven, you are met at the gates by Saint Pete, who has a set of keys in one hand and a washboard in the other, the sacred implement he is said to have played in the Quarrymen.

Being in the Order of John the Father, it was mainly these versions of Beatle Heaven that I heard, although each person had a slightly different idea of what it looked like. No two heavens were ever exactly the same. Some of these heavens sounded great – insane, but great. I envied my colleagues' lunacy. They had a get-out clause from death. Of course, I believed they would get a rude awakening when they actually died, but they could forget about worrying about death while they were alive, and if there was nothing when they died then they would not know about it anyway. They won both ways. Believing in Beatle Heaven was therefore good for your mental health. Unfortunately, I could not make myself believe, so I would, ironically, probably die sooner worrying about death while everyone else lived longer because they were safe in the knowledge of the eternal paradise that awaited them, long conversations with John, meditations with George, singalongs with Paul, time spent with Ringo when he promised not to sing. It was not fair. All I had was nothing. Forever.

# Chapter Ten
## Living in Cyn

It was the next day. Unfortunately, sanity had been resumed. There were no Milligoons when I arrived in the classroom and made my way to my seat. Brother John was sitting on his desk, legs swinging under him. On the blackboard was written the name Saint Cynthia. She was the patron saint of long-suffering women and clearly the topic of the day. When we were all seated and silent, Brother John picked up the Holy Book of the One True Religion and opened it at a page he had marked with a scrap of paper.

"This is from the 'Book of Cynthia'. 'God the Father, seeing that His son was in pain, after the passing of His mother, Julia, with the seashell eyes, decided to send unto Him a woman who would help Him to heal His pain. She was the Lady of the Hoylake, a small seaside town in the northwest of the Wirral Peninsula, not far from the Holy City of Liverpool. She arrived in the presence of John the Father at the Liverpool Art School in the year of our Lords 1957. They circled around each other for some time, with Cynthia feeling only coldness towards the loudmouthed young god. And then the flames from the youthful fire god started melting the ice in her heart and she found herself becoming secretly attracted to John, who, of course, hid His own heart by making fun of this lady from the sea, born in the sacred town of Blackpool. He mocked her, suggesting she was a cold princess, a lady of wealth and class coming from the faraway rich town on the coast. And so they continued to eye each other warily but with secret yearning until they came to the end of their second year at the Art School. John had always had a vision of himself having a passionate affair with a specific woman, his divine intuition leading him to tell us that "I always had this dream of meeting this artist woman that I would fall in love with" and Saint Cynthia fulfilled that role in the time of his great need.' The Great Story tells us that though she was perfect for John at that time, her love being pure and loyal and standing the test of his anger at the world, she was not 'the one' and another 'woman artist' would appear later in his life.

"At the end of this year there was a celebration in the room of one of the learned men of the Art School, his name Ballard, a joke from God that the two should get acquainted in the room of a man whose name was so close to ballad, a romantic song. John had a good friend, Saint Jeff, said to be something of a prophet, and it was he who suggested to John that the haughty lady from Hoylake hid a secret passion for him. John, fortified by wine and encouraged by Jeff, made his approach, but like all good lovers' tales, which must have their ups and downs, Saint Cynthia, although accepting a dance with the object of her affections, with her heart pounding with love from being in such close proximity, informed him that she could not see him because she was promised to another. John replied with a characteristic wisecrack and, though inwardly disappointed, wandered off to rejoin His entourage.

"'Despite her promise to another, she was now fully smitten and that very same night she followed John to a local hostelry, around the corner from the Art School, now a place of worship, then a public house called "Ye Cracke", where the sacred dance of love was performed with the two protagonists studiously ignoring each other all evening while secretly keeping an anxious eye on the other until finally Saint Cynthia made to leave with Phyllis, her lady companion and John stopped her in her tracks by another of His wisecracks and instead they left together and remained together for many years.'"

Brother John put the Holy Book down and looked thoughtful, as if trying to frame the first question to ask about the first important romantic relationship of John the Father. He finally said, "Can you get into pairs and come up with a list of lessons to be learned from the relationship between John the Father and Saint Cynthia?"

I looked around and tried to seek out the least pious John in the room. My eyes alighted on the John who had made several comments that had shown he was on the right side of sanity. I had meant to find him and engage him in conversation to see where he was on the scale of piety, which went from unwavering belief in everything the One True Religion told us to a healthy scepticism of the sillier aspects. He was sitting behind me, to the left, and when I turned around, he was looking at me with a grin that made me think he had similar thoughts. He picked up his chair and brought it to the side of my desk.

"Morning, I'm John," he said with a smile. He was a slight young man with the obligatory round glasses and brown shoulder-length hair, though he had slightly rebelled by growing a wispy beard, something unusual for second year students, beards usually being grown in the last year spent in the Lennonary. He also seemed to actually need the glasses, unlike most of the rest of the class who wore them as an affectation. "I suppose the main lesson we can learn is that Cynthia earnt her sainthood, putting up with John the Father!"

It seemed, on the surface, an almost blasphemous statement. An overt criticism of John the Father. In reality we both knew that this was an exercise about recognising that the relationship was not perfect, especially regarding the behaviour of John the Father. The One True Religion actually held up this relationship as an example provided by God of how *not* to conduct a relationship. It was seen to represent the type of relationship that was prevalent at the time and all the things wrong with it, which included a lack of equality, indications of violence, poor fatherhood and constant unfaithfulness on one side. This was contrasted with the second relationship, which was held up as the right way. The truth was, as always, much more complicated but the church had to simplify and edit the facts in order to make some sense of them and provide guidance to its followers in matters of the heart. As usual, in their not always truthful but well meaning way they had come up with guidance that actually made some sense. At the heart of the matter for me was the usual question of why John the Father, given his divine status, had to make the mistakes before showing us the proper way. It seemed rather unfair on Saint Cynthia.

After we had discussed the lessons for about fifteen minutes, Brother John asked us what we had come up with. A number of hands went up and it was amusing to see the difficulty that most of the novitiates had coming up with criticisms of the behaviour of their favourite Lord in heaven. Brother John patiently nodded his head but it was our pair that seemed to have the most correct answers. He wrote on the board next to the words "Lesson One", "The Slap". He again read from the Holy Book.

"'It was the December before the Golden Decade, the end of the grey fifties, when John the Father confronted Saint Cynthia over some perceived slight that had sent Him into a jealous rage. They were at the Art School when the hand of God descended upon the face of His love and she was found in tears by Phyllis, her lady-in-waiting, who comforted her and railed against such a cruel god. She encouraged her to leave His fiery presence for her own good and safety, and for a while she decided she must do this. But she still loved Him, and when John the Father realised the crime He had committed He came to her with words of love and sorrow and great profusions of apology and most importantly a promise never to do such a heinous crime again. And from that time John was indeed never violent towards her again.'"

Brother John put the book down. "It is, of course, difficult to believe now but in the days of our Lord, violence, both physical and sexual, towards women was not uncommon and so this episode serves as a reminder of those troubled times. It is a reflection of the attitudes of the time, which included an unhealthy view of some men of their superiority over women. As you know, part of a young person's education these days includes intensive courses in healthy relationship skills. We are taught how to communicate effectively and problem solve without resorting to violence, and most importantly we are taught to respect each other and the equal worth of the sexes. The violence was often learnt from witnessing it within the family and this has also been slowly eradicated by education and the message of the One True Religion that violence is unnecessary. John, the Father, in later years wrote a sermon telling us that 'Woman is the nigger of the world'."

A number of hands shot up. Brother John grimaced, as if tasting something sour. "I guess you want to know about the word 'nigger'. Well, we have touched upon this before, but the time of the Beatles was in many ways a dark age, a darkness in which they appeared to shine a light. These were times when people still judged other people by the colour of their skin. I know, it seems completely barbaric, but that was how it was in the time of our Lords, and the word nigger was the most offensive term that could be used by a white person against a black person. It carried with it a venomous hatred and repulsion, especially against African Americans in the old United States, but for the purposes of John's sermon it was basically a term of exclusion, a verbal justification for discrimination, and in this sense could be used for any group that were oppressed. In this sermon He affirmed His belief in equality between the sexes and disavowed His own chauvinist behaviour. In this we must give credit to Yoko, Ocean Child, who taught John the error of some of His ways.

"At the time of the slap, Saint Cynthia knew John should be punished and made Him wait three months before returning to Him. He was rightly shocked at what He had done and although His fiery nature still seeped out in His cutting and sometimes unkind remarks, He was never physically violent again." Brother John paused. "Although we use this first important relationship as providing an example of how not to conduct a relationship, it must be remembered that in the beginning there was love. Saint Cynthia loved John and He loved her, and although His love faded over the years it is important to remember that in the beginning there was love. When John the Father went to the Holy City of Hamburg with two gods and Pete, the patron saint of nearly men, He would write ten page letters of love and affection and go into great detail of their life abroad to His love waiting patiently at home."

Another pause while Brother John wrote "Lesson Two, Faithfulness" on the board.

"Of course, what He did not reveal in His letters was something that Saint Cynthia would have found most upsetting. The God of Fire was having relations with many women. His brother god, Paul, has told us that He would walk into the room and see the naked bottom of John the Father bobbing up and down with a girl underneath Him and know this was a time to apologise and back out of the room."

A hand was raised by the John I had worked with. "Does not the One True Religion allow for multiple partners?"

"Thank you, John. Yes. But we must remember the reason for 'The Slap' was a blind rage caused by the jealousy felt by John the Father. Saint Cynthia had merely danced with another man at a party. There was no suggestion of sexual relations and this mere rumour of a dance had thrown Him into a violent rage resulting in the infamous act of violence that we now use to shock our sensibilities and provide as a severe example of how never to behave. John clearly felt He could do what He liked, including sleeping with many women, but if Cynthia acted that way she deserved severe punishment. It has come to be known as the 'One rule for men and another for women lesson'. There is the parable of the newspapers in Scripture, which tells us of the time that John came to realise the error of His ways."

He picked up the Holy Book and flicked through the pages. "Ah, here we are. 'And in the early days of their blossoming love, John and Yoko, despite this love, would clash intermittently over His sexism. She saw that He did not view women as equals, that they were there to serve tea and sleep with, and in the mornings this came to a head with His expectation to read the papers first because He was the man of the house. And so Yoko shouted at Him, "What is this? I am not supposed to read the papers first?" Eventually it began to dawn on John that she had a point, that this simple act of His reading the papers first was about His belief that it was His due because He was a man. And so John the Father learnt His lesson that there must be equality between the sexes and that He had been guilty for many years of treating women as His inferior.' Thus we learn the lesson that for peace and love to reign in the world, we must have equality between the sexes, that one of the reasons for the violence towards women in the Dark Times was this view held by some men that women were inferior. The other lesson is that we can always learn the error of our ways and change for the better.

"And so the second lesson around faithfulness is about fairness and honesty. As John here has said, it is no sin to have multiple partners, that polyamorous relationships are accepted, but this means the consent of all involved is necessary in order for there to be no hurt for those involved. Of course human relationships are complicated and the example of all our Fathers, the Beatles, tells us that where the heart is concerned mistakes will be made and we must try our best to be honest and fair. But in the end we must be forgiving of mistakes that are made."

# Chapter Eleven
## The Patron Saint of Nearly Men.

---

It was still dark outside. It was near the end of September. A month into the new term. An early autumn English morning. In the time of our Lords, the days would have been just starting to turn colder but now the days were still warm. The whole world was a little warmer. It would not start turning cold, especially here in the south of England, until the month of November, late in the English autumn, a few weeks before Beatlemas, the winter religious festival. As the days turned colder there would begin the vain hope of a white Beatlemas. It was a well-known secret that each order of the gods had their own name for the celebration, and here we greeted each other with a smiling "Happy Johnmas". I am not sure why the date is towards the end of December. It is supposed to celebrate the birth of the Beatles, so logically the day John met Paul makes more sense but it seems that underneath it is a desire to celebrate midwinter, something that stretches back to a time long before the time of our Fathers. Beatlemas Day is therefore celebrated on the twenty-first of December, the shortest day of the year. Thus the birth of the Beatles is seen to coincide with the lengthening of the days, the coming of the light, and Scripture tells us that on this day "unto you the sun of righteousness shall arise and it shall bring healing in its wings". Thus the strange Beatlemas carol sung in midwinter is "Here Comes the Sun", and now we know the Sun is the Beatles themselves, bringing warmth and light into all our lives.

But that was a few months away. As I wiped the sleep from my eyes I could feel the excited buzz from the others in the dormitory. The pious ones were saying the Lords' Prayer. A John next to me was on his knees by his bed and reciting the lines of "Imagine".

I mumbled to myself as if in prayer and quickly wandered off to take a shower. As I left three Johns were giving a rousing rendition of the Beatle hymn "Liverpool".

"And did those feet in ancient times
Walk upon England's mountain green?
And were the holy lambs of God
On England's pleasant pastures seen?
And did their countenances Divine
Shine forth upon our clouded hills?
And was Liverpool builded here
Among these dark satanic mills?
Bring me my bass of burning gold
Bring me my drumsticks of desire
Bring me my guitar, while clouds unfold
Bring me my voice of fire
We shall not cease from mental fight
Nor shall my guitar sleep in my hand
Till we have built Liverpool
In England's green and pleasant land"

It seemed like a strange song to me. The central question seems to be whether Liverpool was built in England. Where did they think it was built, the Middle East?

The singing was another symptom of the air of anticipation amongst the novitiates. We were going on one of our occasional day trips. Some of the other Johns would describe them as pilgrimages because they always involved a visit to a sacred Beatle site. Today we were up early, stumbling about in the murky dawn in order to set off early in our solar-powered magical minibus to spend the day at a sacred site in the Holy City of Liverpool.

Before leaving we all assembled in the underground church that had been built to spend time in contemplation of the Beatles. It was a fact that half of all Beatle churches were built underground as an acknowledgement that the early days were spent singing and preaching underground. Their most famous subterranean place of performing was of course the Cavern but they also met Saint Klaus and Saint Astrid while performing underground in the Holy City of Hamburg. Saint Klaus, describing how he was wandering around the area after an argument with Astrid to clear his head, tells us he was literally halted and mysteriously drawn to the sound of music that was coming from somewhere underground. He was outside the now sacred site of the Kaiserkeller and the sound he heard drawing him to them like a mystical experience was the music of the Beatles. Today we were going to another underground location, the first of the cellars that were full of the noise of the Beatles.

After a quick recitation of the Lords' Prayer and a few moments in silent contemplation we all hurried up the steps of the church just in time to see the sun rising in a sky filled with clouds, a good sign for followers of the Beatles, as John the Father had once asked us to imagine that the clouds were a daisy chain and that we should therefore smile again, and George wrote of Cloud Nine and even Paul told us he had his feet in the clouds. Brother John was standing by the magical minibus urging us to get on.

"Come on," he said with a grin. "The magical minibus is waiting to take you away, waiting to take you away."

We clambered into the minibus, clutching our packed lunches of macrobiotic mush, and settled down for the long drive ahead of us.

I hung back and waited until all the Johns and Johann were safely seated in case I should be joined by one of the pious Johns, which, after all, was most of them, and be forced to engage in conversation about the finer points of Scripture or the religious interpretation of some banal event in the life of John the Father that any normal person would accept at face value but here in the Lennonary had to be given some deeper and divine meaning. I found it extremely hard not to ridicule their sincere but usually nonsensical, if not downright absurd, interpretations of his life. I found myself constantly treading a fine line between being seen as a freethinker with interesting but essentially incorrect views and a blasphemer who could be asked to leave at any time. The order tolerated and even encouraged a certain amount of freethinking, but there was a line that could not be crossed, so I was careful not to get involved in too many discussions with the believers. The truth was that the worst that could happen was that I would be asked to leave, but I was happy at the Lennonary. I loved John and enjoyed studying his life and times and was largely happy with the society that had emerged from the teachings of the Fabulous Four. I was just not convinced that he or the others were the sons of God, and it was this last bit that I had to try and not say out loud. The order argued that they fed and housed us, so it was only fair that our part of the deal was that we believed. It was, after all, a religious order.

As I stood looking down the short aisle, I was relieved to see that all the pious Johns had paired up. There were only two Johns sitting alone. One was the largest of the Johns, a novitiate who liked to tell us he was showing his devotion to John the Father by going through his Fat Elvis period. I think he was joking; it was sometimes difficult to tell. John the Father described one period of his life in the mid-sixties as his "Fat Elvis" period, as he was generally unhappy and overweight and even wrote a genuine cry for "Help" at this time. Devout followers of John have described this as further evidence of his divinity as in 1965, the year of Fat Elvis, Elvis the Baptist was not fat and therefore John the Father was predicting the coming fatness. The less devout and more sane in society tried to point out that John the Father had made these comments much later, in fact after Elvis the Baptist was taken from us after he had gone through his own Fat Elvis period, which went on for much longer and arguably helped kill him. Because of his special place in the mythology of the Beatles religion, he officially died peacefully in bed with a beatific smile on his face having fulfilled his purpose as the man who sent a message via his records to the Sons of God across the water and was happy to be received by God the Father in Beatle Heaven.

Some of his followers had elevated his status to king and believe he died on the throne. A few surviving forbidden texts agree that he died on a throne, if that's what you call the toilet, and if you had looked in his medicine cabinet you would have found a cornucopia of prescribed pills that, along with his bad diet, had killed him, that the constipation-inducing opiates he was addicted to had meant he had died of a heart attack straining on the toilet. It was whispered in the Lennonary that it was God's punishment. An undignified death for his betrayal of the Beatles later in his life. They pointed to the fact that his long road to fat decline began after his meeting with the President of Darkness in the White House in 1970. It is said that he told the president that he thought the Beatles were anti-American and that they promulgated this anti-americanist theme in England. The truth was the Beatles loved America, especially its music, and John the Father made his home there. If they were anti anything it was war and particularly the old USA's involvement in Vietnam. Some Johnnists believe that on hearing this betrayal by the Baptist, God in heaven punished him by destroying his once famous beauty and turning him into a fat parody of himself. Once larger than life he became larger than a house, convinced by mischievous angels such as Bill Belew that he looked good in a jumpsuit, whereas he actually looked like a garage mechanic gone seriously wrong. It was a rumour never seriously quashed by the religion, as it acted as a warning to those who would blasphemously badmouth the Beatles.

I digress. The point was that Fat Elvis John was a nice young man but too large to comfortably share a seat with. The remaining lone John was the seemingly most sane John in the class – that is, if you judged sanity by a person's propensity not to believe any old nonsense they were told. I had had a number of conversations with him since we had shared my desk in class. They took the form of gentle verbal sparring in order to gauge what the other believed, to see where the other drew the line that should not be crossed. A few of my fellow students drew the line at the classroom door; they simply believed everything they were told and that Scripture was the word of God, written in stone. They scared me. There could be discussion, no debate, just blind acceptance. Some of them had a line that was the perimeter of the Lennonary; they were willing to engage in theological debate but it was quite limited and was more about interpretation of Scripture than questioning its veracity. My own line was drawn at the borders of the lands of the One True Religion. Everything was open to discussion and debate, but I believed in the principles upon which we were governed. The principles of peace, love and equality. I believed for the simple reason that they seemed to work.

I sat down next to John with some relief. His line was somewhere outside the Lennonary, though not as far and wide as mine. He seemed to believe in the divinity of the Beatles but could not take seriously much of the Scripture. I had found out that he was politically ambitious and his time in the Lennonary was not due to any strict devotional belief but rather the first step in his roadmap to high office.

We waited until we were underway, so the chatter of the other Johns and Johann and the noise of the moving minibus would provide covering noise for any conversation that might have been frowned upon by the others.

"Morning, John."

"Morning, John."

"Well, John."

"Yes, John?"

We seemed to be the only ones who found the fact that we were all called John faintly absurd. Our customary greeting now used the name as many times as possible to highlight the silliness. Our parents were not blessed with divine foresight. We were given a birth name until the year of our Confirmation, a ceremony which partly celebrated the affirmation of our belief in the One True Religion and partly celebrated our coming of age from boyhood to manhood or from girlhood to womanhood. It was at this point that we chose the name we wished to be called as an adult, usually the name of the person's favourite Father or saint. As it happened I had been called John by my loving but unimaginative parents, and I often wondered if it proved that the name you were given at birth influenced your future life. John had revealed to me that at his birth naming ceremony, which we called a Beatlening, he had actually been Beatled the name Paul. He had explained his presence in the Lennonary and not in an order of Paul the Father by the fact that he had come to the conclusion that the more successful politicians seemed to have spent time here. In the time of our Lords there was a path from the old private schools of Eton and Harrow to the universities of Oxford and Cambridge that seemed to give those students an entry into the world of politics, a path that was restricted to a privileged few, a privileged few whose success seemed based not on talent but a sense of entitlement. That path had been replaced by attending the orders of the Fathers, and John had decided that the Lennonary was the place most likely to allow him to achieve his political ambitions.

He had sworn me to secrecy as although the four names were seen as equally beautiful in the outside world, in the cloistered cloisters of the Lennonary this innocent fact would have meant he would be regarded with a lot of suspicion and not a little contempt by his peers. As it was he was seemingly popular with everybody. He was charming and witty and seemed to agree with everybody he talked to, no matter the nonsense they talked. A born diplomat, you might say. A bit like Paul. He would make a good politician. I say "seemed to agree" because if you listened carefully when he talked to the more piously insane novitiates, he would smile and nod rather than *say* he agreed and would give bland replies which never revealed his true feelings. I occasionally wondered whether I was just another experiment in how to deal with people with different perspectives on his path to political power, but our conversations revealed beliefs that would get him into trouble in the Lennonary, though never, I came to realise, anything that would be unacceptable outside Tittenhurst.

"So what's your big policy?"

"What?"

"Your big policy, you know, your big idea? You want to be a politician, what on earth for?"

"Oh, right. Well, I have a few ideas, but my big idea I'm gonna call my 'All the Lonely People' policy."

I was never entirely sure when he was being serious, and he seemed to think the title of his policy was self-explanatory. I told him it was not. He sighed a politician's sigh. It was the sigh of being pushed for details of a great sounding idea. It usually meant the details had either not been worked out or not thought through very carefully.

"We have solved a lot of problems through economic, racial and sexual equality, but for a religion and political system that has love as one of its three main pillars, there are still an awful lot of lonely people in the world. I'm going to solve that problem. I'm going to answer the question posed by Paul, our other Father, about where they all belong. We've pretty much eradicated poverty. I want to eradicate loneliness."

I was impressed. It sounded insane and there were still no details, no specific policies to explain how this redistribution of love might be achieved, but I had asked for a big idea and there it was. For a society that attempted to be based on the three pillars of peace, love and harmony, (most equated harmony with equality, which they saw as meaning that we should live in peace with the ethos of cooperation, while others, unsurprisingly given the story of the Beatles, argued that this referred to the musical definition of harmony, that we needed to sing in harmony to be in tune with each other in the literal sense. There were, therefore, a minority of believers who emphasised the importance of music and song in everything they did. If they ran a business, they would start each day with a song, and promotions tended to be based on musicality or the quality of their voices. They created what could only be described as a harmonacracy, with differing results for, as you can imagine, the fact that you sing well did not necessarily mean you were good at running a business. It was argued on the other side that this was just another way of saying the same thing, that we achieved the best results when we were in harmony with each other. And so it went on.) This seemed a perfect policy to hang your hat on.

"I've no idea how that works but as a big idea that's not half bad."

"Thanks, I know. I've always wondered at the phrase 'not half bad'. It makes no logical sense, but we know it means something is surprisingly good. There isn't an opposite expression to say something is not half good."

I think he was practising the politician trick of changing the subject from something he was not comfortable talking about, but I persisted with my questions.

"Of course, calling it the 'All the Lonely People' policy tends to suggest it has come from Paul, our other Father, and not John *the* Father."

"Yes, John. I am aware of that. That's why I don't want to shout too much about it at the moment. I had toyed with calling it the 'Yer Blues' policy or even the 'Isolation' policy but they don't sound as good, plus 'Yer Blues' is a bit too bleak, and let's be honest Paul was always slightly better at producing harmonies." He said this last part in a whisper that I barely heard.

"Oh, and I've also been thinking about introducing an extra day to the week and calling it my 'Eight Days a Week' policy," he said, looking pleased with himself.

"Why would you want to do that? Surely most progressives have worked towards reducing the working week?"

"It's not increasing the working week; it's just increasing the week by a day. The sermon suggests there aren't enough days in the week in order to love each other, that joy would be brought if only there was one more day to receive love, so I'm going to provide that extra day."

"Have you just been going through the songs of the gods that have not already been used for various daft policies and made up even dafter policies?"

"No," he said, avoiding my eye.

As the blackbird flew, it was about a hundred and seventy miles to the Holy City of Liverpool from Tittenhurst, but by magical minibus it was forty miles further and it took us, with one stop at a service station for a comfort break, just over four hours to reach the outskirts of that holiest of holy cities. We had, of course, all been there before on various pilgrimages but the feeling of excitement never seemed to be any less every time we approached the famous entrance to the holy city. There were four enormous statues of the Fabulous Foursome at the southern entrance to the city. All the talking had stopped and the novitiates were gazing out the window, their faces varying masterpieces of awe and reverence. Even I could not help but feel the nervous anticipation in the pit of my stomach as the magical minibus approached the holy city where it all began. All those years ago.

We drove past the giant ankles of the four gods, ankles clad in Cuban-heeled boots, dating their immortalisation in these statues to the early 1960s. The Holy City of Liverpool was associated with their early years and was full of sacred sites associated with them: the houses where they grew up, the schools they attended, the public houses they drank in, the church garden where it all began, the many venues where they played. In the time of the Beatles it had been bombed in the war and had seen its traditional industries decline, so many locals left to find work elsewhere as the governments of the time neglected this holiest of cities. Now the reverse was true. It was a thriving city with millions making their pilgrimages every year to stand in the shoes of their gods, to feel the presence of the Beatles in the humble abodes they had lived in as children, all now sacred sites: 251 Menlove Avenue, 20 Forthlin Road and so on. A once shrinking population, forced out to find better opportunities, was now an expanding one, providing hospitality, services and the famous Scouse humour to the hordes of awestruck visitors, who were often made happy just to hear the distinctive dialect spoken that reminded them of the few recordings still surviving of the voices of the gods.

I remember my first pilgrimage as a thirteen-year-old, still in youthful awe of the four gods that so filled the world around me, but particularly adoring of John the Father and starting to appreciate his rebellious streak and his fiery, sometimes snarling irreverence. I was naive and unlearned and at the beginning of my journey of doubt. My father was Englishly religious in that he sort of believed as long as it did not interfere with his true interests, which seemed to consist at the time of old ships and gardening. Thus he had proposed a father-son pilgrimage from our little town to the Holy City of Liverpool on the pretext of visiting Menlove Avenue, the house where John the Father grew up under the stern but always loving gaze of his Aunt Mimi. I remember the sleepless night prior to the pilgrimage, the building excitement as dawn broke, and the beginning of the journey in my father's car. I was so exhausted I fell asleep and was woken up several hours later by my father as we approached the holy city. It seemed, as we drew nearer to those huge statues guarding the entrance, that the very air felt slightly different, tinged with magic and musical notes. Indeed, I felt I could strum the air with my fingers and wonderful music would sound.

"Are we going straight there, Dad?"

A look flashed across my father's face that I could not at first interpret but his words soon gave me a clue that it was probably guilt. "Ah, no, I've got tickets for this afternoon so I thought to, you know, kill some time before the main event, as it were, we could go and visit the Maritime Museum."

My heart sank. I did not share my father's passion for ancient sailing vessels, and the suspicion that he had arranged this whole visit as a pilgrimage to the Maritime Museum rather than as a special treat for his favourite child was slowly working its way through my consciousness. It now became clear why we had set off so early: to give my father plenty of time to look around the Maritime Museum. Liverpool had been famous for its docks, and the century before the Beatles were sent by God, it had been a busy bustling port, one of the busiest and most famous in the world. Unfortunately for the reputation of the holy city, much of the wealth created by this busy port was based on the slave trade.

I stared at the exhibition in the museum of the role of the holy city in the slave trade, completely incomprehensible to my twenty-third-century sensibilities. I was dumbstruck. I felt my belief in a kind, caring, benevolent God, already on the slide, further slide towards profound disillusionment. How could a God let His children, His cherished creations, treat each other this way? It was an inauspicious start to a day that had started with such excitement at the prospect of visiting the childhood home of my favourite god.

My father had only cursorily glanced at this evidence of human cruelty and rushed upstairs to another exhibition. I was left alone to ponder the choice of Liverpool as the holiest city. In order to put God in a better light, it was said that He punished the city for its misdemeanours, that before it had reached its holy status, He set in motion events that would see it go into a steady decline. The end of the slave trade was the beginning of this decline. Although the old docks were revitalised by the building of the Royal Albert Docks in the mid-nineteenth century, this was a brief respite before the great city slipped into further decline. Further punishment occurred in the middle of the twentieth century when, during the second of the world wars, Liverpool was severely bombed by the German air force, as written by John the Father when he told us about Madalf Heatlump (who still only had one). This decline was to continue for decades to come, but at the same time it is said God felt He had punished the city long enough and had decided to sow His seeds in the dirty and dilapidated city in the northwest of England. And so, in the midst of war, He literally planted His sons in the four corners of the city. Centuries later, Liverpool would rise from the ashes of its decline and become the centre of the universe, the holiest of the holy cities, visited by millions of pilgrims every year.

Of course, to any sane individual, none of this could possibly make sense. It did not answer the question of why God chose Liverpool if He felt the need to punish it. The answer often given was a defensive one which did not really answer the question. Find me a city that had no history of blood on its hands, they'd say. Although this indeed may have been a difficult task, it really only highlighted that the history of mankind seemed to be one of them being rather horrible to each other.

"Ah, but don't you see? That is why He sent forth His four sons to show us the way," the church would claim triumphantly. This of course seemed to suggest there was a serious design fault in the children He had created in the first place, and so it went on.

I trudged upstairs to find my father engrossed in an exhibition on some old ship that was famous for sinking on its maiden voyage after being touted as unsinkable. It was called the *Titanic* and its enduring fame seemed to suggest we were fascinated by failure, the more spectacular the better. As we drove into the holy city, I thought of this now as we headed to the district of West Derby and our ultimate destination.

In the distance, as we came into the city, we could see the walls of the independent state within the city: Olive Mount, the old Wavertree district. The city of Liverpool was said to be built on seven hills and it was one of these hills, Olive Mount Hill, that gave it its name. It was the smallest state in the world by area and by population, which currently stands at just over a thousand. The head of this state is the Beatle Pope, presently a woman. Pope Joan Paula III, who had recently replaced Pope George Ringo II. She was also the head of the One True Religion. Officially the Beatle Pope is said to be the direct descendant of Saint Peter, the man entrusted with the keys to heaven by God and John the Father, with John saying to Saint Peter on their last earthly meeting, "You are Peter, and on this rock I will build my church and the gates of hell shall not prevail against it. I will give you the keys to the kingdom of heaven."

However the reality was that when a pope died all the leaders of the One True Religion would gather together at the Olive Mount House and vote on who would be the next pope, the only rule being that the next pope had to be of the opposite sex to the last one. It was recognised that the One True Religion was somewhat male dominated at the top and there was much discussion and debate about whether God the Father was actually God the Mother, a question which was never satisfactorily resolved, the answer to which usually depended on whether you were a man or a woman. The lesbian and gay community believed that god was a gay man or a gay woman, and so it went on. None of this was surprising to doubters such as me, who saw it essentially as an argument over a made-up person, and I therefore believed there could just as well have been an argument over whether it was God the Red-Nosed Reindeer. It was often quoted that God made us in His own image, which ruled out the Red-Nosed Reindeer faction, but just seemed to pose the question, "Yes, but which one of us?" The church was liberal in its approach to these differing versions of God the Thing You'd Like It To Be. It was like bespoke Beatle Heaven – a bespoke God, tailored to your individual needs. It was an all-inclusive religion, and if it made you happy to believe that God looked a bit like you then the church was happy to let it be.

As we drove through the streets of the holy city we passed many signs that had the legend "Anfield" inscribed upon them. The last one I saw had the word "Cathedral" added to it. Although it was neatly written, it was clearly graffiti added by a local wit. Anfield was the home of Liverpool Football Club, and as the graffiti implied, football had become the main rival of the One True Religion. The stadium could now hold over a hundred thousand fans every game. In amongst the many statues of the four gods and the various saints that made up their story were other statues of secular saints, Saints Bill, Bob and Jurgen. I mention this as one of the weaker and less serious arguments that God was a man, and quite possibly English like his sons, was the suggestion that he had given football, the "beautiful game", to England as a gift hundreds of years ago. They point to the fact that this connection between God, football, England and the Beatles was proven by his further gift of allowing them to win the World Cup in the midst of the time of the Fab Four in 1966. Some argued that to punish the English for not being modest enough, after this pinnacle of success he forever cursed them to be a mixture of rubbish at the game and unable to score penalties.

The present Beatle Pope, born Maria Ramirez in Buenos Aires, was the first to come from South America in the hundred and twenty-five year history of the Beatle Pope. She was a lively and vivacious woman, popular with the people and, at forty-five, youthful for a pope, with her wayward husband and two young sons bringing an exotic flavour to the windy and often overcast holy city. After the nine years of steady steering of the Papal State's tiller by Pope George Ringo II, an honourable but unimaginative man from Munich, Germany, who had never married and seemed rarely to smile, the new pope was a welcome change for the masses with her messy family life, her flashing smile and propensity to find most things amusing, which she showed with her instantly recognisable laugh, which was deep and hearty and rather loud. She was also passionately outspoken about injustices. The people, recognising that she represented the spirit of the Beatles much more than her dour predecessor, seemed to adore her. When the novitiates of the Order of John were ordained after their three or four years of training, they were presented with their Certificates of Ordination in a special audience with the Pope. If I ever completed my training I looked forward to this.

After we had spent the morning in the Maritime Museum, my father finally and very reluctantly came and found me in the cafe where I had spent the last hour sipping an orange juice and reading a book, having got bored after about ten minutes of looking at pictures of ships in which I had zero interest. As we drove towards Menlove Avenue in Woolton, my father spoke animatedly about the exhibitions he had seen, clearly not noticing my glazed expression. He seemed particularly taken by the *Titanic* exhibition.

"Didn't you find all those exhibits which were items recovered from the wreckage fascinating?"

"Not really."

"They even had an original chamber pot."

"What's a chamber pot?"

"It's a ceramic pot they used to pee in."

"Right, I must have missed that. Here was I getting all excited about visiting the childhood home of John the Father, the home where God grew up, and I've gone and missed the piss pot."

My father glanced at me, finally beginning to sense my irritation. "I thought you'd be interested in the sea and ships. After all, your favourite deity's father was a seaman." He looked quite pleased with himself for making this justification for our surprise visit to the Maritime Museum.

"I thought his father was God."

"Ah, well, yes, His actual father was, of course, God, but His earthly father was Alf, a man who spent a lot of time at sea."

"Yes, a lot of time at sea and virtually no time with his son. So little time that he wasn't even made a saint."

"Yes, he does seem a strange choice for the surrogate father of a god," my father said, as if noticing this for the first time. "Perhaps he knew, you know, that he wasn't the real father, thought it best to keep out of everyone's way."

My father was not a deep theological thinker. He accepted the religion, seemed to believe but did not really let it take up too much of his time. He seemed quite surprised when I chose to enter the Lennonary. He was a simple but clever man, a scientist who was employed by the government to find new ways of producing energy that did not harm the planet. He was quietly helping to save mankind, although he never talked about it that way. It was just his job which he happened to enjoy. He worked long hours, and outside of work he liked a pint of beer, often that he had made himself, and to read books about ships from times past. He also seemed to love my mother and his children.

I thought about the many hours we had spent together, often working on model ships which he had bought me. I now realised that perhaps the model ships were not really meant for me, but he could have just bought them for himself and locked himself away in his shed. It was his way of spending quality time with his son.

I thought about the contrast with John the Father's father. An absent figure from the age of five, only to be reunited when John was an adult, rich and famous and therefore curious to see his father but always suspicious that he had only shown up for handouts. A young man so full of rage and anger and sadness at his rejection by his earthly parents that to make up for it, for a time, he managed to get the whole world to love him. Surely only a god could have achieved that. That was how I felt at the time, although the doubts were starting to appear like small blots on my horizon.

That day we arrived at the holy site of 251 Menlove Avenue in the leafy suburb of Woolton. The house was called Mendips after the range of hills in Somerset, which had since become another sacred place, much to the initial bemusement of the West Country locals but which they soon embraced when the tourists started arriving in busloads with their pockets full of cash. Thereafter there started various myths about how John the Father had spent time in contemplation in the caves, especially Cheddar Gorge and Wookey Hole, though no one ever found any actual evidence of this. To get in on the act, Glastonbury, a town not far away and famous in the old days for holding a massive music festival where Paul, the other Father, is said to have performed, started its own set of myths. It was said to have been visited in the years after the assassination by a Joseph of Greenwich Village. No one was entirely sure who this Joseph was but it was said he brought with him the Holy Grail, a cup which contained some drops of blood from John the Father that had poured from his wounds. It was an interesting story but again based on no hard evidence. Sceptics of the story asked what this Joseph was doing with a handy cup capturing the blood of the Lord at this terrible time. The story went on to say that this Joseph had been granted lands by some early believers in the divinity of the Beatles, who were said to wander the town dressed in purple and talk about crystals and tarot cards a lot.

Joseph used these lands to set up a proto One True Religion community, legend saying that he had also brought with him a wooden plectrum also belonging to John the Father which he planted in the grounds of the community and which rooted and burst into bloom as a beautiful tree, said to bloom each year at the time of John the Father's birthday. None of this was officially endorsed by the church but it did not stop the legend growing; neither did it stop the search for the Holy Grail, which was said to be the source of great power, or of great happiness and eternal youth. A few sane people suggested these were actually just rehashed legends from many years before the arrival of the four sons of God, but people seemed to prefer a good story over sanity so the legends continued.

My father parked in a car park designated for pilgrims and we made our way the half mile distance to the House of John. We were not alone; there were others making the same pilgrimage, talking to each other in hushed tones, seeming to get quieter the nearer we were to the house where John had grown up. I was not sure what I had expected. I think I expected either something extremely simple – the church often talked about the humble beginnings of the Four Gods – or something spectacular, breathtaking, a palace worthy of a god. I remember being vaguely disappointed. It was neither the simple, lowly place which for some reason I had imagined as a stable or a cave, or the awe-inspiring, cathedralesque building of my imagination, but a semi-detached house that looked quite a lot like our own house back down south. After many years of experimenting with eco-friendly materials to build houses, which had included plastics, sheep's wool, hay bales, recycled wood, earth and cow manure, it turned out that the simple clay brick was just as eco-friendly, so although our house had been built in the last twenty years, on the outside it looked very similar to the House of John. In fact, if it was not for the many signs marking the spot and the group of pilgrims milling about outside, I would never have known which house it was.

There were fifteen of us waiting to go inside and it was clear we were an international brigade of Lennonists. There was a young couple from Italy, on a pilgrimage from Rome to see as many sites as they could fit, in the Holy City of "I Favolosi". The Beatles were venerated in Italy, although they only visited there once in 1965. All the places they played have become sacred cathedral sites: the Velodromo Vigorelli in Milan, the Palasport in Genoa and the Teatro Adriano in Rome. History tells us there used to be another, immensely powerful religion that was based in Rome, in a place similar to the Olive Mount state in Liverpool, but legend has it that when faced with the choice of the One True Religion based on the peace, love and laughter of the Beatles and the old religion, which had strange and frankly bizarre rules around sex and seemed anti-fun, the peace, love and laughter-loving Italians chose the

One True Religion and spent many of the early years of the new religion firstly enjoying themselves without feeling guilty and secondly wondering why they had believed in such nonsense for so many years. There was then, in Rome, a ready-made set of magnificent buildings, such as St Peter's Basilica and the Ringoine Chapel, named after the second Beatle Pope, Ringo the First, with its amazing frescoes depicting the significant times in the lives of the Beatles, which the One True Religion appropriated, simply suggesting that the St Peter referred to had changed. St Peter's Square, the large open space that lies before the basilica, is occasionally filled to capacity with believers or those curious to see the Beatle Pope, who uses the basilica to make important pronouncements or just general blessings at times of religious holidays on her many visits to the eternal city.

The changing from the old religion to the new had been bloodless. Many of those who had dedicated their lives to the old religion, living in splendid hypocrisy behind their gilded walls, simply changed sides and robes. Many breathed a sigh of relief and whispered to each other about how the new rules allowed them to have relations with adults in the open.

Next to the Italians were a group of Australians, a nation not given to whispering their presence, loud and proud and so talking in unhushed reverent tones. They were from the Holy City of Adelaide, a city that had turned out in their hundreds of thousands to glimpse the gods when they visited there in June 1964. It was also home of another massive Beatle cathedral on the site of the Adelaide Centennial Hall, where they played a number of sell-out concerts. These pilgrims had come halfway round the world to see the House of John. I hoped they had other things to do as I looked at the sacred site, which looked to all intents and purposes like a pleasant semi-detached house. Perhaps the inside would be more inspiring.

There is some dispute as to the authentic holiness of the Australian sites touched by the Beatles, mainly disputed by the members of the Order of Ringo, our Starr in Heaven, as he was not there for the whole visit due to a bout of tonsillitis. They were peeved, firstly because he was not there but also because it drew attention to the fact that he had been ill. Those in the other orders, always jealous of their favourite god, asked the question whether Ringo was truly a deity given he was ill. Do gods get ill? Does God the Father in Beatle Heaven ever catch a cold? Does he ever have a touch of the flu, a dicky stomach? A splitting headache? Most of this sniping was quashed when the Ringoists reminded the followers of George, their Sweet Lord, that he had famously had the flu on the day of their first time on the show of Saint Ed in the old United States, the show that sowed the seeds of their triumph in that country then and now. The church therefore came up with the solution that, though the Beatles were, of course, gods, they were in the frail bodies of mortal men and therefore subject to the illnesses that us mere mortals suffer. They also say that God the Father had punished Saint Jimmy, the man who had dared to take the place of Ringo. He was a man who had flown too close to the sun, had had his wings melted and after leaving the Beatles was forever falling lower and lower until he fell so low he disappeared from view altogether.

At the back of the waiting group of people was a family of four who had also travelled thousands of miles to visit the House of John. They were Japanese, mother and father standing in respectful silence as they waited to enter the house where they hoped to feel the presence of the youthful fire god while their son and daughter, who looked around nine and ten, whispered and giggled and with a look of awe on their faces when they glanced at Mendips. Whether they were excited at the prospect of entering the house of a god or, like me, they were in awe of the fact that they appeared to have travelled over six thousand miles to see a semi-detached house was unclear.

Japan was one of the first countries to adopt the One True Religion. After the second of the world wars, this once warrior nation introduced a constitution that many referred to as the "Peace Constitution" with its Article 9 that stated that "the Japanese people forever renounce war as a sovereign right of the nation and the threat or use of force as a means of settling international disputes". Although there were attempts to revise this article it remained in place and provided a perfect platform for the smooth transition to the government and religion that has become the blueprint for Beatle democracies around the globe. And with the fusion of John the Father with his consort, Yoko, Ocean Child, in a relationship that lasted until his assassination, Japan became one of the four major power centres of the One True Religion along with England, Germany, and the New United States.

When the Beatles visited Japan in the year 1966 it is said in that country that the spirit of Article 9 gave them the courage to put forward their ideas of peace. In a conference the Beatles were asked what, after having attained sufficient honour and wealth, did they seek next. John the Father answered, simply, "Peace". This was then echoed by Paul, the other Father, in unison with John, and they then both stated that they wished to "Ban the bomb". It was also in Japan that John the Father, made his first statement about a conflagration that was going on in a small Southeast Asian country by the name of Vietnam. Again, according to the Japanese, suffused with the spirit of peace that the air of Japan contained, after breathing this air, when asked about what he thought about this conflict, he said, "Well, we think about it every day and we don't agree with it and we think it's wrong." Thus, ever since the Japanese have claimed it was the Japanese air that gave them the courage to put forward their thoughts on peace and war and, they add, was it not Yoko who accompanied John in his campaign for peace in the following years?

A strong cultural connection had sprung up between England and Japan as a result of these associations with the declaration of the importance of peace in Tokyo in 1966. The connection was strengthened by the tradition of Japanese women seeking English partners and English men seeking Japanese partners in the "Yoko seeking John" or "John seeking Yoko" tradition that had grown since the advent of the One True Religion, particularly among those who favoured John the Father as their favourite god, though, of course, there were no favourites. The truly faithful would find their partners and make their way to Gibraltar, near Spain, were they would get married, both dressed all in white. They would then have photos taken in front of the famous Rock of Gibraltar, which was said to symbolise the foundation of the relationship. If they were particularly devoted to the One True Religion and each other, they would then honeymoon in Amsterdam, talking in their beds for a week and much else besides.

There was some dissent about how holy a country Japan was from those who closely followed Paul, the other Father, due to a legend that he was deported from Japan in 1980 following a discovery of hashish in his luggage, but it was pointed out that he returned there many times afterwards and was actually very fond of Japan.

Next to the Japanese family and in contrast to the dark-haired and smaller quartet were a young couple, probably in their early twenties, who later told me in their perfect English accents that they were from the Blessed City of Stockholm in Sweden. The prefix "blessed" was given to places touched by the Beatles but not seen as central to their story. Considering that any connection to the four deities tended to bring pilgrims and their wallets and their purses, many places dug deep and found some connection to the Beatles or at least one of the gods. The Beatles had performed in Stockholm in 1964 in front of screaming devotees and there was now a large Beatle cathedral on the site of the Johanneshovs Isstadion in Stockholm where they played. This was actually the second time they visited Sweden and was in the midst of the madness of Beatlemania. The Swedes are quick to point out that Sweden was the first place that the Beatles toured outside Britain when they toured there in October 1963 so, they argue, the whole country was blessed. Of course, the Germans dispute this and point to the fact that Hamburg has been designated a holy city because of its central importance to the Greatest Story and not just blessed as Stockholm is. This has led to many years of theological warfare between the two countries, with much of the debate hanging on the definition of "toured". The Swedes argue that the Beatles just played one venue when they played in Hamburg and that Stockholm should indeed be designated holy, while the Germans argue that, on its own, the amount of time they spent in Hamburg was enough to give it a special prominence in the story. The debates raged to this day, though only in those two countries, and though I say theological warfare it never spilled into anything like actual warfare. The two countries were happy to follow the teachings of peace and love, and the worst the tensions got was that they never gave each other any points in the Eurovision Song Contest, a European contest that involved each country entering a song that was a cover of a Beatles song and which, somewhat bizarrely, Britain had not won for over fifty years.

These claims on the Beatles were mirrored everywhere in the world with everyone claiming their city or country was holy or blessed. Indeed, Sweden had another rivalry with their close neighbours Denmark, who claimed that their capital city should be designated as blessed but had only managed to be officially proclaimed the Hallowed City of Copenhagen, "hallowed" being a designation just below "blessed" and therefore some way from "holy". The Beatles had played there in 1964 but they had gone to Sweden twice and hence the "blessing", and so it went on. Whenever these disputes seemed to be getting out of hand the church talked about invoking the "Imagine No Countries" clause from the Lords' Prayer and the bickering usually stopped, at least for a while.

As Japan had slipped into the rhythm of the One True Religion, given their head start of their "Peace Constitution", the Swedes similarly had a head start with their political system, which fit in snugly with the socially democratic model that the One True Religion espoused. Sweden, along with its Scandinavian neighbours, Denmark and Norway, had for many years topped the equality and happiness charts and it was clear that these two traits were clearly linked: the greater the equality, the greater the happiness. They also figured highly in the Global Peace Index, which, added together with their love of the Beatles, meant they were perfect breeding grounds for the One True Religion. It was a simple formula that had been largely adopted by the countries that followed the teachings of the Fab Four. Although the economic system was based on the workings of free market capitalism, to combat the tendency of this system to create inequality, people were encouraged to be members of strong unions, and a large percentage of the workforce worked in the public sector and there were generous welfare provisions. Citizens paid high taxes but received high quality public goods in return such as health, education and childcare. It was simple but effective and had only stuttered in its progress in the past because of high immigration. Understandably, in the days before the advent of equality for all countries, people wanted to go to the equal, happy, peaceful countries and this put strains on the system. Now that this had been solved by making all countries equal, happy and peaceful and making movement a choice and not an economic necessity, the system seemed to work.

There were some debates as to whether high taxation truly followed the teachings of the Beatles, with some pointing to George, Lord of the Weeping Guitars', sermon on the hated "Taxman" but it was argued that they did not like the high taxes because they believed the money paid for rockets and bombs, and so in the new Beatlocracies the taxes were hypothecated: the government had to tell the people where their money went and any military expenditure had to be put to a vote.

The time finally came for our little group of fifteen to go in. My annoyance at my father dissipated when the guide gathered us in the small hallway and in hushed tones told us we were honoured to be in this place. There was a waiting list of fifteen months and so my father must have booked this last year, which lessened my suspicion that he had arranged the whole thing in order to go to the Maritime Museum.

The tour of the sacred site only lasted fifteen minutes. Truth be told there was not much to see. We seemed to spend quite a lot of time in the kitchen, where the guide pointed out "interesting" objects such as a container which he explained was for bread. I could not help thinking that the fact that it had "Bread" written on it meant such explanations were unnecessary. Although most of the group seemed to be in hushed awe, rarely daring to speak on such consecrated ground, I was left feeling a little underwhelmed at the surroundings. It was only when we trooped upstairs and were shown John's room that I got any feeling of a "presence". Perhaps I willed it into being by my own longing to feel near to my favourite god, but as I gazed at the posters of Brigitte Bardot, I felt a tingling in the pit of my stomach that I interpreted at the time as the Holy Spirit.

In later years I realised it was probably the same tingling sensation that John had felt when he looked at the pictures of Bardot. It made me feel closer to John, but not in a religious way. I realise that visit was the start of my doubts of the true divinity of the Fabulous Four.

When we left the House of John, the next fifteen pilgrims from the four corners of the world were waiting patiently outside with familiar excited looks of expectation. I hoped they would not be disappointed.

I remember the conversation with my father on the long journey home.

He asked, "So, what did you think of the, uh…?"

I understood his inability to describe what we had just seen, so I helped him out. "What did I think of the House of John? Well, it was very much a house, with things in it that you would expect from that time. Thanks for taking me, it was an experience. What about you?"

"Well, it was quite interesting to see the toilet. I've never seen where a god does His business before."

I glanced at my father, unsure whether he was being serious, given his seeming fascination with the chamber pot from the *Titanic* earlier in the day. The question of the bodily functions of gods had never really crossed my mind before. There was nothing I had come across in scripture on the subject. "Did gods defecate" was not a question that had ever come up in Beatle religious studies. Could a god be constipated? It felt slightly blasphemous to even think about the question. It was often said that gods moved in mysterious ways, usually when discussing their actions that made no sense, but whether their movements were regular was never mentioned.

"And the windows were nice."

"What?"

"The windows, they were all stained glass. It reminded me of something."

"A church maybe?"

"Oh yes. Would it be blasphemous if I admitted I thought the *Titanic* exhibit was more interesting?"

"Probably, Dad, but I suppose the *Titanic* story was more dramatic. Would you have been more interested in the House of John if it had sunk?"

It was my father's turn to glance at me to see if I was being serious. When he saw I was grinning, he smiled back and we spent the rest of the car journey describing the things we had seen in the House of John and ascribing magical powers to the most banal of objects. There was a tin of baking powder, a jar of pickled onions, all of which we gave a background story to. Each chair and table, my father pointed out – further destroying any mystery – like most of the objects in the house was in fact a replica of what they believed would have been in the house. This was made clear by the church in order to prevent the continuous stealing of objects that had kept happening when the pilgrims thought they were the originals touched by John the Father. They would later appear in Beatle churches all over the planet as "original" relics, given pride of place to attract people in to expand the congregation.

A decade later, Brother John was parking up. We had arrived at our destination in West Derby, in the Holy City of Liverpool. The place where we were heading was 8 Haymans Green, but it was best known in the Greatest Story Ever Told as the Casbah Coffee Club. The Casbah was a club for young people opened up by a certain Mona Best. She lived in a large Victorian house with her husband and two sons. It was a fifteen-room house with a large attic, but this being the story of the Beatles, the real story, the action, took place in the cellar. It was a large cellar divided into a number of rooms and in August 1959 Mona opened the Casbah and a certain group known as the Quarrymen played the opening night.

The large house was now home to a reclusive religious order that went by the name of the Best Order of All, although outside the community they were usually referred to as the

Second Best Order of All and were devotees to Saint Pete. It was a mixed order; both men and women were welcomed. What united the members of the order was that they had all suffered a great disappointment in life. It consisted of people from all walks of life, politicians who had come a close second in an election, athletes who had been quite good but never made the medal position, writers who had never quite been published or if they had, had sold copies mainly to friends and family; artists, comedians, actors, film-makers, directors, playwrights and the most devout of all the order, musicians and singers.

Mona Best, unofficial saint in the Best Order, was the mother of Pete Best, the patron saint of nearly men and a legendary figure in the mythology of the Greatest Story. The Best Order is reclusive firstly because they want to be – they are, after all, disappointed and want to spend time alone in contemplation of their particular might-have-been – but also because the main church, the One True Religion, are largely ambivalent towards them. They granted Pete sainthood because of his connection to the Beatles in their early days but in this canonisation lay their implicit regard to Pete Best. He was a part of the Great Story but he was not a god. In the secular world there existed some interesting debates to this day as to the reasons why Pete was asked to leave. For the church, the answer is simple. He was simply filling in until the fourth piece of the puzzle in the form of Ringo, our Starr in Heaven, turned up. The other three all knew the first time Ringo played with them that Pete's days were numbered, that they had found what they were looking for. The true and proper Beat of the Beatles.

We followed Brother John to the entrance to the sacred cellar of the Casbah. Not only had the Beatles played there many times but they had helped decorate it before it opened, making it doubly sacred to their followers, touched by their divine sound and also literally by their paintbrushes. Although the three gods had been together for a while, their progress had somewhat stalled at this time so the regular spot at the Casbah was something of a second beginning for the young gods. For John the Father this was a special time of new beginnings. He had just left a summer labouring job, something which the church likes to point to when they wish to give an example of one of the gods glorifying manual labour and the role of workers. The truth seems to have been that he hated every minute of it and never repeated the endeavour. Scripture tells us about this brief and painful interlude in his life as follows:

"And in the hot summer of 1959, John the Father determined that he needed a new instrument to spread His word and gospel. He asked His loving but stern guardian Saint Mimi who smiled and said He would do well to study harder and to forget the guitar, which was alright as a hobby but He would never make a living from it. And so John the Father decided to prove His determination and procured Himself a job at the holy building site of Scarisbrick, where now a temple resides in honour of His labours. For six long weeks He toiled in the searing summer sunshine. God the Father, looking down on one of His four chosen sons, decided to play a little trick on His favourite son by, unusually, making that summer actually hot in England. The sky was blue every day and it was said that this was mirrored by the air around John the Father, coloured by His use of flowery language as He toiled in the searing sun. After six weeks John had proved himself to His strict aunt who finally agreed to help Him with His much desired purchase and accompanied Him to the place now known as the Shop of Many Wonders and Beginnings, then known as Hessys', and along with His hard-earned wages helped Him buy His first proper guitar."

And so it was written that this was a time of three for John: the end of his days of labour, the acquiring of his new guitar and the start of the residency at the Casbah after a quiet period. Some of the secular histories suggest he did not leave of his own accord but was asked to leave. Pointing to his employment card, they argue his reason for leaving was given as "unsuitable". The church ignores this, not wanting it to be part of the Greatest Story that one of their gods was sacked from his job. I think they have missed a trick. They could have interpreted the employment card explanation as a simple statement of fact. He was a god. Working on a building site was surely "unsuitable". Maybe they did not want to upset labourers. All the evidence seems to suggest that John the Father, would have agreed with the assessment. He believed he was destined for bigger things, and the next night John, Paul and George started playing at the place where we were now standing outside.

Above the door was, writ in large, a quotation from Dante Gabriel Rosetti: "Look in my face: My name is might-have-been; I am also called No-more, Too late, Farewell." Brother John rang the bell and we waited until the door to the main building was opened by a tall man I assumed was a member of the Best Order. I looked for signs of disappointment in his face but could see nothing definite. I detected a slight droop in the shoulders but it might have been my imagination, my expectation that he carried the burden of his failure on his shoulders. I wanted to suggest that he took the advice of Paul, the other Father, and not carry the world upon his shoulders but I got the impression that advice from that direction might not be welcomed here. In truth, he seemed quite jovial and welcomed us with a smile and bade us come into the house. The ground floor had been knocked into a large space where the Brothers and Sisters would give a lecture before taking pilgrims on a tour of the Casbah, the sacred site that lay directly below us. Brother Pete invited us to sit down in the lecture room and he told us we would soon be joined by the head of their Order, Abbot Pete, who would give us a brief talk. A few minutes later an older, stern-looking man came in and went to the lectern at the front. He put some papers on the lectern and then looked at us for a few seconds, a look of great suspicion on his face. We were followers of John the Father, so I suppose he saw us as followers of the great betrayers. He was dressed in what seemed to be the official Best Order dress of all black: black leather jacket over black crew-neck jumper. I wondered how you got to be Abbot of this order. Was it on merit, was he good at abbotting? Had he done all the training? Or was he the most disappointed, the bitterest of the order? From his words to come, it seemed it may have been the latter.

"Good morning to you all and welcome to the Holy City of Liverpool and welcome to the sacred building that you now are in. God the Father chose this very place as a new beginning for His sons. I would like to tell you two short stories. The first is of how a saint stepped in to save three young gods and Saint Stuart when they were set to start on the next stage of their Great Story. They had been chosen to go to the Holy City of Hamburg where they were to spend many nights honing to perfection the sound that would become an irresistible call to the whole world, a sound that could only have come from the very heart of God. But at this time they were missing a heartbeat. They had no drummer to provide the dynamism and rhythm so essential to their sound. So it was that they remembered Pete, the son of Mona, with his handsome, moody looks and, perhaps more importantly to them, his drum kit. Paul the Father rang him just a few days before they were due to leave and asked him if he would like to audition. A man of few words, he said, 'Yes.' And so began his important part in the Greatest Story. August thirteenth is a holy day in our Order. It is the day of the audition when Saint Pete proved his worth to the gods and was asked in hushed tones if he would like to join the group and journey into the unknown that was a faraway country and provide the heartbeat that they needed. Saint Pete did not need to think about it. He said, in his succinct way, 'Yes,' and he was in."

He stopped and looked around at us. There seemed a challenge in his look. I was not surprised. I almost choked at this interpretation of the event. As I had read it, the audition was a formality; the young gods were so desperate that as long as he had a drum kit and seemed to know which end to hold the drumsticks then he was in. As John the Father put it, "We auditioned him and he could keep one beat going for long enough, so we took him to Germany." He did not ask if there were any questions. He knew we were from a Lennonist order and therefore regarded us with some suspicion, and I could not help but feel we were in enemy territory and should tread carefully.

"The second short story is a story of the perfidy of the gods, but also a story of the triumph of the individual to overcome devastating disappointment."

John, my brother in doubts, was sat behind me and whispered, "Did he just say the perfidy of the gods? Can he say that? Does he think we don't know what it means?"

"Probably. What does it mean?"

"Betrayal, treachery."

"That's blasphemy isn't it?"

It *was* blasphemy but this was the church of the Beatles and there was no punishment for believing something contrary. There were no burnings at stakes, no blasphemers sent into exile, no gulags or religious prisoners – actually, officially, there was no such thing as blasphemy. George, Lord of the Weeping Guitars, talking about the old, failed religions in the year of our Lords 1966, asked the question why everything could not be brought out into the open. "Why is there all this stuff about blasphemy? If Christianity is as good as they say it is, it should stand up to a bit of discussion." Thus, there was no concept of blasphemy in the One True Religion. Instead, those who would have been called blasphemers in the older, wronger religions were politely ignored by the church. They were allowed to rant and rave all they liked in private but given no platform in public to discuss their contrary views. There were no martyrs in the One True Religion. The result was the growth of all these large and little offshoots. The large offshoots were the Johnnists and the Paulists, the Georgians and the Ringoists. The smaller offshoots were the Stuartites and the Milligoons and the Bests. They tended to cater to the different needs of people: artists, absurdists and the disappointed. Sometimes they overlapped and people might move from one order to another depending on where they were in their life. We were, later in our tour of the building, introduced to a former Stuartite who had come third in the annual John Moores Prize, named after the man who had not only held the exhibition in which Saint Stuart had a painting but who also bought the painting. With some of the money, Saint Stuart had bought his bass guitar and the rest is Scripture. Third place had led to nothing and the Stuartite's disappointment had led him here to the Best Order, or Third Best in his case.

After his blasphemous statement, Abbot Pete glared at us again and waited for some indignant remarks and raised hands. We looked to Brother John for some guidance. He was looking bored and even yawned, so we tried to do the same, feigning indifference.

The Abbot continued. "There is much debate as to the reasons for the treachery of the gods, but there are important lessons to be learnt in the heroic and stoic behaviour of Saint Pete in the face of these events."

As I have said there was not really any official debate. He was seen as simply filling in before the true fourth god, Ringo, appeared, but as usual I could not stop my hand going up to ask a question which was designed to upset Abbot Pete. "Wasn't the reason given that he wasn't good enough? Saint George, the patron saint of making people sound good and not very nice ties, simply couldn't work his magic and make Saint Pete sound any better, and is there not a legal document from Saint George saying he was not good enough, also that he felt he was the odd man out and didn't seem to be a true part of the group?"

Abbot Pete's face went from pale to purple in under four seconds. He thought the Best way to answer my, to him, blasphemous question was to ignore me. Frankly it was a good thing there was no such thing as blasphemy as we would have been exhausted at all the rock throwing we would have to have undertaken. I had read many accounts of the various furores surrounding what the many different religions had considered blasphemous and the threats both verbal and physical that had been thrown at any individual or organisation that had disagreed with or, God literally forbid, made fun of their particular creed. From burnings to beheadings and excommunications to condemnations. All that had been done away with by the openness at the heart of the One True Religion.

But the idea of blasphemy in the abstract survived for the simple fact that humans seemed to believe their particular version of events was correct and those who disagreed with them were presumably sent by Satan himself. Abbot Pete, therefore, ignored my blasphemy and continued with his own. "As the day of martyrdom approached…" Again he stopped and glared at us. I wanted to ask another question about the definition of martyrdom, that in the case of Saint Pete there seemed to be a certain lack of dying involved, that getting booted out of a band due to being rubbish on the drums was not really akin to martyrdom. Weirdly, he answered my unasked question. "No, Saint Pete did not die but he chose to face pain and suffering rather than give up something he held sacred."

He did not go into details but I assumed he meant that he held it to be a sacred truth that he was not a crap drummer. I could think of more noble causes to be martyred for.

"As this day approached, Saint Pete heard rumours but could not believe that the group he had been a member of for two years, through thick and thin, mainly thin but now heading towards thick, very thick, would cast him aside. He was entwined within the very essence of the Beatles, popular with their followers. The entwining included their road manager, Saint Neil, patron saint of doing things for gods. He was sleeping with his Mona, mother of Saint Pete. And Mona had just given birth to a baby brother for Saint Pete and Saint Neil was the father. Oh, perfidy, perfidy. Not one of the gods told Saint Pete to his face. Even gods can be cowards. Faced with the task they turned to Saint Brian, patron saint of managing gods and doing the dirty work of the gods."

There was a certain amount of coughing amongst the Lennonist novitiates. He had called the gods cowards! I felt a primeval urge to pick up a stone and throw it at the blasphemer but then I remembered there was no such thing as blasphemy in these enlightened times and that this was a good thing. Also, there were no stones handy. Saint Brian was an integral part of the Greatest Story, and this was the first time I had heard he was the patron saint of doing the dirty work of the gods. It was clearly an attribute only ascribed to him by the Best Order.

Abbot Pete continued. "And lo, the day of martyrdom came and Saint Pete was asked to the offices of Saint Brian, a man not to be blamed, a man who liked Pete and on this day could not look him in the eye. And he said unto Pete, with much embarrassment and with the words almost sticking in his throat as they stuck like daggers in the back of Saint Pete, 'I've got some bad news for you. The boys and myself have decided that they don't want you in the group anymore, and that Ringo is replacing you.'"

He stopped again, emphasising this moment of great treachery, eyes closed. He opened his eyes and continued. "And though his world was falling apart around him, the noble Saint Pete, in the Best style of the martyr, told Saint Brian that if the others did not want him then he would go. And so he left with Saint Neil, his good friend and kind of stepfather, who could not resist the draw of the gods and despite this treachery stayed with them for time immemorial. Were the gods jealous of Saint Pete's looks? Were they put out by his individualism, his different hair?"

My hand shot up, as if with a life of its own. "Or did they think, given Saint George's assessment of his ability, that he wasn't very good on the drums?"

"And how do you know this to be true?"

"Well, for example, when John the Father was asked many years later why they threw Saint Pete out of the band, he said, 'Because he couldn't play very well.' I would say that was simple and to the point, wouldn't you? And one more question. Was not Saint Pete offered the job as drummer in the Mersey Beats, who also went on to become quite successful, but he turned them down, which would bring into question his judgement. Wasn't it true that when he left the Beatles, he lost everything and they lost nothing and in fact gained a decent drummer?"

Well, he had annoyed me with his constant harping on about the treachery of the gods. I was a little surprised at my annoyance at these attacks on their behaviour. After all I believed I was a cynic, not a true believer, but here I was taking sides.

The Abbot took a deep breath and smiled murderously at me. He nodded to Brother Pete, who went over to an old-style record player and picked the needle up and put it down on the revolving black plastic disc. The record crackled and the Abbot and the Brother bowed their heads as if in prayer. A song started that sounded as if quite a lot of expense had been spared but it was the unmistakable sound of Merseybeat, of which the Beatles were the original gods. Gerry and the Pacemakers were their mere mortal equivalent and this, whoever this was, sounded like some gods breaking wind. The best thing about it was that it was mercifully short, but the Abbot kept his head bowed and maintained a look of blissful happiness all the way through, which frankly made me doubt his sanity or his hearing. The record finished and Brother Pete removed it and reverently put it into a cardboard sleeve. The Abbot looked slightly smug, as if he had just won an argument.

"Well, that was Saint Pete when he was in the Pete Best Four with, I'm sure you'll agree, a marvellous little number called 'Why Did I Fall in Love With You?'. Now, who wants to tell me that the drumming on this record is substandard?"

A number of hands shot up. The Abbot scowled and pointed to a young man at the front. "Yes," he almost spat.

"I just wanted to ask if the Pete Best Four were a success."

He again looked suspicious, clearly wondering if the question was asked maliciously, but the John who asked was not me and therefore asked out of genuine curiosity. The Abbot seemed to sense this and his face softened.

"Not at the time, no. True talent is not always recognised," he said with such feeling that I assumed he was now talking about himself. I wondered what his disappointment was. "Was Vincent Van Gogh recognised in his lifetime?"

There was a silence that could only be described as stunned. Comparing Saint Pete's drumming to the tortured genius of Van Gogh seemed to be a bit of a stretch to say the least. The same hand went up and he asked, again innocently as far as I could make out, "So was his work appreciated and recognised after he died?"

The Abbot frowned. "Well, not exactly. The lesson we learn from Saint Pete is that, like Van Gogh, he was initially so distraught by the treachery of the gods that he felt suicidal. But unlike Van Gogh, he pulled himself up by his bootlaces and got on with life. He watched from the sidelines as the Beatles conquered the world, which in most cases would lead a good man to turn bad or to live in constant despair. But we can see that God the Father did not forget Saint Pete, unlike his four sons who had discarded him without a thought. We can see the clues in what he did after leaving the Beatles. He decided to give up his life in show business and become associated with bread. Bread, after all, is the supreme gift from God and is a sign of the generosity of God towards man."

He did not mention that this association was loading bread into the back of delivery vans, that if this was God showing us that he had not forgotten Pete, that he was still touched by God, then the person who actually made the bread must have been a celestial being.

He continued. "And then God showed his sense of humour by directing Saint Pete, the man who had been deprived of the Best job in the world to become a man who helped others find jobs. So the man who lost his dream became the man who helped others find theirs."

This seemed to be the end of the talk. He did not mention that in Liverpool at that time, which was not the prosperous Holy City it had become since the rise of the One True Religion, there were very few jobs to offer in the proud but economically declining city, that Saint Pete would have spent much of his time telling his clients there simply were no jobs to offer, rather than offering them the job of their dreams. But it was always important to remember that the religious orders told the story they wanted to hear and therefore little things like what actually happened should never get in the way.

I put up my hand. The Abbot tried to ignore me by pretending to concentrate on collecting his papers together, so I coughed loudly.

"Yes," he said.

"I was just wondering if you thought that Saint Pete's bitterness was lessened by the millions he received later in his life recognising his work with the gods?"

It was meant as a rhetorical question but the Abbot seemed to consider it seriously. "Ah, what is money? Does not the One Truish Religion tell us that it is not important? I think all

Saint Pete was asking was to be treated with respect, to be told to his face by his erstwhile colleagues why they no longer needed him. He was not bitter in his later years. When asked what he would say to Paul the Father if they were to meet, his reply was philosophical. "We're senior statesmen now. Our time left on this planet is short. Let us talk about things in general. Let us put a bottle of scotch on the table and let us have a good old bash."

A bit like his drumming, I nearly said.

The Abbot wished us the Best for the future and hoped we would not suffer too many disappointments in life but that if we did we should always remember the example of Saint Pete, who, after his initial disappointment, lived a long and happy life. He then left, telling us he had to sift through a number of applications to join the order and had to decide whether the applicants had been disappointed enough. "You'd be surprised how disappointing some of these so-called disappointments are," he said, shaking his head. I wondered again what his own disappointment was but did not have the courage to ask.

Brother Pete gathered us together and took us downstairs to the cellar, to the "Casbah Coffee Bar", a place writ large in the Greatest Story. We followed him around the nooks and crannies of the sacred ground and he would occasionally stop and explain the significance of a particular area. He pointed to a section of the ceiling that had a now faded array of stripes painted on it and told us that they were painted by the hand of Paul the Father just before the club opened all those centuries ago. He also told us the story of how John the Father had mistakenly painted another section of the ceiling in gloss instead of matt. As stories went I had heard more thrilling; these seemed as interesting as watching the paint he seemed to find so fascinating dry.

The walls were festooned with pictures of the Beatles in their early years. There were many of Saint Pete and try as I might I could find none of Ringo, our Starr in Heaven. For obvious reasons he seemed persona non grata in this place.

My fellow novitiates looked around in awe and seemed to listen to the stories of the young gods painting with wonder in their eyes. It was amazing how a place or an object, however ordinary – or slightly drab and gloomy in this case – could take on a fascinating aura if it had been touched by the gods. Brother Pete stepped back and bade us to wander around at our own pace and take in the delights of this sacred underground place. For me, I had had my fill at looking at what was essentially, if you took off your god-tinted spectacles, a shabby old coffee bar that had only existed for three years as an actual coffee bar. It was as if it had been created specifically for the purpose of being a launchpad for the Beatles and when they left it was no longer necessary, a little like that other sacred underground place in the holy city, the Cavern. So instead I sought out Brother Pete, who was lurking unobtrusively by the entrance.

"Hello," he said. "Do you have a question?"

"I was just wondering, if you don't mind me asking, what your particular disappointment was."

I thought he might be upset. I did not know the etiquette around asking this question. It might have been a serious transgression, an unforgivable rudeness resulting in my ejection from the premises. But I could not help it. I suffered from potentially terminal curiosity. Terminal because, in my younger days I had often been told after an apparently impertinent question that curiosity killed the cat. I had secretly thought "Well, it's a good job I'm not a cat" and persisted with my enquiries. But he smiled and it seemed genuine; the eyes seemed to smile too. The truth was that people were often surprised and delighted that someone had taken an interest in them, that they were not just a person who showed people round buildings or whatever they did. So he answered me.

"Well, I was a writer. I wrote a book about young people who wanted to be famous – you know, writers, actors, poets, musicians, but they weren't quite good enough. It was a comedy and quite funny, which is quite important, you know, with comedies. I was always surprised to read novels described as comedies that didn't seem to be at all funny. Well, I don't really need to tell you the end of the story. I'm here after all. In the house of failures and nearly men and women. It's funny really, this place is full of people who think the world was wrong, unable to recognise their talent. Who knows? Maybe the world was right. The order teaches us that, although it's important to follow your dream, you can be happy without being famous, that the foundations of happiness are friends and family and being able to love yourself as well as others. You've probably noticed that the four gods are frowned upon here because of their treatment of Saint Pete, but their story is also used. It is useful to believe they were gods because it means it's useless to try to emulate them as mere mortals. Their godlike status in their times did not lead to happiness but a life that, at the height of their fame, felt like a prison, and was not fulfilling in itself."

"Will you stay here forever?"

"Oh, no. Not many do. There are a few who never get over their bitter disappointment. Abbot Pete is one. I don't know the nature of his disappointment. It is the subject of earnest debate amongst the Brothers and Sisters. There are rumours he has a set of drums in his sleeping quarters, some say he was thrown out of a band, others say that it is something he keeps as a tribute to the saint he loves. Certainly, no one has heard him play the drums. Some even say he was in line to be the Beatle Pope. But most people leave after a couple of years; they move on to different things or go back to the thing they loved before but with less expectations. I feel ready to move on. I've even started writing again. I realised I missed it, it gave me a purpose. I just don't expect to be the next big thing anymore. Saint Pete seemed a decent enough bloke but he didn't have much to say, so there's not much to study. He really just gives the example of a very disappointed person who gets over it and leads a happy and fulfilled life, eventually going back to being a drummer in his own band and touring the world. There's intensive counselling here which is useful. Some of us were suicidal when we arrived but, you know, we soon realise that being bitter and angry and disappointed all the time is exhausting. Our disappointment is a bit like a bereavement, and we are taught to go through similar stages and usually after a couple of years we're ready to move on."

"And you're ready?"

"Yes, I think so. As I say, I'm writing again. It's a novel about a group of people who have been disappointed in life who find themselves in a community of disappointed people who come to realise that their disappointments are just a part of life and help each other to move on." He laughed when he saw my face. "Well, they say write about what you know."

"And if it is unsuccessful?"

"Then I will remember all the lessons I've learned here. That failure is just a part of life, nothing to be ashamed of, something to learn from and move on, that if you haven't failed in life you've probably never tried to do anything. And I can always come back here."

He winked. After the suppressed anger of the Abbot, he was a breath of fresh air, and I felt that this was a good place, a useful place, that the Greatest Story seemed to provide a place for everyone.

What he had not mentioned was that because of the nature of the gods, their divine creativity, the society that emerged from the One True Religion encouraged creativity. I have already mentioned the important positions of the Art Schools, the encouragement of the fine arts, but other areas of creativity were encouraged and supported by the government and the church. The most sacred area of activity was of course the creation of music, but the Beatles spread their touch to other areas. John the Father had three books published, so writing was also seen as a semi-divine activity. Brother Pete may well have gone to the writing schools set up to provide a place for writers to gather, learn from each other and their tutors and to write. Or he may have attended one of the religious orders dedicated to the writings of John the Father, such as the Order of the Spaniard in the Works or the Skywriters. As well as studying his works, they were also places where budding religiously devoted writers tended to go to write. After leaving the schools and religious orders, grants were available for writers to continue their writing on production of evidence of a manuscript. Of course, all of this meant that there were a lot of books produced and there was no guarantee that the buying public would want to read any of it. Often, the stories were ill-disguised autobiographies of the writers, who thought their lives and thoughts interesting enough to write about. Sometimes they were, but more often, they were not. Sometimes the uninteresting lives were saved by the skill of the writer, who could write in beautiful prose or in a way that made you laugh. The most popular were escapist fantastical tales with monsters and humans with magical powers or supernatural beings that were sometimes good or sometimes bad. Writing had been democratised. If you wanted to write then you could and do nothing else for five or six years with the blessing and support of the church and the state. Not everyone wanted to be published; for some it was a process they went through before moving on to something else. Every book written at the special schools or religious orders would be made into a solid hardcopy book, but whether it would end up simply as another book in their growing libraries or published for public consumption would be decided by the committees of those institutions – an unsatisfactory method that tended towards the pushing of more conservative texts, but no worse than the more traditional method of pot luck that some agent or publishing house might pick up your work. Brother Pete told me he had tried both with no luck. I wondered if what he wrote was literary gold or just plain rubbish. If all the people supposedly in the know, in the business, were telling you no, perhaps you should take up something else to pay the bills.

I did not tell him my thoughts or suggest he take up plumbing, but instead I wished Brother Pete the best of luck and made my way to the exit. Brother John was calling us to gather together. We were going to the next sacred spot.

# Chapter Twelve
## The Holy Trinity of Disappointment

---

We all climbed back into the minibus. Most of the others seemed deep in contemplation, as they often were when they had visited a holy place, especially a place connected to John the Father. It was a place where he had once stood, had once played his holy instrument and sipped coffee. It was often an emotional moment for them to stand where gods had once stood. I sat down next to John in our seat and we said nothing but glanced at each other and raised our eyebrows, which said a thousand words. Brother John took us into the centre of the holy city and we found a car park, which I assumed was also holy, being in the holy city, but I did not ask, not wanting to sound facetious. We clambered out and followed Brother John, who was looking at a street map. Our destination was a secret. Brother John just looked enigmatic when asked where we were going. This being the holy city there were a lot of holy sites.

We walked for ten minutes through the immaculately clean streets, kept spotless by the devotion of the followers of the four gods, which seemed slightly ironic as the few pictures I had seen of the holy city in the time of the Gods were decidedly dark and dingy and a little rundown, the only life in them, or so I imagined, brought by the wit and energy of the people. Some called them the chosen race; others simply called them Scousers.

They were a nomadic group of people who had often been forced into exile by the lack of opportunity in their place of birth. Liverpool, a once great seaport driven to despair by bombs from abroad and neglect from the government at home. One of the famous demons sent from the devil to sow despair and discord in the country of the four gods had become prime minister of the United Kingdom. She was a demon who had stood on the steps of Downing Street and had told the unsuspecting nation that where there was harmony she would create discord, where there was truth she would bring lies and where there was hope she would endeavour to bring despair, and unlike most politicians in the age before the coming of the One True Religion, she kept her word. Indeed, during her reign, things had gotten so bad that the people rioted in parts of the Holy City, particularly Toxteth. She sent one of the few saints in her Cabinet of Grotesques, Saint Michael, a man who was later to bring her down, who argued for massive investment in the declining city. But Thatcher, the demon of greed and inequality, laughed and said, "Let us say no more, but I think we will let this city decline. They after all refuse to vote for me."

There is also the tale in Scripture of the husband of the demon prime minister, a man said to come from a long line of goblins, who went by the name of Denis, of the time when Paul, the other Father, was invited to Downing Street to a party with other notables. Scripture tells us that "Denis perused the list with his goblin eyes and they fell upon the name of Paul the Father. 'No, no, no and thrice no,' he said to his minions, much displeased. 'Strike his name off and this man too,' he said, seeing the name of Saint David of the natural world, an Attenborough by name. 'They have criticised my wife, they must not be given the honour of a visit. But make sure this man comes,' he said. He was pointing to the name of Rolf Harris, a renowned ogre from the underworld, who had earlier inveigled himself into the world of our gods, who was later, after the reign of the demon was over, to be arrested on charges of sexually abusing young girls."

And so the city was left to rot for years and the chosen ones did not feel very chosen, and many left to create a diaspora of Scousers around the country and around the world. They were often demonised as thieves and chancers. In the time of the emergence of the One True Religion, but before it came to dominate the world, the Scouse people were seen as a threat by the old religions and some governments and myths grew up against them, that they sacrificed children, that the very nature of the Scouser was immutable and destructive, an alien presence that grew in the midst of the host nation like a parasite. In some nations, all the ills and problems of the country were, ridiculously, blamed on the Scousers. Some even passed laws against them, often using a famous forgery, 'The Concords of the Elders of Merseyside', a plainly made-up load of rubbish purporting to be evidence of a worldwide conspiracy of the Scousers desire to take over the world. There were even attempts to taint the Scousers by saying the murderer of John the Father, was a Scouser, despite him being born in Fort Worth, Texas, and having no connection to Liverpool. Such was the madness of the times before the coming of the One True Religion, when hate seemed an easier answer to love and understanding and peace.

The most famous exiles, of course, were the gods themselves. John in New York, Ringo in Los Angeles, George in Henley-On Thames and Paul in London and Rye. Since the rise of the One True Religion, the tendency for the Scousers to move away to find more opportunities had completely reversed. The house prices in the holy city rocketed, as many tried to move there, many just to have their child born in the sacred perimeters of Liverpool. There has also grown up an industry around the teaching of how to speak in the Scouse vocabulary and accent. Children with accents which were once seen as posh from the south of England are now sent to elocution lessons to try and speak in the language and the voice of the gods.

We had been walking for about ten minutes through the pristine streets, listening to the conversations of the locals on our way, always excited to hear the sacred Scouse tones, of which there was a wide range, from pleasantly musical to completely undecipherable, when Brother John stopped by a street sign which told us we were in Slater Street.

He pointed to it and asked, "Anybody know the significance of this street?"

Everybody knew. Many hands went up. It was the subject of a religious song that told the tale of the early years of the Beatles. In tribute to the work of John and Paul, the Fathers, who had written about the places of Liverpool in Penny Lane and Strawberry Fields, there had grown up a canon of religious songs about the significant places they had been associated with. This street and the song were called "Slater Street". Like "Penny Lane", the song referenced businesses that were there at the time of the gods, such as the line "On the corner is Billy Gunn's selling beer and wine/ And further down is a watchmakers once upon a time." It was this former watchmaker's shop that was the focus of the song and the place we were heading towards.

Brother John pointed at a student John. "It's the street where the Jacaranda is located, a coffee bar opened in 1958 and owned by Saint Allan of Bootle, patron saint of giving gods away. It's part of the Greatest Story because John the Father would visit there, often with Saint Stuart, and they would end up playing there and Saint Allan would become their first manager. I think Scripture says 'And Saint Allan met John the Father and Saint Stuart while they were at the art school and so he set them a task that involved painting and was so impressed that it was the beginning of his short but important association with them.'"

My hand was still up. Brother John smiled and nodded towards me.

"I think the task was painting the ladies' toilet," I said innocently. "And apparently he thought they did a terrible job," I added.

There were a few frowns. The more devout novitiates thought I was being facetious, suggesting that a god might have to paint a toilet. And also how could he do a bad job? We had by now arrived at the entrance to the Jacaranda, now converted to be part museum, part place of worship. We were escorted around the building by a curator and ended up in yet another cellar where there was a sermon in progress. There was a man at the front on the stage reading from Scripture.

"And so the Beatles asked Saint Allan, who had come to like them – for who could not resist the charm of the gods? – 'Will you be our manager?' And Saint Allan replied that he would be honoured to be their manager and set about finding them work to spread their words and songs." He paused and shut the Holy Book. "And he did indeed find them work around the Holy City of Liverpool, including the sacred ground you are now sitting in, the cellar of the Jacaranda, and also gave them their first taste of a tour outside Liverpool with a trip to Scotland supporting Johnny Gentle all in the year of our Lords 1960." He opened the Holy Book again. "And so in the summer, in the year of our Lords 1960, Alan Williams, a small man destined for smallness, found the three gods and one saint a variety of work. He was a vessel of God but not touched by the divine vision of the man who was to take his place, the man who believed in his heart that Elvis was just the Baptist, and that the Beatles were the direct descendants of God in heaven. Saint Allan even persuaded the four to play at a club he owned with the nobleman Lord Woodbine of Trinidad, now known as Saint Harold, patron saint of calypso. Here they performed with Saint Janice, patron saint of those who make gods blush. They played their instruments and she removed her clothes in an ancient rite performed for a strange group of men who were from a tribe known as the Perverts, who for these occasions would dress in their traditional garb of dirty raincoats. God in heaven was not pleased with Saint Allan for making his sons blush. He cursed him and let him become one of the Holy Trinity of Disappointment along with Saint Pete and Saint Dick, the patron saint of massive misjudgements. He was to later whisper in the ear of His sons that it was time to move on."

He again paused and shut the book. "We are told, then, that he displeased God by not recognising that they were gods destined for greatness and by making them play with a stripper, but he was made a saint to acknowledge his vital role in the Greatest Story.

"It was early August when the next big thing happened in their story, the next step in their inexorable climb to world domination, and it was all down to Saint Allan. They were in the Holy City of Liverpool when the call came through that would eventually send them to the Second Holy City of Hamburg."

# Chapter Thirteen
## The Holy City of Hamburg

We were back in class. It was the next day. There were eight of us sitting facing the front, eight Johns. The ninth member of our class, Johann, was standing at the front, looking nervous but pleased with himself. Brother John was sitting to his right in his teacher's swivel chair, waiting for us to settle down. When he had our full attention he announced, "You all know Johann, and you all know he is from the Holy City of Hamburg. Yesterday we visited two sacred sites that were touched by the feet and sound of John the Father and we heard about the role of Saint Allan. We all know the next part of the Greatest Story, and I thought it would be nice for a native of the second holiest City to introduce us to the time that our Lord John spent there."

He nodded to Johann. Johann shuffled some papers and coughed nervously. He was a tall young man in classic second year Lennonary clothes of a suede jacket over a black polo neck jumper, his blonde hair shoulder length and brushed forward in the style of the devoted. Outwardly, he was all coldly orthodox, the perfectly devout novitiate. But in a candid conversation one day, I'd learned he had a troubled past.

As a teenager he had been wild, a non-believer, scoffing at the teachings of the One True Religion. His mother had died when he was young of a rare form of cancer, one of the few types we had not found a cure for, his father descending into despair and drink as a result, so most of the safeguards of the egalitarian society that had emerged had not helped him. Johann had gone off the rails in his pain and anger at the world. It had all ended in a serious suicide attempt. The long sleeves of his polo neck jumper hid the hideous scars that were a constant reminder of his former life. While in hospital recovering, he was visited by a member of a strict Johnnist religious order and became a born again Johnnist. It was not a great leap for him to see the parallels between his and John the Father's painful childhood. He explained to me that he had been saved by John. John the Father was seen by this order as the God of Sin, sent by God to show that we were not perfect, that it was human to err, but that we could always redeem ourselves, we just had to try to be better people. This order also believed that John died for his and our sins, that his murder was the cleaning of the slate if we were just to allow John into our life. From the moment that Johann took John into his life he believed that all his sins were cancelled and he could start anew. Thus he believed he was offered salvation from his past mistakes and the longer he walked in the path of John he was offered present salvation, that he grew in holiness and finally he would be offered a place in Beatle Heaven so his future was also saved. I did not say, but it sounded like the ravings of a lunatic to me, though it seemed to work for him. He had gone from a life of reckless, nihilistic self-destruction to a life of quiet contemplation. A life in which he did no harm and a little good. Who was I to destroy that? In his new way of thinking, his mother was safe and happy in Beatle Heaven, waiting for him to join her when he had finished his time on earth. Of course, like a lot of religious types he did not dwell on the question of why the gods had taken his mother so early and so painfully in the first place.

He removed his glasses so he could read his notes better and began. "As I'm sure you know, I come from the Holy City of Hamburg. It is, indeed, known as the second holy city after Liverpool. Why so holy? Well, it is the place where the Beatles played the most times apart from Liverpool. It is where they honed their skills, perfected their music, shouted and sang their message, where they lived and loved and fooled around as young gods will do before becoming older, more mature gods, ready to take on the world and win. It is known by some as the Playground of the Gods. Here the three gods met the missing piece of the puzzle, the fourth god, who would sit in for the first time whenever Saint Pete was not around. It was here that Saint Stuart returned to his first true calling, his art, met his true love and died his true death, all essential elements of the Greatest Story. It was in Hamburg that the gods made their first record, which allowed God to send one of His angels, a young man by the name of Raymond, into a record shop in Liverpool, where he asked a man who we now know as Saint Brian, patron saint of managing deities, about a record called 'My Bonnie'.

"It is the city of my birth, the city where I lost my way and the city where I was saved. I was lost and then I was found, I was alone and then I was not alone. I had found John the Father and I was born again. John had whispered into my ear the word. He let me know that in the beginning, I had misunderstood, but now I understood that the word was good. The 'word' was, of course, love. Brother John has asked me to read from scripture the passage that describes the moment that marked the beginning of their time in Hamburg.

"'And so it was in August, in the year of our Lords 1960, when the young gods were beginning to despair of their future, that a call came through to Saint Allan that would set them on the path to greater things. The call was from Germany, from Bruno of Hamburg, a man like Saint Allan, who owned establishments that entertained the people with music and pleasure. "I need something special for my new place of worship," he told Saint Allan. Saint Allan, not a man to say no to a business deal, replied, "Not to worry, my German friend, I have something very special in mind for you." And not long thereafter, the three gods and Saint Stuart acquired Saint Pete to play the drums and found themselves with Saint Allan and his noble friend Lord Woodbine ready to set forth to a new and exciting world.'"

Johann gathered his papers together and shuffled back to his seat.

Brother John stood up and seemed to gather his thoughts. "And so John the Father, still only nineteen years of age, was on the verge of a great adventure, one day seemingly going nowhere, the next day given a week to get ready to go to a foreign land thousands of miles away. What could stop him?"

A smile played on his lips, so I knew he was thinking about his favourite subject. I put my hand up and said simply, "Aunt Mimi."

"Yes. She knew John was special, had known since the day she had set eyes upon him in the hospital. What she did not know was that the source of that specialness was the very guitar she hated and thought was the barrier that was blocking his true path. One of the gospels has her on her knees begging John not to go and refusing to give her consent, which was needed as he was still considered a minor. At that point I am certain that if asked, she would have laughed and said, 'Messiah? No, he's a very naughty boy!' And so against the wishes of his stern aunt, John the Father was determined to go on this trip of destiny, knew his destiny lay with his guitar, and stormed out of the house on Menlove Avenue on that fateful morning in the middle of August 1960. He went to the passport office and pleaded with the official that with a dead mother and an absent father how could he possibly get adult consent? There is now a statue to that official in the Holy City of Liverpool we all know as the 'unknown bureaucrat'. We assume now that God the Father was guiding his hand when he handed the precious passport over to a jubilant young god. And so three gods and a number of saints set off from the Holy City of Liverpool in a humble minibus of questionable roadworthiness to Hamburg, sailing from Harwich on what has become the famous pilgrimage journey made by millions of the devout, arriving in the Holy City of Hamburg two days later. Can you describe the Holy City of your birth, Johann?"

"Yes, it is not unlike Liverpool, a port city, now with gleaming spires, clean streets and everywhere you look a sacred place where the Beatles touched. The religious centre is based in the St Pauli district, where there are now two huge cathedrals and one religious order on the sites of the clubs where they played: the Indra, the Kaiserkeller, the Top Ten and the Star Club. Walking down Grosse Freiheit is a similar experience to walking down Matthew Street, you can feel the presence of heaven in the very air."

Brother John nodded. "I have made the pilgrimage, I have been there. It does have the feel of the divine, but... was it always so? What did the gods behold when they tumbled out of the minibus on August seventeenth?"

"Good John, no," Johann replied, smiling. "The young gods had arrived in the Reeperbahn, in the year of our Lords 1960. It was not the holy place of worship and meditation visited by millions of pilgrims today. It was known as 'the most sinful mile', the centre of Hamburg's nightlife, where every kind of entertainment was provided. There were restaurants, nightclubs and many bars but also strip clubs, sex shops and brothels. It was haunted by gangsters, prostitutes, pimps and thieves. John the Father said later that He may have been born in Liverpool but He grew up in Hamburg. It was a place seen as separate from the rest of Hamburg, a place where respectable German parents warned their children to avoid."

"And how did the Beatles feel about their new home for the next two months?"

"Well, Brother John, it is one of the reasons I love the One True Religion. The gods cared for all types of people, not just those who saw themselves as righteous. As George, Lord of the Weeping Guitars, told us, 'Everybody around that district were homosexuals, pimps, hookers, and it was good fun.' Those rejected and vilified by the many were accepted by the gods. There were no sinners and no righteous in their eyes, just people. There is, of course, the famous story of John our Father, who on a day off from performing in the Indra, where they played six nights a week, came across a small crowd who were haranguing a woman in a street. They were jeering and moving closer as if to strike her, some had weapons in their hands. John the Father, young though He was, stopped and intervened, asking what was going on. He was told the woman was a prostitute who had wandered out of the red light district into their respectable district and they did not want her polluting where they lived. John stood in front of the terrified woman, holding up His hands, protecting her. The crowd slowly quietened and they stood, still angry, but waiting for Him to speak. When they had stopped their curses, He spoke into the silence. 'Fine, let those among you that have committed no sins strike the first blow, I know I cannot,' he said. The small crowd at first reacted angrily but then, shaking their heads, slowly dispersed, knowing the young man from another land had spoken the truth. He then escorted the woman back to a place where she would be safe."

He finished speaking. He had that look that the devout had when their devotion transported them to another place, a place I had never found, his shining eyes and saintly smile telling me he was in that place reserved for angels or idiots depending on your point of view. I had heard the story many times before and read about it in the Holy Book, but could find no reference to it in the history books. I wanted to ask in what language had he spoken to this German mob but knew I would get patronising looks that would suggest that God speaks all languages and would have passed his linguistic skills on to His favourite son (though of course, He had no favourites). The Holy Book also did not mention the name of the god, vagueness being the ally of religion, and the different orders tended to believe it was their favourite deity who had assisted the sex worker. At the Lennonary it was assumed it was John the Father. I believed he was certainly the most likely to have come across a sex worker, but not necessarily in the role of saviour.

Brother John carried on from where Johann had left off. "And so the gods and saints found themselves in this den of iniquity and made themselves at home amongst the so-called sinners, the prostitutes and the pimps and the gangsters and thieves. And did they live in the lap of luxury?"

It was like a double act, a call and response between Brother John and Johann.

"No, they were initially given no accommodation, but after some discussion with Bruno Koschmider, their new employer, he allowed them to stay at the back of the Bambi, a little cinema he leased. It was not the lap of luxury. It was a pigsty, a hovel, a hole, a dump. There were two rooms which had been used for storage. A dump which was accompanied by the sweet smell of the cinema toilets next door, which they had to use as their bathroom. This was their home for the next two months. They were living in a pit, they were playing in Koschmider's second, smaller venue, but it was a chance to hone their playing and singing, six nights a week, six, sometimes eight, hours a night. The spark was already there, Hamburg was where the flame ignited."

We could hear the pride in his voice when he spoke of his home city as if the very air of the place had contributed to the sound of the gods, had nourished them and turned them into the prophets they would become. I did not say, but I certainly thought that many other acts had played there. Some went on to become famous, others disappeared into obscurity – only the Beatles conquered the world, and if they were divine then surely they would have done so whatever their history. But I understood that we humans love a story, that storytelling was a fundamental part of being human, and the Beatles were a great story, especially if you did not always let the truth get in the way. It was a narrative with a beginning and an end, heroes and villains, romance, happy endings and tragedy. Stories allowed us to pretend we had some sort of control over the world, to see patterns where there was chaos, meaning where there is randomness. That was essentially what religion did for us, so it was not a surprise to me that the story, the Greatest Story, was so central to the One True Religion.

"It was here the young gods forged their bonds. In such close quarters they would either end up with ties that bound them together or an explosion would occur that would shatter them into a thousand pieces. We know, of course, it was the former. There was, however, an outsider in this tight-knit little group of five. Saint Pete was not always to be found with the other four, leaving them to do his own thing, quietly, as ever. And Saint Stuart always knew he would leave the others, to go back to his true love of painting. There was also the fact of Paul, the other Father's, niggling attitude towards him. He knew he could not withstand the jealousy and wrath of this determined young god." Brother John paused and looked at Johann. I wondered if they had actually rehearsed. "Were the Beatles an immediate success?"

"No, Brother John, but they built up a following and were soon too big and too good for the Indra club. Note the name

– the Indra was an ancient Vedic deity. It is seen by many as yet another sign, a hint, from God the Father of the true nature of the Beatles. Indra killed the great symbol of evil, Vritra, who stood in the way of human prosperity and happiness. Look at us now in the time of the One True Religion, as prosperous and content as humans can be."

I put up my hand. I had been quiet too long, and it was time for some mischief. "Is it not also true that they had to move because an old woman who lived upstairs at the Indra complained about the noise?"

Brother John smiled as usual and Johann answered. "It is said an angel in disguise was sent to encourage Koschmider in his decision to move the Beatles to his bigger club, the Kaiserkeller. But they had earned their move. Their music, their charisma and one can only assume their divinity had meant that they had seen the formation of their first following, young men and women who saw something in them that would soon be repeated on a worldwide scale. Not only were they moved to the Kaiserkeller, but they were offered an extension to their contract."

The Story again. An angel? Why had God sent an angel? Why could he not just have directed Bruno Koschmider to let them play at the Kaiserkeller from the start? It was the Story. They were young and fresh and needed to prove themselves, to go from having no fans to a small following. From the Indra to the Kaiserkeller. They were getting better, edging towards greatness, a small move from one crappy basement to another. If you wanted to see it as divine destiny then it was easy to do so. But all successes would start from small beginnings and reach the heights; it was only in hindsight that it would seem like destiny. But even I had to admit, it *was* a good story.

It was Johann's turn again. Brother John seemed to provide the facts and Johann the religious context. "And so the gods and saints had spent forty-eight days in the wilderness; the Indra had been far away from the bright lights and the other entertainments. They had played there and fasted, living mainly off cornflakes, still considered by some to be the food of the gods. Now they were to come in from the wilderness, and on the fourth of October in the year of our Lords 1960 they played their first night in the Kaiserkeller. And it was here that, as the Holy Book says, 'Amidst a Storm and a Hurricane two worlds collided and the three gods met, for the first time, another god, the fourth piece in the puzzle. A Starr had travelled from Liverpool, guided by the hand of God, and from that day forth, though he did not know it, it was clearly written in the Starrs – Saint Pete's days were numbered and with Saint Stuart's mind more and more returning to his art, the band of gods and saints was not far from becoming exclusively a place for divine beings only." He paused, his eyes ablaze with holy fervour and pride in his holy city. "And so the three gods, born in the Holy City of Liverpool, were forged in the Holy City of Hamburg amongst the downtrodden and rejected of society, and it was here the three became four. A truly fabulous four."

Brother John added, "It is, of course, interesting to note that they were called fabulous even in their own time. Many took the term fab to mean they were extraordinary, extremely good, which of course they were, but it is obvious now that the second meaning also applied, was a clue that even in their own time people subconsciously knew they were more than human, fabulous meaning fabled, legendary, mythological… and it was in the Kaiserkeller that the gods were destined to meet more saints, German saints, that were to also shape their destiny."

This time, Johann read from the Holy Book. "This is from the Conversion of Saint Klaus. 'And following an argument with his beloved, Saint Klaus decided to wander the streets of Hamburg and found he was being guided by a spirit, a force beyond his understanding, until he found himself outside a place of entertainment. It was a place this sensitive young artist would normally have avoided, but having been drawn there by a strange guiding hand, he was now held to the spot by the sound of music emanating from the cellar below. He hesitated, determined to move on, to return home, but he found he was continually drawn back to the entrance of the building from which that exciting sound came. Despite his misgivings, he plucked up his courage and descended the stairs. Saint Klaus sat transfixed in a corner watching the group on the stage. He was particularly impressed with the drummer. A light seemed to shine upon him, he seemed a Starr in the making, different from the others. He enjoyed the music but was aware that this was not the music that had drawn him into the Kaiserkeller in the first place. He discovered he was watching Rory Storm and the Hurricanes, who would take it in turns with the other group during the night. And then the other band appeared and a light was turned on in the mind of Saint Klaus; he had indeed seen the light and, more importantly, now heard the sound. "When I saw them I was left speechless," he said years later. It was the start of a long relationship between the German saint and the English gods.'"

Johann looked up from the Holy Book. "And this is the famous notion of the Hamburgene moment, which comes from this time of Saint Klaus undergoing his famous conversion on a road in Hamburg. As the scripture says, 'As he sat there a light from heaven flashed around him and he heard a voice say "Klaus, Klaus, why do you not believe in us?" and Saint Klaus, fearful at first, replied, "'Who are you?" "We are the Beatles, now get up and go into the city and tell the world of the wonders you have seen." And so Saint Klaus, filled with his new mission to spread the word, went out into the night, a night that now seemed new and filled with possibilities and he knew the first person he must tell us was his love, Saint Astrid. He made his way to her house with wings on his feet, arriving there in no time and awaking her from her slumber. She was annoyed at first as it was late. "Are you crazy, ringing the bell at this time of night?" she said when she saw who it was at the door. But she saw the new zeal in the eyes of this usually taciturn young man and was moved by his words and the emotion in his voice. And so the next night Saint Klaus, Saint Astrid and a third saint, Jurgen, patron saint of looking French and hip, made their way to the Kaiserkeller and joined the sailors and prostitutes and gangsters and pimps in the audience, and the two new young people were also converted, and it was a sign that all who saw and heard the Beatles, no matter their background, would eventually love them.'"

Johann closed the Holy Book and put it down. He looked up at the class. "And I myself had a similar Hamburgene moment when lying in a hospital bed in that very city, visited by a follower of John the Father, and it is true that on that day I felt John was in the room, and so I let him into my life and have been guided by his positive energy ever since."

I wanted to ask whether he had been given some powerful medication at the time, whether he had also seen a Plasticine porter with a looking glass tie, but did not. There was always that central question for me that if the One True Religion was essentially harmless, in fact, seemed to create a better world, what did it matter if it was all made up nonsense? Religions of the past had faltered because of their lack of tolerance, that if a particular tenet was divinely commanded then there could be no argument, as it was literally the word of God, whereas the One True Religion made tolerance one of its central tenets and did not want to kill everyone who disagreed with them, did not call people infidels, heathens or kafirs. Many of the rules of the different religions were often based on the perceived needs of the times and look, in retrospect, insane. There was an obsession with sex: no masturbation, no sex before marriage, no contraception. With sex as a major driving force of human behaviour, this made no logical sense. The One True Religion made no rules; you just had to be an adult and consenting and you could do what you liked. The fact that the One True Religion came about through a desire to build a new peaceful world after centuries of war and disease had wiped out half the population of the world meant that many of the tenets had the aim of creating peace between peoples and nations and then maintaining that peace. They had, either through luck or foresight, been light on the methods but firm on the outcomes, which meant that although the aim of peace was always central, the methods could be adapted to a changing world, thereby bypassing the problems of the old religions, which were over-prescriptive and soon became ridiculous and outdated.

Johann seemed lost in a reverie, presumably thinking back to the moment of his conversion, his Hamburgene experience when his life changed forever. Brother John took up the narrative. "And so the three German saints soon became close friends to the divine visitors from Liverpool. Indeed, there is some debate as to their exact nature as John the Father described them as 'Stuart's angel friends'. Angel or saint, Astrid and Stuart soon found that they were in love with each other and it was time for Saint Stuart to leave the Beatles and go back to his art. 'I've loved before but never so tenderly and intensely,' he wrote of his love for Astrid. And it was time for the Beatles to leave the second holy city and return to the first. Bruno Koschmider, who was never made a saint despite his association with the gods, had had enough of their rebellious ways, which included leaving him and going to work for Saint Eckhorn, patron saint of offering gods better places to play, so called because he was a Peter and there seemed to be growing list of Saint Peters and it was frankly getting a little confusing. So they were given notice to leave, stating the reason as being that George, Lord of the Weeping Guitars, was under eighteen. And so the Beatles had to leave Hamburg, first George, then Paul and Pete, until only one god was left: John the Father, who left in December, with little money and only His precious guitar and amp for company.

"He arrived back in the Holy City of Liverpool on December eighth, a fateful day in the calendar of our Lord. He was penniless and disheartened. Where would He go?"

I knew he could not keep her out of the story for long. I raised my hand and said simply, "Mimi's?"

"Yes. It was at night, the lights were out when John arrived back at Mendips, and the young god, who had left a teenager and returned a man, had to throw stones up at His aunt's bedroom window until she eventually came down, and although she would have put on a stern face to greet her wayward nephew, her heart would have been glad and full of love to see Him again, returned to her, for where else could He go?"

Brother John paused, seemed in the same reverie when he spoke of Saint Mimi as Johann when he thought of his conversion. Then he looked up and continued. "It was a time of reflection for John the Father. He may have grown up in Hamburg but He returned with nothing, having lived in squalor and been surrounded by seediness during His time there. So He spent a week in contemplation, with Saint Mimi encouraging Him to be sensible for once in His life. He was waiting for a sign. He asked himself, 'Is this it? I thought hard about whether I should continue.' He did not even contact the other gods. And so He sat in His room and thought and thought. He continued to wait for a sign. As we now know this was known as the Time of Doubt, as John the Father said, revealing His own knowledge of His true religious nature, 'I just withdrew. You see, part of me is a monk and part of me is a performing flea.' We now use John's example to show that to doubt is a part of being human. It is not a sign of weakness but a sign of our humanity. Of course, there was only going to be one outcome, the sign came and the decision was made to carry on. Saint Mimi was to be disappointed. The world was not."

I wanted to ask if John's doubts showed us that if it was only human to doubt, surely if he was a god he would have no doubts and therefore his doubts brought that divinity into question. If to doubt was to be human then surely he was a human and not a god. I did not. I believed the response would have been shock followed by a volley of stones in my direction. Given my aversion to pain and desire not to be stoned to death I kept my question to myself.

"And so John the Father contacted the other gods and told them He had received a sign and that they were destined to reach the toppermost of poppermost and Saint Neil, patron saint of looking after gods, declared to the holy city that the gods had returned by printing a poster that read simply 'The Return of the Fabulous Beatles'. We were there recently and it was the hallowed ground of the Casbah that they made their first appearance since their return from Hamburg. And the people noticed they were good. Very good. They had returned from Hamburg transformed, something to behold, something to take notice of. The Second Holy City had played its part but we must remember other groups from Liverpool went there and were not so transformed. It was the combination of the time spent in Hamburg and the magic of the gods that meant upon their return the people came to see them and were now transfixed by their sound, by their appearance, by their very presence. Usually the people would come to dance whoever the group were that happened to be playing, and now when the Beatles played they stopped what they were doing and found they were drawn by an irresistible force to the stage to watch the young gods. The year of our Lords 1960 ended with them playing in the Litherland Town Hall, now a cathedral to the One True Religion, and it is said a miracle happened here. To quote Scripture:

"And the young people came from miles around to see out the old year and bring in the new year. But all this was forgotten when the curtains opened and they beheld the Beatles. Although they did not realise it they were indeed seeing out the old and bringing in the new.'"

# An Interlude
## The Cellar of Cellars

It was lunchtime. Brother John had told us we were to return to the second holy city in the afternoon, as the Beatles had returned in April in the year of our Lords 1961. I did not feel like any macrobiotic mush so I set off for my favourite spot, the bench by the lake that John the Father was said to have walked upon by those that believed in that type of thing. I had once seen a picture of him with his Lady Yoko in a boat on the lake. There seemed to be no photographs of him on the lake boatless. To stave off my hunger pangs I had picked up a couple of apples, the sacred fruit of the One True Religion. They were particularly sacred as they were Granny Smiths, the apple chosen by the gods to represent their organisation, which was doomed to failure for being ahead of its time and ignoring the contemporary mores of the serpent that was capitalism. I took a bite and hoped that I would attain the wisdom it was said to impart. I waited a moment but still felt fairly dim so I took one of the books that was frowned upon by the order from my bag, put it inside the covers of an orthodox text and opened it.

It was perhaps an unnecessary precaution. It was now late autumn; the days were becoming cooler and the dark clouds above threatened rain so I was unlikely to be joined by any of my colleagues. The truth was I quite liked the intrigue. The reading of the forbidden texts in the hallowed grounds of Tittenhurst added a thrill to what was an extremely thrill-lacking existence. I liked the ritual of finding a secluded spot and hiding my forbidden reading matter in the pages of Holy Scripture. Remember, the One True Religion was a tolerant one. The worst that could happen would be that I would be asked to leave the Lennonary; there were no gulags in this world. Rather than being sent into exile I would be sent into the world, expected to do something useful, the worst punishment the disapproving and disappointed looks that would have sent me packing from the Order of John the Father.

The book I was reading was not particularly controversial. It was merely unofficial, not recommended by the church. I had had a drunken conversation with the other sceptical John in our class the evening before, on this very bench, with a bottle of wine. We had discussed the importance of cellars in the Greatest Story. We had visited the Casbah and the Jacaranda in the Holy City and we knew about the Indra and there was also the most famous cellar of all, now the site of a sacred church in the Holy City of Liverpool. The church acknowledged the importance of cellars, had made most of those touched by the gods places of worship, had even built some new churches underground, but I could not find in any of the texts the *significance* of this fact, that the formative years of the gods had been spent playing in cellars. We had argued back and forth about the meaning of these subterranean beginnings. I passionately argued, as a person can only passionately argue about something they do not really care about when they have finished a bottle of wine, that it signified not the literal meaning of underground but the political one, that of a movement secretly organised to work against an existing regime.

The other John scoffed at this, arguing that it was hardly secret, that if it was a secret why did they put up posters advertising where they would be playing? He then put forward his idea that there was a psychological element. That it was a representation of the inner room that lay beneath the surface of our normal ideas. The Beatles were about to make changes on the world and you needed to be taken underground to make the changes to those structures and beliefs; it was a way of communicating that the old way of doing things had to be re-examined in order to make way for the new world to come.

I laughed out loud, and after a while he joined in. "You don't really believe that, do you?" I said.

He shook his head. "You started it," he said. "'They were an underground political movement,'" he said mimicking my earlier statement in the voice of a pompous buffoon.

"'They represent the need to go underneath your house to find the things that you buried in order to make a new society,'" I said in a high-pitched lady's voice. "And it's where we keep the wine."

"I don't speak like that."

"Well, you started it. I don't sound like a pompous buffoon."

"You do. There was a survey of all the novitiates and you came out top as the number one pompous buffoon."

"Did I? How come I didn't get a vote?"

"Because I just made it up, you berk. You'll believe anything."

"Ah, if only that were so. It would make life in general, and specifically life here in the order, so much easier. I've been reading some novels of the time of our Lords to try and get a feel for their time. I've just started reading a novel written in the midst of their meteoric rise, 1965, by a woman whose name caught my eye given that John the Father, was a fire god. Her name was Spark and I lit upon the line of one of the characters who believed in one of the old religions before the One True Religion came to dominate, an old religion called Catholicism, one of those ones obsessed with sex and not in a good way. You know, their priests were not allowed to have sex and they were surprised that they were continually rocked by sex scandals. I mean, what type of person would be attracted to a job where sex was not allowed? Either very devout people or sexual deviants, as it turned out. Anyway, this character believed in her God and put it that she was 'endowed with the beautiful and dangerous gift of faith, which by definition of the Scriptures is the sum of things hoped for and the evidence of things unseen.' The beauty and the danger, wonderfully put I think. I lack the beauty of that feeling of security, the knowledge that there is a heaven and I will have immortal life in the paradise of Beatle Heaven but lack the danger of not believing in things that are patently nonsense, the danger of 'knowing' something that is essentially unknowable. So we don't know the significance of the role of cellars in the Greatest Story?"

"How about they played in a lot of cellars because that's where the work was?"

Those words were now playing over in my mind as I opened the book that described what came to be known as the cellar of all cellars. The cellar most associated with the young gods, the last cellar before they burst out into the open and into the sunlight. The Scriptures described it as "the holiest of cellars, the place where the first followers in the Holy City of Liverpool could come and worship their new gods for the first time on an almost daily basis. It was made most sacred by the 292 appearances of the Beatles." This was, of course, the Cavern, the holiest cellar of all. From the description I was reading it did not seem sacred or holy. Located in Matthew Street in the middle of the Holy City, surrounded at the time by fruit warehouses, you would descend the seventeen steps and find yourself in a dark and sweaty atmosphere, high, vaulted pillars obscuring your view of the stage, the damp literally dripping down the walls. When once, and only once, Saint Mimi ventured down those famous steps to see where her beloved nephew "worked" she must have felt she was descending not into a place of worship, not sacred ground, but the depths of hell. But in these less than propitious surroundings, the people who saw them grew to love them and it could be seen in this increasingly fanatical following what was to come. Whether you believed they were divine or not, you could not ignore the effect they had on virtually all who saw them.

I thought about my lack of faith. My religious instinct was extinct, but it was alive and kicking in countless millions around the world and I felt just a little glad that they had fastened onto the Beatles as their latest gods. They had grown tired of the old gods who seemed intent on telling them not to do the things they desired most. They would have been disenchanted by all the rules which had been passed down through the centuries and seemed to make no sense in modern times. Would the same happen to the One True Religion? I felt like a spy in the House of God.

The dark sky which had been threatening rain for some time now made good on that threat, cutting short my lunchtime interlude and mirroring, a little, the interlude of the gods on their return from the second holy city. John the Father had spent a week in contemplation, coming out of his room in the full certainty of what he was to do with his life. The Beatles had played and the people, once indifferent, now sat up and took notice of this new, exciting sound which saw them rise above the other groups. And they had played in the cellar of cellars, the Cavern, where they were introduced by Saint Bob, patron saint of disc jockeys and cave dwellers, who would welcome the growing numbers of worshippers of the Fab Three plus Saint Pete by announcing, "Hi, all you Cavern dwellers; welcome to the best of cellars." Some of the less pious said, behind their hands, that he was also the patron saint of those who got battered by gods, which related to an incident between him and John the Father. It seemed to me quite a specific and very small group of people to be a patron saint of.

I hurried back to class. The rain had come and I needed to run and hide my head. I did not feel that I might as well be dead. That seemed a bit extreme. It was only rain.

# Chapter Fourteen
## A Message from Across the Ocean

Johann was waiting for us at the front of the class when we returned from lunch. Raindrops were dripping from my hair and I sat damply in my seat. Brother John sat to the side of Johann looking off into space, happy to let his German student do his work for him. Johann still had the gleam in his eye from earlier, the gleam that told me he had been granted that beautiful and dangerous gift of faith that I had been denied. Instead there had been a mix up in the post and I'd been sent a package that contained a large dose of scepticism. The history of religion and politics – well, history full stop I suppose – seemed to back up Voltaire's statement that "Those who can make you believe in absurdities can make you commit atrocities." The absurdities in the One True Religion seemed harmless; it was a religion that had as its ultimate goal the creation of a peaceful and violence-free world, so there were no suicide bombers, no martyrs and no holy wars but there always remained the possibility of it mutating into something less than wholesome if you got carried away with the absurdities. After all, communism came to power with the goal of creating a workers' paradise on earth and somehow managed to end up murdering millions in the process.

Johann looked piously on the verge of insanity but far from murderous as he looked up from his notes. "There are a number of pilgrimages that are undertaken these days to honour the Greatest Story. We have mentioned the first trip to Hamburg, which many pilgrims replicate in a minibus. There is a second pilgrimage route to honour the second journey to Hamburg. There is a special night train which leaves the Holy City of Liverpool from the sacred site of Lime Street Station, now called the 'Hamburg Express'. There is also now a spring religious holiday in Hamburg which is based around their return to the second holy city. John the Father and George, Lord of the Weeping Guitars, set off together at the end of March, taking this night train and sailing partway to Hamburg to be met by the lover saints, Stuart and Astrid, at Hamburg train station. The next day, the thirty-first of March, they were out in Hamburg having a good time with Saint Jurgen. This has come to be known as Good Friday. There was however a shadow hanging over them as they were waiting for Paul, the other Father, and Saint Pete to join them after they needed permission from the German authorities following a mishap in their last visit when they accidentally nearly burnt down the cinema where they were staying. The Scriptures tell us that divine intervention allowed them back into the country and they arrived in time to be playing on the Sunday. This has therefore become known as Resurrection or Beatle Sunday, and now thousands of the faithful gather at the site of the Top Ten Club to celebrate that momentous reunion. We also give gifts of chocolate guitars to each other and families come together to have a large Beatle Sunday brunch in order to thank the gods for their beneficence."

"Thank you, Johann." Brother John had stood up. "The Beatles were to stay in Hamburg for three months in the year of our Lords 1961. Who can tell me the significance of their second stay?"

A particularly pious John, which given where we were meant he was extremely pious, put his hand up. "The Scriptures tell us that this was the time when the gods realised that Saint Allan, who had steered them to Hamburg, was not the man to lead them into the light and relations between them soured. They knew they needed someone greater and more dedicated to them and their shining future so, like the message that Elvis the Baptist had sent to the gods with his records, sparking their love of music and setting them on a course that would see them crashing into each other and exploding into one blinding flash of divinity, they made a record and set off a chain of events that would lead them to that man, already waiting and dreaming in their home city, the Holy City of Liverpool."

Brother John nodded. "Thank you, John, very colourfully put," he said, seeming to suggest he may not have put it in those words himself. "They made a record with Saint Anthony of Norwich, patron saint of singing with gods before they were famous. And so it was on June twenty-second, in the year of our Lords 1961, that the Beatles, the three gods plus two saints, entered a makeshift recording studio for the first time and sent their message, their 'Bonnie' as it turned out, across the ocean. The record was produced by Saint Bert of Hamburg, patron saint of getting to number one with terrible records. The message would take its time in arriving, a few months in fact, but when it reached its true destination, it would be heard loud and clear by the recipient. Johann?"

"Thank you, Brother John. The Beatles stayed in Hamburg for three months. They composed their message with Saint Anthony, to be sent through the ether to the coming man. They played every night, they got even better. When they left, the five Beatles became four. It was time for Saint Stuart to leave them and return to his true calling, his art. He had spent eighteen eventful months with the Beatles but now it was time to return to his painting. But perhaps he had spent too long, too close to John the Father, the God of Fire, for his, as we know, was to be a tragic ending. His seemingly ascending star cut down by cruel fate."

Of course, he did not ask why this was. He did not ask why God, in His infinite wisdom, had decided that Saint Stuart had to die in his prime, in his blooming young adulthood, with all before him, love, life and art. He also did not ask why John the Father, his best friend, allowed this to happen or even, in all his godly power, did not *resurrect* him from the grave. Saint Stuart was the man he wrote romantic, almost lovelorn sounding letters to. "Goodbye Stu don't write out of – er what is it? Well not because you think you ought to, write when you feel like," he wrote. The young man who had closed himself off behind a barrier of sharp wit and snarling anger sounding like an uncertain lover hoping his friend in his new world with his new love would not forget him. "So goodbye (from John, you know, the one with the glasses)." How could Saint Stuart forget him? And later, in the same letter, revealing himself, not as a god full of certainty about who he was and his destiny but as an achingly vulnerable young man. "I can't remember anything without a sadness so deep that it hardly becomes known to me."

I had asked Stuart in the Stuartite community his thoughts on the death of his favourite saint. He thought for a moment then explained in a low voice that it was an unsaid but firmly held belief in the community that Saint Stuart was such a bright-burning star that he would have taken attention away from the Greatest Story so had to die, his purpose served. I was not surprised at this interpretation by the Stuartites, that he had to die so as not to outshine the gods. But they did not seem to question what this may have said about God and his sons, if true. Your point of view tended to reflect your religious bias. There were many in the Order of John who whispered that the death of Saint Stuart was indeed due to jealousy, not from God the Father but from Paul, the other Father, who was always at war with Stuart and therefore demanded his sacrifice to appease his wrath. Of course, this made no sense to people who were not insane. Stuart had left the group, which was what Paul would have wanted, whether through dislike or because he was a bit crap on the bass or maybe both, we will never know. This theory also seemed to ignore the fact the whole religion was based on peace and love, yet was happy to believe one of the gods, who just happened to be their favourite god's main rival, was happy to see his fellow god's best mate die an unpleasant death. I had said nothing but tried to let my incredulous face imply that the only obvious answer was that we lived in an absurd, pointless world where these things happened all the time and could not be explained. In truth, it was a difficult face to pull off.

# Chapter Fifteen
## Saint Brian

---

It was the end of October. The nights were drawing in. We were hurtling toward Beatlemas, the winter holiday season, a time of pantomimes in which people dressed up in silly clothes and made terrible jokes. The order always put a pantomime on, the more chaotic the better, in honour of the gods who had performed their own shows, then called Christmas shows after one of the many messiahs that were followed at the time. Ours was called the Johnmas pantomime and included music and skits in the tradition of the Beatles. The tradition included having a compere who was a baddie, usually with a top hat, cape and moustache, though no one was sure why that was a baddie costume, but sometimes in full demon costume. This was to commemorate the original compere, who was said to be sent by the forces of darkness to corrupt the Four Gods. His name was Rolf Harris and had advertised his cruel nature by his command to tie his kangaroo down, sport, tie his kangaroo down. The legend has it that the gods became aware of his true nature, and when he was onstage, John the Father, who was backstage, questioned what he was saying so all the audience could hear. "I dunno about that, Rolf," he would say and the audience would laugh uproariously. The demon from down under was furious and went on to commit various crimes despite the warning from the gods.

For their second and final Christmas show the following year, the dark forces were determined to undermine the gods, so they sent their most powerful demon in their legions. He was a white-haired devil who smoked cigars and went by the earthly name of Jimmy Saville. His strong dark magic allowed him to commit many crimes in plain sight but he was no match for the Beatles, who simply decided to not do their end of year shows anymore. It is said that the next year the dark forces were all set to send a young man by the name of Paul Gadd, who later changed his name to Gary and was to finally prove that all that glittered was not gold.

It was also the time of year that we sent each other Beatlemas records. Apparently, in the old days, people would send each other cards with greetings wishing each other happy holidays and good new years. Now at Beatlemastime small recording studios were opened around the country and people would go in and make a short record to send to friends and relatives. You could say anything, but the main aim was to be amusing and anarchic in the spirit of the Beatle messages they would send to their followers at that time of the year.

But that was all to come. Today was the 28th October, which was known in the calendar of the One True Religion as Angel Ray Day.

# A Parisian Interlude
## From the Scriptures

"John and Paul, the two Fathers, set off for Spain at the beginning of October. They stopped by to see their friend Saint Jurgen, their friend from Hamburg, who was now living in Paris. The gods had but little money and ended up in the seedier part of the city late at night trying to find accommodation as there seemed no room at many of the inns. Although they were destined for Spain, some force kept them in Paris for the whole trip, and one night it came in a vision to the both of them that their hair, which was brushed back in the style of the Baptist in a quiff, must change to a new style. They must have their own look. And so they visited Saint Jurgen at the now sacred site of the Hotel de Beaune in the Saint-Germain-des-Pres neighbourhood of Paris and told him of their vision from the night before. He listened and argued, saying he liked their hair as it was, but they said "We command you to cut our hair in this new style." Who could refuse the command of the gods? So in a lowly inn in the middle of Paris was born the haircut of the gods. When they returned to the holy city, the gods who sounded like no one else now looked like no one else."

The guest lecturer shut the Holy Book. Brother John had briefly introduced him before wandering off to do whatever the Brothers did when they were not teaching. I imagined him poring over obscure documents and references to Saint Mimi, making notes and filling volume after volume with information on the woman who loved John intensely in that peculiar English fashion that did not allow for outward shows of affection. He had mentioned the possibility of turning his doctoral thesis into a book. I had the feeling it was one of those books that filled a person's life, was continually added to but was never actually finished.

He told us the guest lecturer was called Brother Brian, an Epsteinian from the Order of the Life of Brian. Brother Brian was a dapper middle-aged man who was wearing an immaculate dark grey suit and tie with a crisp white shirt. He looked around the class.

"Good morning to you all and happy Angel Ray Day. As you've just heard from the Holy Book itself, the gods returned from Paris with their new look. George, Lord of the Weeping Guitars, quickly followed the example of his two friends. Only Saint Pete maintained his hair in the old style. His days in the group were numbered, whether because of this failure to go along with the hair revolution as the Hairists tell us or because his drumming was not up to standard, I will leave for you to decide."

Although his tone of voice was serious, he had a way of looking over his glasses at you when he said something slightly silly that seemed to suggest he was saying it with his tongue in his cheek. I was not sure there was such a group as the Hairists. I definitely did not know the ideology of Hairism. I did know that the Hotel de Beaune had become another place of pilgrimage, where devout followers of the One True Religion would end up after a weekend in Paris, drinking coffee in cafes by the Seine as the two Fathers had, with their hair carefully quiffed up in the style of 1950s rockers, indeed like Elvis the Baptist. They would end up at the Hotel de Beaune where they would, in a deeply religious ceremony, have their hair cut and styled like the gods, John and Paul, had done in Saint Jurgen's room, for a small but significant fee, of course. There was also apparently a small gift shop where you could buy a few items such as ceremonial scissors, icons with the images of the two gods, one on the back before the haircut and the front showing the new brushed-forward style as if this change was a miraculous transformation. They would also sell very small bags of god hair said to have been left behind by John and Paul and kept by the concierge, a deeply religious woman, who was said to have initially been annoyed to have found the hair hidden under Saint Jurgen's bed but then had felt there was something miraculous about this hair when shortly after putting it in a bag, having handled some of it, she found her arthritis had cleared up. I could find no evidence of this in the history books and the supply of hair never seemed to end, making me suspicious as to whether it was really the hair of the gods and could have been the hair of a dog. Perhaps it continually regenerated itself; it was the hair of the gods after all. But people bought it with the belief that it had curative properties. There were many stories of people who claimed they had recovered from various maladies after buying God hair from the gift shop, from hangovers, which they even called having the hair of the god, to more serious illnesses, although the One True Religion did not endorse it as a product.

Brother Brian paused and looked around the class. "As we know, the gods had sent their message, their Bonnie, across the ocean and were waiting for a reply. Scripture tells us that God the Father, to make sure the message reached its target, sent an angel called Ray, from the magical land of Knotty Ash, to a shop in the Holy City of Liverpool in order to guide the man he met there, the manager, in the right direction. Angel Ray asked the man, the man we now know as Saint Brian, the patron saint of revealing greatness to the world and unhappy relationships, if he had 'My Bonnie' featuring the Beatles. Saint Brian had a policy of obtaining any record that a customer asked for and it was this moment that was the beginning of his advent into the Greatest Story. It is said that the gods had been in the record shop, which was called NEMS, short for North End Music Store, listening to records in the listening booths, though rarely buying them. Saint Brian would have been aware of the Beatles, he would have seen their faces on posters and would have read about them in the new magazine that had been started in the Holy City of Liverpool by Saint Bill to spread the gospel, which he had called 'Mersey Beat'. But it was the angel Ray that really sparked the fire of his interest. After several questions from the curious saint, he told Saint Brian, in no uncertain terms, that the Beatles 'were the most fantastic group you will ever hear', and this left Saint Brian with a gnawing curiosity to see these young men perform. Note the description 'fantastic' – it was another hint from God the Father, a word that could, on the surface, mean very good but, like that other word associated with them, fabulous, had another meaning, fantastical, that implied beyond the real, make-believe, illusory, imaginary, beyond this world. As indeed they were.

"Saint Brian had always been fascinated by the world of entertainment, especially the theatre, and had even gone to acting school in London. He had returned to the Holy City of Liverpool and taken over part of the family business, making a great success of the record store, but now he was bored and ready to take on a new challenge. And so on the ninth of November, further proving the mystical importance of the number nine in the One True Religion, especially to you Johnnists, Saint Brian, with his personal assistant, Alistair Taylor, ventured into the teeming, steaming, seething, straining, loud and pungent underworld that was the Cavern. A well manicured, beautifully attired young man amidst the teenage mayhem, Saint Brian, immediately stood out. He watched them that lunchtime session, and like many others before him, he was smitten by them. 'They were fresh and they were honest and they had what I thought was a sort of presence,' he was to say. Even at that early stage he was already thinking about managing them. He knew in his heart they were destined to be together. Their star quality and his burning ambition for them merging together to conquer the world. Everyone knew that Elvis the Baptist was the first, the man that exploded onto the scene and amazed the world, but only Saint Brian knew that, though he was important, he was only the harbinger of the true gods to come. From the very beginning he would tell everyone he met that they would be 'bigger than Elvis'.

"That night, Scripture tells us, Saint Brian had a dream." He picked up the Holy Book and opened it and started to read. "'Saint Brian, having been visited by the earthly incarnation of the Angel Ray, was that night visited by the Angel Ray in his natural form with his wings spread, causing much concern to Brian who supposed he must be dreaming. The angel said, "Do not be afraid, Brian, for you have been chosen to undertake the special task of introducing four divine beings to the world and they shall be called John, Paul, George and Ringo. You will have the task of spreading joy and gladness and many will rejoice at their entrance upon the world's stage and they will be filled with the Holy Spirit and they will tune many of the children of the world to a new religion." And Brian answered, "How shall I know this, for I am but one man, and though I have seen the light and know their greatness, how will I show them to the world?" And the angel laughed and replied, 'I am Ray, I stand in the presence of God and I was sent to speak to you and bring you this good news. You do not believe this so you will remain mute about the matter until this prophecy comes true and then the awesome power and glory of the Lord will come upon you." Saint Brian awoke in the morning and knew what he had to do. It was the word of God. And a small part of him wondered, when he thought about the words of the angel, who was this Ringo, for he knew the names of John, Paul and George but thought the other was a Pete, and he noted this part of the prophecy.'"

Brother Brian put the Holy Book down. I looked around me at the others, who seemed to accept this story as gospel, which of course it was. I wanted to ask why there seemed to be lots of saints and angels in the time of the gods but they had gone very quiet since, apart from the occasional claim of a miracle at various sacred sites that had been touched by the Beatles.

Brother Brian asked an unusual question. "And how do we know of this visitation?" he asked.

"Because it is written in the Holy Book." This came from one of the Johns who I knew believed the Holy Book was actually written by God the Father himself and not a committee of early followers of the One True Religion in the year 2210, as an unofficial history I had read suggested.

Brother Brian gave him that look over his glasses which seemed to imply he thought he was in the presence of an idiot but smiled and replied. "Yes, but there is no mention of it anywhere else. It has, though, been given as a reason for his untimely death, that he was filled with the sense of his mission and the awesome power of God and could not cope with the knowledge. I do not know about that. He was a troubled man.

"And much of that trouble was not of his own making. As you know I am from the Order of the Life of Brian and that we revere him because of his role in the Greatest Story, but also we are an order that celebrates the diversity of sexuality that exists in the world. There are now twenty-three different types of sexuality that are recognised. Of course, these always existed but in the time, in the life of Brian there was only one that was recognised before the law. Saint Brian was a gay man and this was a status that was 'illegal' at the time." He paused to nod his head at our astonished looks as we tried to imagine a time of such barbarity and intolerance. "And although this changed under the law in the time of our Lords, the government of the time introducing an act in the UK in 1967, it was just the start of the battle for the rights of equality for the gay community. The act was passed in July of that year, and Saint Brian was to pass away the next month. We in the Order of the Life of Brian strongly believe that the gods chose Brian to be their manager because he loved them and would do his best for them but also because he was gay and to show the world he was blessed by their choice. Because of the discrimination of the times, Saint Brian tried to keep his sexual nature a secret from the gods but of course they knew, they were gods after all. The sad fact of the matter is that because of his sexuality, Saint Brian, in his brief life on earth, was subject to brutality and blackmail and the intrusion of the forces of law into his private life.

"So what were his qualifications to manage the Beatles?" he asked.

The same pious John as before answered. "He was chosen by God, as the Scriptures tell us."

"That seems as good an explanation as any, as he had no experience in the role. He went to see the Beatles play several more times before being formally introduced to them to ask about their record, their message, their Bonnie. 'What brings Mr Epstein here?' George, Lord of the Weeping Guitars, said at their first meeting. And so Saint Brian had the thought from the very beginning, perhaps inspired by the visitation of the angel Ray or perhaps from the boredom setting in with his role as record shop manager, to manage them. It is said that before taking them on he spoke to Saint Allan, their previous manager, who had fallen out with them over money who, the Scriptures tell us, 'Warned Saint Brian of NEMS against the gods, saying he must always keep between them a distance of a large stick or he would be burned.'"

I had read that he had indeed said "not to touch them with a fucking bargepole" but I kept that nugget of information to myself.

Brother Brian continued with the story of the coming together of the gods and Saint Brian.

"And so we are told that Saint Brian arranged a meeting in late November to propose his plan to manage them. But the gods were in a playful mood and were determined to test Saint Brian. They even turned up with Saint Bob of the Cavern, who John, our Lord, mischievously introduced as his father who was not in heaven, Wooler be his name. They were also a little drunk having visited the now holy site of the Grapes, then a public house, a purveyor of fine ales and, to particularly test the punctilious Brian, they were late. But Saint Brian was not to be put off. Not only had he had his vision, his angelic encounter, but he had seen them, was as smitten as the increasing numbers of others were smitten and had recognised their celestial star quality. 'I sensed something big,' he told Saint Brown, patron saint of helping gods get married in Gibraltar near Spain, who was also known as Saint Peter but there seemed to be a lot of them already and it was, frankly, getting confusing.

"And so they returned a week later on the holy Sunday now given over to Saint Brian's Day, which occurs on the first Sunday of December. Paul, our other Father, still tested the patience of this saint by being late again. George, Lord of the Weeping Guitars, explained He was having a bath. Saint Brian tried to control his anger and was helped by Lord George pointing out with the cheek of a young god that, yes, He was late but He would be 'very clean'.

"And so it was decided that night on the say-so of your Father, who art in Woolton, Lennon be His name, God of Fire and Honesty who told the world, in his honesty, 'I make a lot of mistakes, character-wise, but now and then I make a good one... and Brian was one.' And so He said the immortal words, a plain and simple command. 'Right then, Brian, manage us.' What do we call this part of the Great Story?" He ended by asking the class.

Many hands shot up. Brother Brian looked over his glasses at a John to his left.

"It is known as the time of the End of the Beginning."

Brother Brian nodded. "Yes, there are saints and there are saints, and Saint Brian was saint amongst saints. His arrival into their story, the Greatest Story, led to the start of their inexorable rise to world dominance. Perhaps God, the Father, had learnt from the mistakes of the past. Perhaps He had sent down sons and daughters before but they had failed to make an impression because, although these prophets and messiahs had gained followers and admirers and disciples, He had forgotten to provide them with a decent manager to harness their power and appeal."

Some of the Johns were nodding their heads as if this thought had just occurred to them and was a moment of enlightenment. Brother Brian was, however, doing that look over his glasses that I was sure meant he was not entirely serious. I had kept quiet all morning and thought it was time to throw a spanner in the works. I raised my hand.

"Are you saying, Brother Brian, that without the guiding hand of Saint Brian, the Beatles, the four gods would not have been revealed to the world?"

"The four gods were the raw material of divinity and God the Father sent them help in the form of the saints we now revere. There is, of course, a hierarchy of saints, and the two at the top are Saint Brian the Manager and Saint George the Producer. I am not going to argue about which was the most important, we are above that kind of thing in the One True Religion." He looked right at me over his glasses and with the trace of a smile. "But, of course, it was Saint Brian."

I persisted. "But they were gods, could they not have organised themselves?"

Again the look and the smile. "I would imagine it's a full-time job being a son of God. You would probably need someone to take care of the details."

I could feel the disapproving looks and hear the tutting of some of the other Johns, who became very uncomfortable whenever the teachings or the logic of the church was questioned. So I bit my tongue. I was going to suggest that being all-knowing was part of the job description of a deity, but it would only lead to complaints about me to the order's higher-ups and besides, I liked Brother Brian, who seemed to be subtly subversive in his approach. As his next comment seemed to underline.

"And I have a note here from your tutor, Brother John, who asks me to mention that after they had agreed that Saint Brian should become their manager, he went to visit their parents to reassure them. As you know, Brother John is an expert on the life and times of Saint Mimi and he has reminded me that Saint Brian went to see her and she was the most difficult of the guardians of the gods to please. This was, of course, her character; she was the fierce protector of John the Father and she questioned Saint Brian about his dedication to her beloved nephew and asked him straight out if it was not just a momentary distraction for him that would soon fizzle out whereas this meant everything to John. But, of course, Saint Brian proved himself to her, and when he died she wrote that he 'would be sorely missed as a good friend and advisor to them. It was a great shock to me also, I knew him very well.' So he received the blessing of Saint Mimi, no small matter, especially according to Brother John, who sees her as *the* saint amongst saints. But it's not a competition, is it?" He paused, did his look and said, "But if it was, Saint Brian would win."

All the other Johns and Johann were furiously taking notes. Only myself and the other rebel John laughed nervously, and I was not sure but I think he winked in our direction.

"And what happened next? After they had made the decision to let Saint Brian manage them? What immediately started happening?"

A number of hands went up, but it turned out to be a rhetorical question for he immediately answered his own question.

"*Things*, my dear boys, *things*, started to happen. The Beatles were a fantastical, fabulous, magical mix of ingredients. Depending on your point of view, your ingredients will change in number. I number them as six. With the addition of Saint Brian, four of those ingredients were now in place. All that was needed was one more god with a drum kit and one more saint with a studio and a penchant for producing gods.

"We will talk about the *things* that began to happen after the arrival of Saint Brian into that magical mix this afternoon, but I think we should first get out of the way a simple observation. You are members of the Order of John and I am a member of the Order of the Life of Brian and we revere the saint and the gods and you revere the god and the saint, but I hope you will acknowledge, and it is indeed why I am here, that it was John the Father who had the closest relationship with Brian of all the gods. They liked each other, maybe they loved each other. Years after the tragic lonely death of Saint Brian, John the Father would describe him as a 'beautiful guy', and of course He meant beautiful inside. There is indeed much speculation on the exact relationship between Saint Brian and John the Father, but essentially we in the order do not care either way. We know that John was close to Brian because He Himself told us this later, saying that, 'In the group I was closest to him, and I did like him – he had great qualities and was good fun.' High praise and from the mouth of God Himself. Of course we have no favourites amongst the four gods. We love them equally." Once again that look over his glasses. "But if we did have a favourite, it would be John the Father."

He clapped his hands theatrically. "Enough, enough. It is time for lunch. I will let you go eat your dreadful mush while I go and eat something marvellous. Saint Brian liked the finer things in life and we followers, however much a hardship it may be, really should follow his lead."

# Chapter Sixteen
## *"Things* Fall Into Place"

---

**"**It is the year of our Lords 1962. It is the year that the final two ingredients of the saintly and the divine fall into place.

We were talking before lunch – did you enjoy your brown rice and vegetables by the way? It's no good nodding – John the Father was about honesty, remember. And yes, although you haven't asked, I enjoyed my lunch enormously and the Chateau Pape Clement was simply divine. Anyway, we were, or at least I was, talking about the *things* about to happen, largely as a result of the introduction of the enthusiastic Saint Brian into the holy mix, the fourth ingredient, if you like. Can anybody tell me what these *things* might be, that occurred in this annus mirabilis?"

Everybody put their hand up. We were good students, we knew our stuff. Brother Brian nodded at one of the Johns.

"On the first day of the year of our Lords 1962, the gods, who had travelled down to London the day before, recorded the sacred demo known as the Decca audition."

"Very good, very good. And did this audition lead to them being taken on?"

The same John answered. "No, Saint Brian and the gods were turned down by Saint Dick."

"Yes, Saint Dick, the patron saint of those who turn down gods. The third in the Holy Trinity of Disappointment: Saint Pete, Saint Allan and Saint Dick. There is a little known order, known as the Order of Dicks, which is home to those who have made catastrophically wrong decisions, who run a course in 'How to avoid being a Dick in the future' and another course similar to the twelve-step approach in which the first step is admit that you are, indeed, a Dick." Again my colleagues were furiously scribbling this down as if it was the very word of God, while he was looking at them over his glasses and barely suppressing laughter. I wondered how much wine he had consumed over lunch.

"Of course, it is an integral part of the Great Story that they were rejected. It shows us even the gods have to struggle, that we need to put our heart and soul into our dreams, that as Ringo, your Starr in Heaven, explained in his plain, some would say, simple language, 'It don't come easy.' They had been together for over four years before the word really started to spread. They had perfected their sound and their sermons on the stage and now they needed a wider set of followers. Saint Brian and the gods were, of course, disappointed by the decision of Saint Dick of Decca but these disappointments can destroy you or they can make you stronger. It was simply not in the stars for Saint Dick to see the light. Indeed, some have argued that he later saw the 'dark' when he signed the anti-Beatles, the Rolling Stones, to his label. But that is another discussion for another day.

"And so the legend has it, the Great Story tells us, that Saint Brian trudged his weary way around the streets of London, clutching his recording of the gods under his arm and proclaiming to anybody that would listen that his boys would be bigger than Elvis. The Great Story tells us that at every meeting he was turned down with a scornful smile, was told that the people were not interested in a group with more than one singer with guitars, that the people wanted singers like the prophet known as Cliff and his faithful Shadows. But Saint Brian knew otherwise. Had he not been visited by an angel?"

The other Johns and Johann nodded vigorously to give their assent to this fact, but Brother Brian gave his look that suggested to me that angelic visitations were, to him, the stuff of fevered religious imaginations, nice embellishments to a story but nevertheless, nonsense. But perhaps that was just my interpretation of his look. I was, after all, surrounded by this sea of faith, always on the lookout for the desert island of a sceptical mind.

"What else, in this magical year?"

My friend John had his hand up with all the others and Brother Brian nodded at him.

"Saint Brian made the gods wear suits."

Brother Brian smiled, perhaps guessing the hidden facetiousness behind the answer. "I was not thinking of this, but yes you are right, young man, very good. The savage young gods had worn leather jackets and jeans and so their appeal was to the young, who did indeed adore them. Saint Brian convinced them to spread their word to the young and old, the near and far, told them they must discard their leather and adorn themselves with suits and ties. How did John, your Father, take this suggestion?"

A pious John answered. "He was not best pleased, but He saw the wisdom in the idea and wanted the words and the songs of the Beatles to spread far and wide so He accepted the decision."

I resisted putting my hand up and suggesting that in one of the books I had read, one of the many frowned upon by the order, it was said that he was indeed not happy with the change in appearance but had, at the same time, stated to Brian, "Yeah, man, all right, I'll wear a suit – I'll wear a bloody balloon if someone's going to pay me." The church did not like this kind of thing. It seemed ungodly and did not show him in the best light, made it sound like he would do anything for money, when the religion tells us that there were so many things more important than money. When I brought up the sermon that John the Father sang in the early days that was simply entitled "Money" in which he sang repeatedly "Money, that's what I want", the Brothers would mumble that this was not a sermon written by the gods and that John was singing it in a sarcastic way, that he actually meant the opposite. They would also point to the sermon "Can't Buy Me Love", which stated that they did not care too much for money, that, after all, money could not buy you love.

"So yes, Saint Brian made certain changes to the gods' behaviour and appearance to make them appealing to a wider audience. It again makes you wonder if only certain earlier would-be gods and messiahs had had the foresight to engage a manager with a flair for presentation, perhaps they might have been more successful in their own time."

I could not stifle a laugh at that, and Brother Brian looked at me, not with a frown but with the merest nod of his head, as if glad someone appreciated his sense of humour. "You, young man with the giggles, what else happened this year?"

"Well, you've already told us really. It was the year, as you said, that the last two ingredients were added to the mix, which meant that the Beatles became totally divine as opposed to only three-quarters divine and they met the saint who would be the medium through which the world would hear their messages. The three gods were joined by a fourth, Ringo, our Starr in Heaven, and they met Saint George, patron saint of those who wear ties disliked by the gods."

I was pleased by my efforts to make it all sound religious. I had not even cast aspersions on the gods for their shabby treatment of Saint Pete. He had been with them for two years but he had never really been one of them. The official explanation, of course, was that he was simply not a god. How could he be one of them? But unofficially it was whispered he never really fit in, sacrilegiously failing to brush his hair forward and, most importantly, being crap at drumming, which for a drummer was always going to be a hindrance in your drumming career. But he had still been with them for those two years, those long nights in Hamburg as they got better and better and people started to take notice of them. As they grew into the biggest thing in Liverpool and were set to take the country by storm and then the world. Even if he was a crap drummer he was popular with their followers. And, being gods, you would have thought they would have the courage to tell Pete he was not the Best drummer in the Beatles, that he deserved some respect for the times they had shared. Surely, John the Father, the leader of this group, the first amongst equals, would have had the courage to tell Saint Pete to his handsome face that it was the end of the line. Instead, they got Saint Brian to do their dirty work.

Brother Brian was nodding. "Good, very good. Saint Pete had been bashing away behind the gods looking mean and moody but never quite fitting in, never quite being good enough, and the three gods knew they were missing a piece of the puzzle. And they had met this piece in Hamburg, had played with Him several times and it had felt right and He had felt like one of them. And so the gods bravely got together and faced up to the difficult task of telling Saint Pete he was out. They girded up their divine loins, stood tall as only gods can and with much courage, asked Saint Brian to tell Saint Pete." He looked at me and I am sure he winked again. The others were too busy taking notes to notice. He continued. "Saint Brian, being a saintly type, was horrified with the task the gods had set him. He was very upset; he liked Pete and was not sure about their choice of replacement. But the gods knew; He was after all, like them, a god. On the odd occasion He had played with them they had exchanged knowing looks. So Saint Brian, patron saint of telling drummers they are sacked, rang Ringo, our Starr in Heaven, who was playing with Rory Storm and the Hurricanes in what the Scriptures tell us was a holy holiday season in the Holy Town of Skegness in the summer of the year of our Lords 1962 at the then popular church of Butlins, and asked Him if He would join the Beatles. Ringo, our Starr in Heaven, is said to have replied on this sacred Wednesday, now celebrated in August, especially by the close followers of the fourth Beatle: 'No, I've got to play this gig in Butlins.'

"There followed a long pause, a pause in which Saint Brian wondered how he would tell his boys about this refusal, and then Ringo continued, 'But I'll be free Saturday.' Scripture tells us of a 'visitation' by John and Paul in the holy seaside town. They appeared to Ringo after the end of a show and said unto Him, 'Hail, Ringo, mighty drummer, we are come this night to ask you to be one of us. It is written that to be whole we need to follow a Starr in the night which will lead us unto glory.' And Ringo replied, 'Hail John, Hail Paul, through this hard day's night, I have been waiting for this summoning and though I cannot foresee the future for tomorrow never knows, I have always known my destiny lies with you, so my answer is yes.' And the four became one."

I wanted to ask if he could not see the future, how could he know his destiny lay with the Beatles? That surely this was a contradiction in terms. But when reading this part of the Scripture for the first time some time ago, it actually made some kind of sense to me. It was laying down the personality of the fourth element, the fourth ingredient, the fourth god. We had John the Father, the clever one; Paul, the other Father, the sweet, pretty one; George, Lord of the Weeping Guitars, the shy, serious one and Ringo, our Starr in Heaven, the most endearing of the gods, the god that came across as a lovable buffoon, the Clown God . He was the divine glue that stuck them together.

"With Saint Pete removed, booted out by those winklepicker Cuban-heeled Beatle boots, which must have been quite painful, there was only one last piece of the puzzle left. I will not go into details of the life of Saint George; I believe you are being visited by someone from the Order of Saint George, so I don't want to spoil his thunder. It will suffice for me to tell you about the meeting of those two saints amongst saints, the saints at the top of the tree of saints, remembering, of course, that they were humble servants of the gods and that it was not a competition, though if it was, Saint Brian would be right on top of the tree.

"After the rejection by Saint Dick, patron saint of, well, Dicks, really, Saint Brian and the three gods were devastated but determined and so, on yet another fateful day, a day now celebrated by the two orders of the two saints, the Brianistas and the Georgians as the Two Saints Day, Saint Brian met Saint George. It was the thirteenth of February, in the year of our Lords 1962. Saint George was impressed with Saint Brian, his manners, his well-spokenness and his immaculate dress sense. We in the Order of the Life of Brian believe it was this good impression that was the spark that interested Saint George. For, although Saint Brian played him some of the music of the gods, he was mightily unimpressed and the meeting ended with no firm commitments from the record producer. But the spark had been lit, the blue touchpaper had begun to fizzle, and though Saint Brian left the meeting heavy-hearted with no good news to tell his boys, a train of events had been set in motion. It was time for the gods to intervene, and a mixture of an angel from heaven and the music of the gods combined to force the hand of Saint George.

"The Gods had written a song called 'Like Dreamers Do', which was heard by the angel Kim, sent by God the Father to aid his favourite sons, and so the angel Kim went to EMI and pushed for this group from the north to be given a recording contract, and so it happened that the boss of Saint George suggested, in such a way as to make it clear there was no choice involved, that he should record the Beatles. Oh, the hand of God moves in such mysterious ways."

Mysterious? Bloody mind-boggling. Why did everything have to be so roundabout? Why could Saint George, having heard the recordings, not just have signed them, then and there? Why did God have to intervene with angels and demons? To a person of little faith it was almost as if the world was a random, slightly absurd place and that the significant events in the lives of the gods were explained by the use of tortuous religious sillinesses with the wonderful gift of hindsight. I did not put this into words for the ears of my fellow students. They did not appreciate that kind of thing. The kind of thing that brought into question everything they had ever believed in.

"Anyway," Brother Brian continued, "the second meeting of the great saints happened on May ninth that year and Saint George was able to pass on the joyous news that he was willing to offer a recording contract to the gods, who still included, at this moment in time, their saint on drums."

A hand was raised. It was a pious John. "Can I just ask? You are telling us that Saint George had his hand forced to accept the gods by his boss. Surely Scripture tells us that Saint George, after hearing the voices of the gods was"—he looked down at his notes—"'filled with a wondrous feeling of love and freedom and the whole room seemed illuminated with the brightest of lights as if the glory of the Lord shone down upon him and he knew his life thenceforth must be dedicated to the reproducing of these voices so that the world could enjoy a similar awakening'."

"Yes, it does say that. It also says that in his youth Saint George had joined the navy and slain a sea monster of enormous proportions. It is all interpretation. As long as we see the hand of God, it is surely all the same. We in the order tend to emphasise the importance of the influence of Saint Brian on Saint George; they thought very well of each other. Some emphasise the command of the boss of Saint George insisting he take on the gods after a message from the Angel Kim. The boss, a Mr L.G. Wood, was said to be displeased with Saint George as he had discovered he had been having an affair with his secretary, Judy Lockhart Smith, and made his displeasure known, thus making it impossible for Saint George to refuse his request for him to take on the gods." He paused, seeming to enjoy this salacious detail. "Or you can believe the literal word of Scripture, which tells us that Saint George was filled with joyous ecstasy upon hearing the voices of the gods, which history seems to suggest is not really the case, but suffice to say if he did not know he was listening to the voice of God, he heard something.

"After that short meeting the future of the gods was sealed. Saint Brian sent a telegram to the gods, who were again in the second Holy City of Hamburg. Saint Brian, *the* saint of saints had in six months achieved the Holy Grail of a recording contract. Now it was down to the gods. And how could four gods fail?"

Several hands shot up. Brother Brian just perceptibly raised his eyes, presumably to his favourite saint in heaven and said, "And here endeth today's lesson. Tomorrow we shall look at the meaning of the word rhetorical."

# Chapter Seventeen
## Daytrippers

---

It was the end of November. The nights were drawing in and we were still hurtling, helter-skelter, towards the winter holiday of Beatlemas. There was a chill in the air, and on this particular morning as I looked through the window of our dormitory I could see it was raining. In the past the English had grumbled about the rain and the weather in general, the cold and damp leading to many dreaming of warmer, drier climes, but now we welcomed the rain – indeed, were extremely thankful for it. This was in part due to the One True Religion, which celebrated the rain, pointing to the sermon by the gods telling us we should not mind the rain, that even when it was raining the weather was fine. It was also due to the climate crises that had just been averted from being a complete disaster for the planet. So when it was chilly and damp, people gave a collective sigh of relief. Religion and politics came together, especially under the influence of the third god, George, Lord of the Weeping Guitars, who warned the world before it was trendy to do so that we were making the world uninhabitable by our actions. He was also a member of the environmental group Greenpeace. Of course, he is only known as the third god in the Order of John, who take the common way of referring to them as John, Paul, George and Ringo as the order of importance.

John the Father did not say much about the environment, which is always useful for the church and the government as they can then imply what he would have felt, which they will, of course, skew to their own agenda. Fortunately they have tended to say that he would have been very concerned with the environment and was simply too busy with the rights of women, people of colour, the poor and other groups to have time to save the planet from our pollution. So, he left it to George to save the planet on behalf of the gods. They also point to the work of his firstborn son, Julian, who spent a lot of his time campaigning to save the planet and working with organisations that were dedicated to coming up with ways to allow us to live more sustainably. George wrote a sermon entitled simply "Save the World" in which he entreated us to save the world because someone else may want to use it and in which he warned of the planet's rape and how we've abused it and how we were endangering the rainforests, the birds and wildlife in general.

Of course, at the time, like the call of the gods to give peace a chance, to listen to the pipes of peace, George's call to save the world was largely ignored, his dire but accurate warnings derided until after his passing, as all things must pass, when it was almost too late. Extreme weather events followed, extreme heat in some places, severe flooding in others, and all this, coupled with centuries of conflict, civil wars and not so civil wars, had left the people and the planet feeling battered and bewildered.

Now we lived in balance with nature. If we used trees for any purposes then they would be replaced, wildlife was respected and revered, our energy was clean, provided by the wind, the sun and the vast quantities of water that had always been there while we burnt fossil fuels and dangerously warmed the planet. Businesses' first directive was now not to pollute, before even the profit motive. Farming was organic; food was produced and eaten locally. Equality, one of the central tenets of the One True Religion, was seen to have been seriously harmed by climate change, especially across countries, with the poorest countries most adversely affected. Thus the church and the governments across the vast territories that were now under the guidance of the One True Religion had an overarching policy that was called "Equality and Sustainability Across the

Universe". History told us that "Across the Universe" was a song donated by John the Father, to Saint Spike of the Goons for an album of songs to promote the charity the World Wildlife Fund, which sought to protect endangered species and to reduce the human impact on the environment, and so hinting at John the Father's unspoken concerns, all those years ago.

So the drizzle outside the dormitory window was accepted with an almost religious reverence, and it would, anyway, have been difficult to dampen the spirits of the novitiates this morning. We were going on another day trip, our first since our trip to the holy city. This time we were not going so far. We had got to the stage in our studies of the Great Story where the focus changed from Liverpool and Hamburg to the place where they produced their moments of divine magic for the next seven years of their mortal time on earth. We were going to London, a place so steeped in Beatle history that it had been deemed "the eternal city of a thousand and one Beatle places". They had all lived there, some of them longer than others. They had performed there, songs and pantomimes. They had appeared on radio and television shows broadcast from there; they had visited clubs and pubs and art galleries. John the Father had even been arrested there, and today we were going to visit one of the most sacred sites of the One True Religion. A place that had been immortalised in their own lifetimes and was now a multi-purpose community that had taken over much of the surrounding area, where people came to worship and study and, if they were deemed worthy enough, where they came to make music, like the gods before them. We were going to the sacred site of Abbey Road.

We piled into our solar-powered magical minibus and Brother John, after a quick headcount, drove off down the Tittenhurst drive and out onto the open roads. We were heading towards John's Wood in London. It used to be called St John's Wood, but it turned out that Saint John was not a saint of the One True Religion but some other obscure religion and therefore deemed to be made-up nonsense. It seemed to be true that the victors did indeed write history.

There was an excited buzz amongst the novitiates. Even I felt an unexpected thrill at the thought of visiting this most sacred of sites. It was said God the Father created the world in just seven days. Many took this to be evidence of his almighty power. I personally thought it might explain all the mistakes that had happened throughout history, especially concerning his creation of man, and that maybe next time he had the urge to create a whole new world perhaps he ought to think about taking more time over it, as it seemed like an ill-thought-out rush job in hindsight. The four gods, mighty like their father, had created their first album in just one day, beating their dad by a full six days. And we were going to the place where it happened.

Abbey Road was a former nine-bedroom Georgian townhouse. Another confusion. It was now run by the Sacred Order of Saint George, who were known as Georgians, but the term "Georgian house" apparently related to the name of the monarch of England at the time it was built. Apparently there used to be a quaint custom whereby the head of state of the United Kingdom used to be decided by a certain family being given the title of monarch and you would be chosen as king or queen if your mother or father was king or queen! I know, madness, but apparently very popular with most of the people of the country. The Georgian period ran from about 1714 to 1837 after the death of William the Fourth, whose name – and it might just be me – did not sound much like George. He had succeeded his brother George the Fourth, a much more George-like name, who, in turn, had succeeded his father, George the Third, again very Georgy. George the Third had reigned for sixty years, a very long time, and for the last ten years he was completely insane, which apparently did not prohibit him from remaining the head of state and meant that forever after the qualifications for becoming head of state remained very basic. The bar had been set and it had been set extremely low.

The newly United Republic of Britain now had an elected president, which seemed a much more grown-up way of doing things, except we had a strange tendency to elect the sons and daughters of former presidents as if we missed the hereditary principle we had abolished. We were a "newly" United Republic after the Scots had rejoined us not long after the emergence of the One True Religion. They had gained independence in the middle of the twenty-first century as we had gained independence from Europe after seventy-five years of peace had led us to question what benefits we derived from our membership and following rumours that curved bananas were to be banned. Scotland, a proud and canny nation, had left us after years of misrule when the old United Kingdom had elected a long succession of idiots as their Prime Minister. This proved a wise move as it allowed them to remain neutral and watch on with Celtic disdain as England involved itself with all the wars that followed in the coming centuries until, battered and bruised physically, emotionally, psychologically and financially, it emerged a hundred and twenty-five years ago as the birthplace of the gods and became, somewhat by accident, the centre of the religious world. The Scots, also economically devastated by the madness that had engulfed the world and a canny nation that always knew which side of their bread was buttered, saw the writing on the wall. England was the new centre of the world; it was the home of the gods and England was milking it for all it was worth. Scotland too had some claim on the gods. John the Father had fond memories of childhood visits there to see Aunt Mater and Uncle Bert, and it is said he had his first vision there. The church has since told us that this was his first premonition of his divine status.

He was on a mountain walk with his Aunt Mater in the beautiful and rugged terrain of the Scottish Highlands. She lived in a croft in Durness, a village in the northwest Highlands of Scotland with her dentist husband, Bert, and John the Father would visit every summer as a child. On this particular walk he was overcome with a feeling of completeness that he was unable to describe. He felt he was almost hallucinating. He said later, "You know, when you're walking along and the ground starts going beneath you and the heather, and I could see the mountain in the distance, and this feeling came over me. I thought this is something. What is this? Ah, this is the one they're always talking about, the one that makes you paint or write." This was to be his first great revelation, which he interpreted to mean he was special and destined to do great things. The church, of course, tells us gleefully in Scripture that it was his personal revelation of his sacred destiny.

This place had now become yet another place of pilgrimage, thousands flocking to this out-of-the-way village to see if they would experience a similar revelation. Many said they did. Perhaps they did, perhaps it was just the power of faith or wishful thinking, perhaps they were descendants of George the Third. It was a place of dramatic beauty, the kind of place where one might expect a revelation or two, a place where you might convince yourself that any breath of wind, the appearance of a wild animal, a sudden rain shower, a cloud formation, was a sign if you wanted to. There seemed a high correlation between someone having an intense faith in the One True Religion and the likelihood of them having a revelation. In the past it seemed that only believers witnessed miracles of the old religions, and now the more devout your belief in the One True Religion, the more likely you would have a revelation or see a miracle.

One site of a miracle was not far from the place we were going to visit today. In the same area of London as the sacred site of Abbey Road was the place said to be the site of many miracles of healing known as Lords. A former arena for the playing of a quaint old English game called cricket, it had been destroyed in one of the many wars before the advent of the One True Religion. Bombs had made craters in the once famous playing arena, which had filled with water, and in the early days of the new religion a young girl called Bernadette, a young girl who was well known for her devotion to the four gods, had been playing near the largest water-filled crater and claimed to have heard a sound like the sudden gusting of a strong wind but when she looked around, all was calm. When she looked up she saw, on the far side of the crater, a man dressed in white with long hair and a beard, and round glasses, smiling at her. She then saw a man in a black suit with a big nose, a handsome man who, although he wore a suit, had no shoes and a fourth man who also had long hair and a beard but was dressed all in denim.

Although it was a dark grey day in February, there seemed to shine behind them a bright white light. She later said she knew she should be mortally afraid but was instead filled with an inner light and though her hands trembled she moved closer to the four shimmering men, who were all smiling and gesturing towards the water-filled crater. She felt impelled to take off her shoes and socks and dip her feet into the murky brown water that filled the crater. When she pulled them out she noticed that her feet, formerly covered in blisters and corns, were now in pristine condition. She returned to the site several times and saw the visions of the gods twice more. The third time she brought a friend, who did not see the vision herself but was convinced that Bernadette had seen them.

And now Lords was yet another place of pilgrimage, where the devotees of the religion came and bathed to cure whatever ailment plagued them. Many people claimed they were indeed cured after a dip in Lords' holy Beatle water, which appeared to all intents and purposes to the less holy-minded as a mixture of rainwater and the water from an ancient burst water pipe. These miraculous cures were proof positive of the existence of the gods, if you so believed, or the power of the mind if you believed in something enough, if you were a little more sceptical.

No one in the church seemed to question that this seemed a strange manifestation of the gods. All four of them coming down to cure a young girl of her corns – perhaps they could have put their powers and time to a better use, perhaps curing someone of a more lethal malady. In the time of the earthly Beatles, at the height of their adoration, they would find disabled children were brought to their dressing rooms by their parents or carers as if they expected the Beatles could lay their hands on them and miraculously cure them. The church, of course, used this as evidence that even then people knew they were divine. They did not mention they did not cure anybody and were all appalled when this happened. It was slightly airbrushed out of history that John the Father, the sometimes cruel Fire God, was often seen to mock the disabled. The church had many times put an ingenious spin on the behaviour of the gods that appeared unworthy to our contemporary uber-egalitarian eyes, but this seemed beyond them so they simply pretended it never happened.

The church did not talk about the many pilgrims that had not been cured of their various ills, and it was a badly kept secret that a few of those who had drunk the holy water of the Fabulous Four had suffered severe stomach upsets and there were now prominent signs that asked people to not drink the holy water. After news broke of the holy site of Lords and the miracle of its dubious healing qualities, other sightings occurred around the world of the gods together or a single god in a place which became a holy shrine for one reason or another. There was, for example, a statue of John the Father in a church in Sicily in Italy which became famous for its tendency to weep tears of holy water. There was a site in Knock in Ireland where Paul, the other Father, had been seen repeatedly and was now another place of pilgrimage, despite a few locals claiming that there was actually a young man who lived in the area who did look a bit like Paul McCartney. And so it continued. The power of faith. Sometimes I thought the world was mad. When I read these stories I knew it.

Although Scotland had Durness, the site of John's first revelation, and the historical fact of their first tour with Johnny Gentle there was not much else (the Order of John tended to ignore the fact that Scotland was important in the life of Paul, the other Father, who'd owned a farm there). However, they saw the coming windfall of the association with the One True Religion and so rejoined England after much negotiation to negate the possibility of having to suffer the silly decisions of the annoying Sassenachs to their south, which had led them to leave in the first place. The egalitarian aims of the Beatle religion and politics were also more in tune with the collectivist Scots, again making the decision easier. Across the sea, the Northern Irish had finally realised they were indeed Irish and rejoined their southern neighbours, a decision again made easier by the introduction of the One True Religion, which replaced the religious hatred of the past. They now got together over a pint of stout and laughed at the old days when they had worshipped the same God, the same messiah, but managed to turn his message of love into a bloody civil war. They now marched together in their bands, playing the songs of the new gods who had, in their time, sang songs which had made plain their wishes in regard to that country. John the Father with his sermon on "The Luck of the Irish" and Paul the Father with his fairly unequivocal demand of "Give Ireland Back to the Irish".

Our United Republic, with its state within a state, the Holy Liverpudlian Empire, was thus not much changed since the days of the gods, with Wales still looking across at their English neighbours with a mixture of affection and disdain, with the disdain increasing the further north you went. They too tried to secede in the times of war and madness before the coming of the One True Religion but once the new religion had asserted itself they too saw the benefits of close association with the new gods and started finding all sorts of connections to the Beatles which became instant tourist hotspots for pilgrims from around the world. The village of Portmeirion became a special place of pilgrimage after it was revealed to be one of George, the Lord of Weeping Guitars', favourite places to visit and where he spent the anniversary of his fiftieth year on earth. It was also a favourite haunt of Saint Brian, who famously went there to convalesce after coming down with glandular fever in the year of our Lords 1966 and is therefore said to be worth visiting for its healing properties. And of course the gods were in Bangor in Wales, another holy Beatle town in modern times, to listen to the Maharishi Mahesh Yogi when tragedy struck.

We had recently elected our new president, the popular Jacky Frances King, affectionately known as "JFK" to her loyal followers. She was the daughter of a former popular president of twenty years earlier – as I have said, the Republic, after finally ridding themselves of the outdated monarchy based on the hereditary principle, seemed to enjoy electing the sons and daughters of former presidents. The role of president was largely ceremonial and mostly involved opening things, giving state dinners and appearing at a moment's notice when a tragedy happened, looking suitably attractive and sombre. Although the church and state were nominally separate, you had to be a follower of the One True Religion to have a chance of election, and Jacky was known to have spent four years studying in the Order of Paul the Father before emerging like a butterfly and spreading her wings in every direction in seeming preparation for her destiny. She lived with her husband John, the First Man, and her two children at Windsor Castle for half the year and Balmoral the other half. Her choice of Paul as the god to study made her unofficially unpopular in our order, even slightly traitorous to some, but she was very popular with the general public, young and attractive with a sharp wit, and rumours of serial infidelities only added to the public's fascination.

I liked her. She laughed a lot and was wise enough to not make it obvious who she most revered when it came to the gods. The only hint was her love of animals and strict veganism. She was good friends with the Pope and the Prime Minister, another woman who had recently been elected to the leadership of her party. This female triumvirate were occasionally seen together, heads bowed in deep conversation, plotting the feminisation of the world. When a journalist questioned President King about the three most important roles of the Republic being in the hands of women and their plans, she smiled a smile that contained a number of very sharp daggers.

"It's funny how you only ask that question when three women are in power, that it still goes unremarked when the roles are held by men. Even after all this time, even after Scripture tells us through the words of John the Father about the need to question how the world is organised, you ask what we are 'plotting'. Well, I tell you openly, that the 'plot' is to make the world a fair place for the other half of the sky. Besides," she said, smiling sweetly, daggers withdrawn, "we will always have our four fabulous gods in heaven – all men, if I'm not mistaken – so it seems only fair to balance it out with a feminine touch here on earth."

There seemed no answer to that. She had pointed out the permanent imbalance in heaven and made it sound almost inevitable that it should follow that women should get their share of power on the mortal side of things.

"We are, after all, only implementing the wishes of the Boys," she said, using Saint Brian's phrase for his favourite charges.

***

We were all aboard the magical minibus. From the early rain it had turned into a November day of brilliant sunshine, cold in the shadows, warm in the sun. There was tremendous excitement running through all the novitiates. Even me and the other sceptical John, sitting together at the back of the bus, huddled together in meek rebellion, smiling at the childish wonder of our fellow students, were caught up in the enthusiasm for our destination. Unlike our previous destination, the Casbah and the Jacaranda – which were, after all, really just places the Beatles had played – whatever you believed about the One True Religion, today's destination, Abbey Road, was a place of undoubted magic. It was the place where the gods did what they did best. They produced their sermons and songs, their masterpieces, in these hallowed grounds. The only time they went elsewhere, in the end times of the Get Back sessions, the magic faded, became less powerful. It still shone through; they were, of course, still gods. But the place was special, magical perhaps. Something they proved when they returned to finally record the swansong of the gods which they knowingly entitled, in an acknowledgement to the place where it had all happened, simply "Abbey Road".

Unlike the Casbah, which was staffed by the bitter followers of Saint Pete, a small cult dedicated to feeling hard done by, we were going to a holy different set-up. Abbey Road was run by the Order of Saint George, the top order below those of the gods, only rivalled by the Order of the Life of Brian. It was the toppermost of the poppermost of the orders of saints, especially to the Georgians, who saw themselves pretty much as permanently top of the charts when it came to saints. Brother Brian had begged to differ and like most things in life it depended in which camp you stood. Apart from this petty rivalry no one really questioned the importance of Saint George in the Great Story. The Great Story, like all great stories, was one of interweaving connections, a dance to the music of time as one author who lived in the time of our Lords had put it rather nicely. Saint Brian had been in Hamburg when the Beatles were playing there before he met them. John's call to arms, to fame, to the other gods about going to the toppermost of poppermost was a phrase invented by no less a person than Saint Dick, patron saint of massive blunders, and Saint George had a ready-made connection that was guaranteed to impress the gods.

Saint George, like the gods, loved the Goons. However, he not only loved their manic sense of humour, he had actually worked with them in the studio as individuals, a fact that was likely to create an immediate connection with the gods, especially John the Father, the god most attuned to the wisdom of the need to laugh at the world.

Saint George, the patron saint of England, the patron saint of pianos and oboes, a saint amongst saints, rivalled only by Saint Brian in his importance in the Greatest Story. Saint George's Day was June the sixth. That was the date he met the gods for the first time in the sacred recording studios of Abbey Road. Studio number two to be precise. He was not there when they first arrived. He had not yet crossed their paths, was unaware of exactly what he had in his studio. The session was instead started by Saint Ronald, patron saint of being assistants to more important saints. According to the Gospel of Saint Mark, after hearing the Beatles perform "Love Me Do", Saint Ronald was overtaken by a feeling of rapture and summoned his boss, Saint George, and he came at once to listen in, and in the words of Saint George himself, "it was love at first sight". The truth was that he was not overly impressed by their music, but was extremely impressed by them as people. He said that just being with them "gave me a sense of wellbeing, of being happy". Even I could not help feel that he sounded like he was in the presence of a group of individuals that were perhaps not mere mortals.

We arrived an hour after setting off. The Abbey Road studios had been just one large house at number three. The church had slowly bought the rest of the houses in the road and now owned virtually the whole road. They were not slow to point out that an abbey was, of course, a religious building, to be precise a building that had housed monks or nuns. The church told us this was yet another hint from God the Father about the true nature of the Beatles. We walked past the Abbey Road zebra crossing, which was being used by pilgrims to recreate the famous picture of the gods crossing that very same place. Always a popular place for the followers of the Beatles, it was now a sacred site, so popular that you had to book months in advance in order to walk in those famous footsteps. We arrived at number three and Brother John, who was in the lead, led us up the famous nine steps to the front door. There was a rumour that there were originally eight steps but the church had added another step as part of the legend of the sacred significance of the number nine. The door opened and we were greeted by a smart-dressed man with slicked-back hair who introduced himself as Brother George and greeted us all individually as we trooped in, in the famous Georgian greeting. "Hello," he said, smiling. "I must say I'm not too keen on your tie." And we would all return the greeting with the traditional, "Greetings, I'm not too keen on yours either." I felt extremely foolish. I was not wearing a tie, for a start.

We were ushered into a large room which had the legend "Studio Two" above the door and all of a sudden we were inside the place where it had all happened three hundred years ago. The excited chatter of the novitiates stopped as they entered. We were all silenced by the sheer weight of history, the atmosphere of intense holiness and the numerous signs that said "Quiet, please". I looked around and took in the massive room, the high ceiling, the wooden flooring, the huge piano standing alone in the middle of the floor, the many microphone stands lined up along the walls, the clock on the far wall that had reminded the gods of the passing time, and the famous twenty steps up to the control room. It had been lovingly restored to its full glory of the time of the gods. The building itself had escaped the destruction of the many wars since then. It was another favourite miracle espoused by the church that all significant buildings that were touched by the Beatles survived intact through the many wars in the time between the passing of the mortal versions of the gods and the emergence of the One True Religion. I knew this could not be true. Many famous arenas had been destroyed in the Third Civil War in America. Shea Stadium, the Hollywood Bowl and many other famous venues associated with the gods, all lost in the conflagration of the third and most terrible internal conflict of the old United States before the advent of the One True Religion and a semblance of sanity.

There were ten chairs set up on one side of the auditorium and we all sat down and watched as Brother George stood in front of us and unfolded some pieces of paper. I hoped we would not spend too long talking about the tie incident. He fiddled with his own tie and looked at us with a smile that let me know I was going to be disappointed.

"It seems only appropriate that I read from the Holy Book about the description of that first meeting on what we now call Saint George's Day, on June sixth, in the year of our saint 1962." He glanced down at a piece of paper but I got the impression it was not necessary, that it was a passage burned into his memory. "And the gods were gathered in the control room, and Saint George, who, although he was not yet fully aware of their divine status, nevertheless, felt himself warmly "embraced" by their very presence, asked them after a discussion of their experience in the studio, "Is there anything you don't like?" There was a long silence in which the three gods looked at each other and was finally broken by George, the Lord of the Weeping Guitars, replying, "Yeah. I don't like your tie." And though Saint George was a little put out as he liked his tie, there was much laughter and the spell of silence was broken and the connection was made between gods and saint.' And so I would like to repeat how much I dislike your ties and hope that the same connection can be made."

There was a chorus of replies from the more devout novitiates around the theme of not liking Brother George's tie. *For John's sake,* I thought and briefly wondered what would happen if I put my hand up and told him that, actually, I rather liked his tie.

Brother George continued with a question. "Along with the connection with the gods, what else of significance happened at that first meeting? There is a clue in the number of gods mentioned in the passage from the Holy Book."

As usual a number of hands shot up and Brother George pointed to a John in the first row.

"Saint George told Saint Brian that the drummer, Saint Pete, was not good enough."

"Yes, it was the final nail in the coffin of Saint Pete's time as a Beatle. Saint George remembered him as being very handsome, very quiet and very bad at drumming. He did not know at that moment but he was in accord with the feelings of the gods, who had already decided to replace Saint Pete, a mere saint after all, with a god, Ringo, the Starr in Heaven. Saint Pete had served his purpose, kept the beat, however badly, for two years, and now God the Father had other plans for him."

He did not say what they were. Presumably because there was no easy answer. A lifetime of thinking "What if?" would be my best guess. But Saint George had noticed not only that he was not good enough on the drums but was also quiet, sullen even, whilst the others were not quiet, that they were funny and charming and that that was the thing that most attracted him to them, even more than the music. Saint Pete was about to leave the Greatest Story, exit backstage.

Brother George continued. "The other decision Saint George made that day was around the idea of who would be the leader, the focal point of the Beatles. As we have said he was not yet aware of their divinity but had gleaned there was something special about them, yet he was looking for a group in the image of the most successful English star up to that point, Saint Cliff, patron saint of summer holidays and bachelors, and his Shadows. He wondered which one to make the star, not yet getting the basic fact that they were all stars – indeed, with the addition of Ringo, they were all gods. Time spent in their company made him realise there could be no separation of one from the others, there could be no shadows in this group, that they were, indeed, a group. He had narrowed it down to either John Lennon and the Beatles or Paul McCartney and the Beatles, but as Scripture tells us it came to him as if it was a revelation, which of course it was. In his own words, he said, 'And then suddenly it hit me that I had to take them as they were.' A flash of inspiration from heaven itself. Though, of course, the gods would not have had it any other way."

Brother George droned on for another half an hour, giving us a potted history of his favourite saint. How he had been born in 1926 in Drayton Park, North London, that despite his clipped accent, his posh-sounding voice, his beginnings were decidedly humble. He let us know how humble by telling us in hushed tones that in the building where he grew up there was just the one lavatory between three families. He dramatically paused at this point to let this amazing fact sink in. We were, of course, religious scholars, well versed in the life of the saints. None of this was particularly new to us. While my fellow novitiates politely listened in rapt attention to the well-trodden tale of the life of Saint George, I sneaked looks around me. Even I, who seemed to lack the spiritual gene of my colleagues, could not help but feel the holy spirit of this place. The ghosts of the gods seemed to crowd in on us. This had been their place of work, now transformed into a place of worship. In each corner had been placed the sacred instruments of the gods. In one corner was a set of Ludwig drums with that most familiar name written across the big bass drum. In another corner was a number of Hohner bass guitars as played by Paul the Father, along with less familiar bass guitars that he used, such as the Rickenbacker basses, on later recordings. The other two corners were filled with many electric guitars favoured by John and George with the odd acoustic thrown in. You could tell George's corner by the small selection of Indian instruments. And in the middle of the room that magnificent grand piano. Apart from the piano they were all, unfortunately, roped off and festooned with signs saying "Do Not Touch". I did not know whether they were the original instruments of the gods but it seemed a shame that these instruments, once responsible for producing the most potent magic of the gods, should be seen simply as holy relics, to be looked at from a distance, never to be touched again. I wondered whether the Georgians got together when no one was around and played the instruments in homage to their gods. But then I thought it would go against their own saint, that he was the producer, not the performer, that surely they would need four young men to play the instruments and then try to produce something worth listening to.

I closed my eyes and I could hear Paul the Father say those magic words that counted in "I Saw Her Standing There". That simple "One, Two, Three, Four". A simple count into the song, perhaps a count of the number of gods in the room. Like everything, it depended on your point of view.

I opened my eyes and tuned in to what Brother George was telling us. He had got to the part in the story of Saint George, so important to him and his Brothers, peripheral to us, who, as Johnnists, if we were honest, were really only interested in the part of the story in which he appears. He had just played a piece of music by Debussy, "L'apres-midi d'un faune", and explained it was Saint George's first message from God the Father. It was a piece of music that had touched him in a way, that made him curious about how to create such magical sounds. It was, according to Brother George, God's way of starting him on the path to be what he later became, the producer of the gods. He experienced an epiphany and he recalled that 'I thought it was absolutely heavenly. We should note that "heavenly", the One True Religion likes to tell us. He was, of course, right in his description, and from that moment on his life became a search for that sound, that music that would reach the core of a human being and awaken their spirit by its aesthetic power. And God the Father was to deliver to him the means to deliver this very sound in June 1962, when His four sons from the Holy City of Liverpool showed up at Abbey Road.

Brother George was telling us about the second message from God. This one came in the form of the "Epistle from Oscar". I smiled at the language. It was funny how letters sounded more religious when they were described as an epistle.

Brother George explained, "Saint George himself believed he had what he called a 'Fairy Godfather' in the form of Sidney Harrison, a man who provided a helping hand in important stages of his career. Fairies were mythical beings who took human form and had magical powers. He was, of course, half right – we believe that fairies are demoted angels, living their life here on earth, ready to serve God the Father in the eternal hope of getting promotion back to full angel status. This Fairy Godfather had helped Saint George get into music college when he was at a crossroads in his life and now he intervened and pointed Oscar Preuss, who was looking for an assistant, in the direction of Saint George and so, seemingly out of the blue, but actually part of God's careful plan, Saint George received his 'Epistle from Oscar' asking Saint George to work for him, and on the 'Epistle' was the address of the organisation in Abbey Road.

"And so Saint George, for the first time, was made aware of what has become the most famous road in the world. And when he arrived he found he was to be the assistant to the man in charge of the record label also soon to become known around the world. Parlophone, second only in importance to the Apple label in the Greatest Story. Do we know the origin of the company?"

It was like asking a room of mathematical geniuses if they knew their times table. Many hands shot up. Brother George, appropriately, nodded at Johann.

"It was a German company. It is suggested that it was chosen by God the Father because of the symmetry of the importance of Germany in the early years of the Great Story. It was part of the Carl Lindstrom Company and the logo was a version of L for Lindstrom and not the pound sign as most people believe—"

Brother George, who had been fiddling nervously with his tie which we did not like, interrupted him with a cough. He'd guessed that Johann may well have gone on for some time, quite possibly telling him things he did not know himself and bringing into question the point of his lecture. It was the opposite of the blind leading the blind; it was the well sighted leading those with twenty-twenty vision. "Yes, thank you, very good. Of course, when Saint George arrived there in the year of our Lords 1950, it was owned by the British company EMI.

It was seen as the not quite so successful sibling of their other labels such as Columbia, who had Saint Cliff and his Shadows. Saint George was just twenty-four when he joined and within five years he was the manager. Scripture tells us that his Fairy Godfather, his fallen angel, had come to see him and told him, 'George, congratulations on your new appointment. I need to tell you that you have seven years to prepare yourself for the most important task that you will be asked to perform in your lifetime.' Saint George was perplexed by this statement and begged the man who had guided him in the direction he had travelled to tell him what he meant. But Sidney, who knew he had pleased God by his work and felt he would soon be an angel again, just smiled and said, 'Learn all you can of your craft and you will be ready when the time comes. And I know you will be worthy of the task set for you.'

"And so, as time passed, Saint George was forever on the lookout for the arrival of this great task, of this work of God. He would sometimes look at the night sky and search for any signs of the coming of the Lords. He had, unknowingly, given himself a clue in his young piano-playing days belonging to a group known as the Four Tune Tellers, which became George Martin and the Four Tune Tellers, thus providing a description of the time to come. Sidney Harrison had given him just one clue, that the arrival of a Starr from Heaven would signal that the time had come for his life's great work. And so he would occasionally search the skies for this star. He thought he saw something in July 1957, standing on the roof of Abbey Road and staring at the night sky, when he saw two stars collide in the sky. Of course, he did see something, but it was the birth of the Beatles, five years before he was to meet them. Even when he met them, he did not realise the significance. He had fooled himself by thinking that the star would be in the skies. He did not realise that the Starr would simply walk through the door of his studios one day. And so, although it is obvious to us now, he did not realise, at first, that the time had come. We believe that God did this on purpose, that although he knew at a subconscious level, he fooled himself and therefore could provide his best service to the gods without being too nervous."

I stifled a laugh. According to Scripture the sign that Saint George had been waiting for was the person of Ringo, our Starr in Heaven, a heavenly body on earth not in heaven. When Ringo walked through the door of Abbey Road Studios bells should have been ringing, heavenly choirs should have been singing and fireworks should have been going off in Saint George's head, but instead he was so unaware of Ringo's divine status and so unimpressed by the nervous god's performance that the next time the four gods entered studio number two, there was someone else in the studio. Who he was depended on how religious you were and which god you most admired. For the followers of Ringo, our Starr in Heaven, on that day there appeared nothing less than a demon in the studio, sent by the dark forces to spread discord amongst the saints and gods present in the studio that September day. To the followers of the other Gods, to us Johnnists, for example, it was a "test" of the strength of the new union between the group who had been diluted by the presence of a mere saint in their midst and were now a purely divine foursome. For the more sane among us, and there seemed to be precious few, his name was Andy White, a proficient session drummer included by Saint George because not only had he failed to notice that Ringo was a god but was not sure he was a good enough drummer from his first hearing of Ringo's playing.

He was wrong, of course, and the rest is history. There are rumours though that the followers of Ringo have never forgiven Saint George for this early slight to their favourite deity. We Johnnists were not surprised. We rather snobbishly believed that if you took away Ringo's drumming, there was not much left to follow in terms of sacred beliefs. It was whispered that the Ringoists had their own Saint George's Day, September 4th, when they would build large bonfires and burn effigies of Saint George and the demon, Andy White, although no one seemed to have any idea what he looked like. This meant that he would be depicted as having horns and hooves and a long tail, seeming to imply he was the very devil. They even pointed to the fact that he was struck down by God later on with a severe stroke as punishment. When I looked up the details outside of the Ringo-worshipping literature, it turned out he had lived to the ripe old age of eighty-five, and if he was struck down by God, He had taken a while to find him and then struck him down by what looked like suspiciously natural causes.

Johnnists secretly believed that this was another example of God punishing not Andy White but the runt of His litter, Ringo, our Starr in Heaven. They whispered that He had exhausted all his top energies on His most perfect creation, John the Father, and there was a slackening off as you got further down the line of gods. Paul the Father was next, George third (not *the* third, as he was insane, if you remember) and Ringo a not very close fourth. This, they argued, explained the differences between the gods. Ringoists would point out, with a logic difficult to argue with, that Ringo was actually the oldest and therefore would have been God the Father's most perfect creation. Sane people asked how come God the Father, the omnipotent being – omnipotent literally meaning having unlimited power – could "get exhausted" and produce inferior gods. In reply Johnnists would usually cough and change the subject.

Brother George spent the next twenty minutes standing next to a table with a record player on it and placing the needle on a variety of records. They were all examples of records produced by Saint George in the BB years (Before Beatles). The included a number of "comedy" records by Saint Peter and Saint Spike which Brother George found hilarious but which we listened to and looked at each other nervously, not quite getting it. These were favourites of the gods after all, particularly John the Father, but after thirty seconds of a song called "Any Old Iron" by yet another Saint Peter, patron saint of bright pink-coloured big cats, we were beginning to wonder if we were missing some divine insight. The devout were looking particularly worried, apart from the most devout John, who was smiling and nodding his head as if he understood why this was a funny record. We called him Pope John because he was so devout; he believed the Scriptures were the literal word of God and there was no room for debate in his closed mind. He had a quote from the One True Religion for every occasion, no matter how irrelevant. We did not get on and I suspected that John the Father would have found him insufferable. Now he was chortling to himself at humorous records from the mists of time that were frankly puzzling to the rest of us, presumably because he had read that the gods had found them funny. He had clearly never read the sermon by George, Lord of the Weeping Guitars, where he exhorted us to "Think for Yourself". Brother George was now playing a record about someone digging a hole in the ground by someone called Saint Bernard, who was not a dog. Mercifully, he picked up the needle from the record before it finished and turned to address us once more.

"That was a few examples of the exemplary work of Saint George before he met the gods in that miraculous year of 1962. As we have seen, he saw that there was no one person to take the lead, that they were a collective, a group. In our teachings that has become known as the second important decision of Saint George, the first being the booting out of Saint Pete.

"I would like to now tell you about the third important decision of Saint George, made that same year. Saint George was not yet convinced that the songs of the Beatles themselves were good enough for public consumption. Indeed that year there was a recording made of the Beatles in the Star Club, Hamburg. Although there are no surviving copies of that recording we do have a track listing which lists twenty-six songs, and the remarkable thing about that list is that out of those songs only two were composed by the gods themselves. Saint George, still not yet fully aware of exactly who he had in his studio, decided he needed to choose a song for the Beatles to record that would be a hit. And so after listening to a song called 'How Do You Do It?' he decided this was the song he wanted them to record. In the Gospel According to Saint George, he writes that he was convinced that it was the 'song that's going to make the Beatles a household name, like Harpic.'"

He waited, a look of expectation on his face. We did not disappoint him.

"What's Harpic?" a John asked.

"Exactly," Brother George exclaimed triumphantly. "Who knows? Harpic has been lost in the annals of time, like the song he wanted to give the gods. There is some discussion that it was a popular instrument of the time, related to a harp, producing heavenly sounds and thus worthy of being compared to the Beatles."

I wanted to raise my hand and say that there was evidence that Harpic was the name of a toilet cleaner and that "How Do You Do It?" was a number one hit for Saint Gerry and his Pacemakers so maybe Saint George was right about it being a hit for them, but there was something in his claim that something mysterious happened, as he went on to explain.

"He insisted they record it but as we know something happened to the gods at this time, something we cannot understand through earthly reasons. Just two of their own songs out of twenty-six, remember, in their live sets in that same year, and suddenly they came to Saint George with what can only be called a command. They came to him and said, 'We want to record our own song.' They had had an epiphany. It was as if that up to this point they had been simply rehearsing for this moment using the songs and sermons of others and now they had reached the point where they could speak to a much wider audience, they started to reveal their true divine nature. They knew it was time for their words and not the words of others to take centre stage, and so they reluctantly recorded the song that Saint George had offered them but then commanded that they record their own material. And this was the third important decision of Saint George. He agreed. He was annoyed that they did not want to record the song he had chosen but a voice inside his head told him not to argue, told him to go along with these four young men and their enthusiasm. It can only be another example of divine intervention in the Greatest Story. How else can we explain the all-powerful manager of Parlophone records being told what to do by these young upstarts from Liverpool?"

It was a rhetorical question and most of the Johns were nodding in agreement, that surely it must have been the voice of God advising Saint George to listen to His children. I had been quiet all morning so thought it was probably time I asked a question. Brother George acknowledged my hand.

"Could it not have been that he realised that the songs they wrote themselves were actually quite good?"

He was in a slight quandary. He could not say that the songs were no good – they were the songs of the gods, after all – but it undermined his narrative that Saint George had a direct line to God, that the voice inside his head was God. If Saint George had this direct line he would be that much more powerful a saint, not only carefully chosen for his task but spoken to by God the Father at important times. It was at times like these that I saw the religion as one big competition for a piece of the story; the greater the claims, the greater the status given to that order. It seemed to me that Saint George had a pretty good claim to being a vital personage in the Great Story without adding dubious claims of divine visitations and voices, but it was a religion after all and without these extras some more secular-minded individuals might suggest that he was simply the right man at the right time for the Beatles.

Brother George responded diplomatically. "Of course he was impressed by the words and music of the gods, but we believe only divine intervention can explain his three important decisions. It is written in the Scriptures after all. It is made quite clear who influenced the decisions."

Yes, but who wrote the Scriptures? Officially they were written by one source, the person who became the first Beatle Pope, who took the name John Paul George Ringo the First. He is said to have written the Scriptures after intense studying of the history of the Beatles and a long conversation with God the Father which allowed him to fill in the bits where God had intervened. The more sceptical suggested these were the bits he made up. I always found it amusing that at the beginning of any new religion there seemed to be lots of interactions between God and the founding prophets and that afterwards God seems to disappear. A slow fading from the scene until He or She is never seen or heard from again.

Brother George turned back towards the ancient-looking record player. There were so many other, arguably better, ways to listen to the music but this was seen as the sacred way as it was how the followers of the gods listened to them at the time. He lifted the needle and held it just above the spinning record.

"Now, if you would bow your heads in a little prayer, we can go back to where it all began, many years ago."

We bowed our heads and closed our eyes. I heard him carefully place the needle on the record. There was a moment of delicious crackling and then it began, the harmonica wailing, the drum beating and then the voice of God, or one of the gods at least, as John the Father, like all gods before him implored us, pleaded with us, commanded us to love, love him do. Like the first commandment in one of the old religions, God was said to have commanded that we should have no other gods before him or, as some translated this, "Love God more than you love anything else", so the four new gods, in their first plea to the world asked us to love Them, love Them do, as we knew They loved us.

We had indeed spent the whole of the previous day going through the words of this song with a specialist scholar who was visiting down from the Holy City of Liverpool, where she spent her days studying every word that was produced on record by the gods. This was no easy task as a lot of the material did not seem to be particularly profound, especially the early writings. I found it quite good fun to listen to the torturous efforts made to interpret the words in a religious context. In the end the church sensibly suggested that not everything the gods produced was to be taken as a sacred text, that at the time they were wary of upsetting the existing religions, needed to dazzle the world before slowly putting across their true message. But "Love Me Do" was the first release by the four gods, and so the church had to try and interpret it as an important statement. Hence the visit of Sister Georgina. She was a pleasant middle-aged woman who was treated with hostile suspicion by most of my fellow students as she had clearly committed the sin of being educated in the Georgist Order at Friar's Park. She was essentially in enemy territory, though of course we had to pretend we loved the gods equally. I felt sorry for her and so did not ask any awkward questions, of which I had many, given the dubious nature of the interpretation of the words of "Love Me Do".

The main thread was, as I have indicated, the request of the Gods for us to love them, that this was all we needed to do and everything else would fall into place. I had to sit with a straight face while Sister Georgina went through line after similar line. An example of the lesson went as follows:

"So you see, they ask us with force to love them – note the double use of the word 'love' at the beginning of the song. They command us, not just to love them but to love, love them do. And this command is followed by the line that can only fill us with joy. 'You know I love you.' Thus they are commanding our love but in return they are offering, for nothing, their unconditional love. It is already there, so obvious that we 'know' it."

Her enthusiasm was so infectious that I almost felt, at that moment, she might be right. Then at the end of that first chorus, she pointed to the humility of the gods. "They have just told us that they will 'always be true', the covenant is made, we just have to love them as they loved us and they would always be true, and to finish off this simple command they finally ask us to love them politely – they use the word 'please'. Imagine God asking us to *please* love them. How humble."

I was impressed not only by her enthusiasm but also her ability to stretch out the meanings within the song for a whole day. We discussed what it meant to love the gods and what their love for us meant to us. She also spent a good deal of time on the theme of the importance of love itself in the One True Religion. She told us that the seemingly simple song contained the word love at least twenty-four times, twenty-five if you listened carefully right to the end. By doing this they were not only asking us to love them but underlining the importance of love. This was a theme they would return to again and again, with the sermon "The Word", the word being of course "love", and the commandment that in life "all you need is love".

I kept my questions to myself. I wanted to know why they were not singing "Love *us* do" and "you know *we* love you". There were four of them after all. I did ask, as respectfully as possible, whether the song was not a simple love song, a plea to a lover rather than the gods asking us for our love.

"Oh, my sweet Lord," she said, smiling sweetly. "Of course, it can also be taken as a request for love from one person to another. You notice there is no clue as to who is being asked. It could be everybody, as we take it to mean, or it could be specific. A lover, male or female, or a friend, or a mother, daughter, father or son, the important point is that they are asking to be loved. It is the sustenance that makes us whole, the source of our strength; without it we wither and fade. Oh, give me love, give me peace on earth, sayeth the Lord. They are the two strands of our great religion and you cannot have one without the other."

We talked of love in its many forms and she won over the class, despite her constant Georgist exclamations, with her infectious enthusiasm about the beauty of love and how it had saved the world. We even found ourselves joining in with her as she led us in a Georgist chant about a man called Harry. Even I felt enlightened by her passion for the world and all who lived in it. She told us about her love for the gods and her love for her husband, a veritable saint to put up with her, she laughingly told us, though he was not perfect of course, none of us were. And then she told us of her two children, a boy and a girl, teenagers now and therefore somewhat of a trial, a test of her love. But she knew she had provided them with the love they needed to thrive as human beings, both she and her husband patiently waiting for the storm of teenage hormones to pass, seeing beyond their little rebellions, to the good people they would become, the blueprint of love stamped upon them.

Listening to her, it all seemed so simple. Perhaps it was. My sceptical brain had many questions, but even if what she had told us was naive nonsense it was pleasant nonsense, harmless maxims about the power of love. I doubted that all we needed was love, but at the same time I was not anti-love, preferred love to hate, and so kept my counsel. I was learning the importance of picking your fights. Ironically the only people she seemed to lack the capacity to love were the members of the Order of Saint George.

We told her we were visiting the sacred studios of Abbey Road the next day and she sniffed and said, "Well, you can tell the pompous buffoons from me that they are a bad judge of character to follow such a bad judge of character," in an outburst that left us wide eyed with shock, before regaining her composure and wishing us a pleasant time. It turns out that in the Gospel According to Saint George he had described George, along with Ringo, as a subsidiary talent to John and Paul. Therefore in the eyes of the Georgists he had relegated George, Lord of the Weeping Guitars, to a subsidiary god and they had never forgiven him for the judgement. Of course, the fact that he had elevated John and Paul meant he was very popular in the orders that followed them.

Back in Abbey Road studio number two and the record was fading with the gods imploring us to love them do. Brother George opened his eyes and watched as the needle slowly settled back into its place and the record stopped spinning. He nodded his head and said the refrain, "We do love you." This was repeated by the students, some with tears in their eyes. This was a sacred place and listening to that record had been overwhelming for some of the more devout amongst us. For me it seemed almost like a religious experience, and I guessed for them it *was* a religious experience.

The solemn look on Brother George's face slowly broke into a broadening smile. He even rubbed his hands together. "Now, of course, we spend our time studying the life of Saint George and his part in the Greatest Story but we are also, all of us here in the order, record producers. Who wants to come into studio number three and make a recording?"

It will not surprise you to learn that all of the students could play guitar, some could also play the piano and there were even two who could also play the harmonica. The guitar was the instrument most closely associated with John the Father, so it was seen as a way of getting closer to him, to understanding him, and now we were being offered the chance to play in the same studio as he did all those many years ago. We each took turns to play a song on an electric guitar, a copy of one that John would have used, and then would troop into the control room and listen back. It would have been nice to have played as a group, but no one could play the bass, or at least no one admitted being able to. It was the instrument of the other Father and therefore secretly frowned upon. It goes without saying that no one else deigned to touch the drums and when I did try them, despite the disapproving looks of my colleagues, I found it was not as easy as it looked.

We finished the day back in studio two discussing the "miracle" described in the Holy Book in the chapter entitled "Genesis". This is the story of the miracle of the creation of the first long player of the gods, "Please Please Me", which was recorded in just one day. This was celebrated every year on February 11th as Creation Day. There were a lot of religious festival days in the calendar and people tended to pick and choose or they would be exhausted from all the celebrating, and there was even such a thing as RCF or religious celebration fatigue. The church was fairly understanding that the followers would select which days they chose to celebrate, often depending on the importance to them of the event. Everybody celebrated Beatlemas; it was a tradition of a winter holiday that everyone enjoyed, breaking up the long cold nights with some festive cheer, the exchanging of the recorded greetings and some also gave each other gifts, although they were not entirely sure why. Creation Day was big among the Order of Saint George as it was a day in which he had played an important part and I now knew it was probably largely ignored by those who had chosen George, the god, as their star in heaven – not to be confused with Ringo, *the* Starr in Heaven, though as I have said, it is rumoured he was also not best pleased with Saint George, as he had brought in that session drummer in the early days and had had the temerity to ask Ringo, a god, after all, to play the tambourine!

Creation Day itself, for those who celebrated it, consisted of the playing and recording of ten of the songs on the first album of the gods, starting at ten in the morning and always ending with a rendition of "Twist and Shout" at ten at night when the singer was exhorted to "let rip" with their vocals in an effort to get into a state of communing with the gods. This caused some argument in the church. It seemed that in all types of society you would get traditionalists and progressives, whether it be in politics, the church or whatever institution you cared to be a member of. The traditionalists in the One True Religion saw it as sacrilegious to record the music of the gods. They were gods, and to try and emulate them was pointless and frankly blasphemous, they argued. How could you better the gods? The progressives argued that to make it a living and vital religion, the joy of playing and listening to the music was fundamental, was an essential way of getting closer to the gods. As the Beatles were in their time a challenge to the old order, it seemed strange for them to have followers that were not progressive but it simply seemed the way of the world. If everyone was a progressive we would be continually changing and moving on to the next thing, which sounded exhausting even to my progressive-minded ears – plus just because something was old did not mean it was always bad. Those in the middle, known as the Third Wayers, suggested that the Beatles sounded best when they sang and worked in close harmony and it was their aim to marry the best of the old ways with the new thinking of the progressives. There seemed also the simple fact, to me, that if you became over-progressive in a church you might just progress yourself out of existence! So the traditionalists pored over the words of the Gods and spoke them reverentially in the form of prayers while the progressives sang them at the top of their voices and hinted that not every word of the gods could be interpreted as holy writ, that if you tried to interpret them as such it would eventually drive you insane, that sometimes it was just as important to listen to the songs as simple expressions of life-affirming joy. The traditionalists agonised over "I Saw Her Standing There" and held long debates over the age of the girl – she was just seventeen, after all – while the progressives took joy in that introduction to the world of that youthful, exuberant shouted "one, two, three, four" that started the first song on the album, that introduced the listeners to the promise of a new world.

Even the traditionalists were split between the ultra orthodox, the born again One True Religionists who believed that every word the gods had said, wrote or sung needed to be interpreted in a mystical way and the traditionalists who accepted that this was difficult, to say the least, and argued that many of their early recordings were often attempts to draw the world in, to dazzle them, to gain adoration, to make the world ready before the more important messages about peace and love which appeared later. It was therefore seen as a strategy of the gods to make the world love them and then unleash their true purpose to the world once this had happened. And so it was not until later that John the Father told us to give peace a chance, Paul, the other Father, sang his famous hymn to "Let it Be", George, Lord of the Weeping Guitars, reminded us that although we were living in the material world there was much more beyond this material world, and Ringo, our Starr in Heaven, told us he would like to be under the sea in an octopus' garden.

It was the end of the day. Brother George had just played us "Twist and Shout" and I could not help but think of some born again One True Religionist beavering away in some tower of his own making, divorced from the real world, interpreting the words to that song. They were, thankfully, a small minority, made up of those people who would always take their beliefs that little extra step beyond the realms of reason. They existed in religion and politics and were a dangerous breed because they took every word of whatever gospel they followed deadly seriously and brooked no argument. They were a type never to be allowed too near the levers of power as they did not understand tolerance and debate and could only maintain themselves by creating hideous societies. "Pope" John was one such ultra orthodox novitiate in our class, who, unsurprisingly, concentrated on the words and life of John the Father. We had nothing to say to each other. His mind had a permanent "closed" sign in the windows of his eyes and I was careful what I said around him because he was the sort who would report you to the Brothers for any remark he found inappropriate, which was pretty much everything I said. Hence I said next to nothing when he was around. Most of the Brothers would listen politely to his complaints and then send him away with a plea to concentrate on his own studies. He soon learned to go to those Brothers who were more sympathetic to his ultra beliefs and so I watched what I said. He was one of life's natural informers and I had once made the mistake of having a glass of wine too much and telling him that he was the sort of person that John the Father would have utterly loathed. I could see in his little piggy eyes that were much too close together that I had turned him into a sworn enemy from that moment on.

Brother George was summing up for the day before letting us go. "And so Saint George, the saint amongst saints, had recorded the gods on Creation Day. They had exhorted us to love, love them do, for they were gods, and in return they would love us back; we *knew* they would love us and then they exhorted us to please, please them, which we did, initially, by adoring them and now, as the wishes of the gods became clearer, we try to please them by living honest lives of peace and love. Saint George was either a genius for his three big decisions, especially the decisions to let them sing the songs they wanted to sing and to let them be the group they wanted to be, a collective with no obvious frontman, or he was touched by God, maybe it was both, but either way he has a special place in the Greatest Story. As Scripture tells us, 'All of the people who came into contact with the gods were struck as if by a thunderbolt from heaven,' and indeed they were. First Saint Brian and then Saint George were afflicted by this thunderbolt and when the two of them introduced them to the world, then the whole world fell at their feet.'"

His voice had risen to the level of a clergyman exhorting his congregation and a couple of the novitiates, piggy eyes included, were swept up in a religious fervour and said popular end-of-prayer phrases like "carry that weight" and "I call your name", and I thought of John the Father in Beatle Heaven, or more likely rocking and rolling in his grave and laughing at his disciples.

# Chapter Eighteen
## Their Satanic Majesties

It was December, a month of two halves for the Order of John the Father. The first half was a traumatic time as it was, of course, the month of the Assassination. The first week of the month was a time which we were encouraged to spend in quiet contemplation of the teachings of John and how he died for us. That is a celebration of an ending, and so I hope you will forgive me if I leave it for another time, nearer the end of the Great Story. And so December is a schizophrenic month in the unlearned meaning of that word. It starts with quiet contemplation and mourning for the loss of John the Father and is immediately followed by the joy of Beatlemas, the winter holiday of the One True Religion. We have to shed our tears and then quickly forget our mourning and go straight to rehearsals for the annual Beatlemas show put on in honour of those December shows in which the gods featured in the years of our Lords 1963 and 1964. There is much dressing up and singing of Beatlemas hymns such as the sacred song from the pen of John the Father, "Happy Beatlemas, War is Over". Every year we sing the song and ask each other, in all solemn seriousness, and so this is Beatlemas, and what have you done? We tell each other, rather unnecessarily in my opinion, that another year is over and a new one has just begun. And we must list our achievements for the year and also what efforts we have made to ensure that there is peace in the world, that war has not begun, that war is over.

But amidst the joy and merrymaking of Beatlemas there is also another tradition. This is a tradition that has a dark side. It is a tradition that includes the telling of ghost stories, a tradition that the BBC, the Beatles Broadcasting Company, perpetuates by showing a ghost story every Beatlemas Eve. Another part of this tradition in the Order of John the Father is that it is a time when we look, just for a couple of days before we break up for the holiday, at the story of the anti-Beatles. The days have become colder, the daylight hours are the shortest of the year, and so it seems appropriate to discuss in whispered tones the group of men sent, depending on your point of view and level of sanity, as agents of the devil himself up from the depths of hell. Or alternatively, given that the One True Religion did not actually believe in hell on the grounds that it seemed unreasonably cruel to condemn people to burn for eternity, they had been expelled for bad behaviour from the heavenly paradise of God the Father to spread chaos and disharmony in the world that the gods were trying to bend to their will for the opposite purposes of peace and harmony. Some of us believed that their place of origin was a place called Dartford, just outside London.

And so some people believed this group of young men, known to the world as the Rolling Stones, were the anti-Beatles, part of a prophecy that referred to people who opposed the Beatles and were intent on substituting themselves in place of the Beatles. In the Scriptures we are warned that there are those who "deny the Father and the sons". Thus, not long after the appearance and inexorable rise of the four gods there appeared on the scene this group of young men, headed by their chief sprite, Mick, Father of Darkness, and his acolytes, two of who seemed to be the embodiment of whirlwinds of chaos in the persons of Brian, Lord of Mischief, and Keith, Son of Dionysus, the god of wine, insanity, ritual madness, festivity and theatre. Those who believed this sort of thing tended not to talk too much about Charlie, who seemed quite quiet and his main hobby seemed to be collecting antique firearms, or Bill, whose hobbies included metal detecting and archaeology.

But as with all religions, the question was why spoil a good story by looking at the actual truth?

And so every year, while getting ready to celebrate Beatlemas, we take a peep at the dark side. It was, after all a part of the Great Story; the anti-Beatles were contemporaries of the Gods and it is written in the Holy Book that they, this band of demons and sprites, the Rolling Stones, were given a helping hand by the gods themselves. It is written that the gods, generous in their nature and unaware of the true nature of the Rolling Stones, set them on their way to success. Scripture tells us "God the Father was much displeased with the great dragon, that ancient serpent, who is called the devil or Satan, or Mick to his friends. This deceiver of the whole world was thrown down to the earth and his angels were thrown down with him. And so finding themselves in London in the year of our Lord 1963, somewhat dishevelled from the throwing down from heaven, they looked around themselves and saw, as not everyone saw, the new prophets from Liverpool, who were more than prophets, and set themselves the task of usurping them from the pinnacle they had reached. And though changed from winged angel and tailed serpent to ordinary men, they decided to stay looking dishevelled and immediately caused a stir by the way they looked and they also learned from the gods and imitated them and their hair was a tiny bit longer and the mothers and fathers saw this and feared for their daughters."

And further on in the Scriptures, we are told, 'The gods, all-knowing but innocent in their awareness of the darkness in the world, were instrumental in the rise of the anti-Beatles. It so happened that the man who had been chosen by God to turn down the Beatles, the man who some call Saint Dick of Decca, patron saint of stating that 'guitar groups were on the way out, Mr Epstein', had spent all his waking hours since that time trying to make recompense for that decision, indeed, trying to find the next guitar group. As a result he found himself in the Holy city of Liverpool desperate to find the next Fabulous Foursome, an impossible task given that there could be no others like them, judging a talent contest with none other than George,

Lord of the Weeping Guitars. The magnanimous George, as unimpressed by what he was seeing at the contest as Saint Dick, mentioned to Saint Dick that he should check out a new group called the Rolling Stones that he could see in Richmond. When George turned to speak to Saint Dick again, the chair was empty; Saint Dick had vanished. He was already on his way, with much haste, back down to the south of England to see this new phenomenon as recommended by the word of God."

I liked that "all-knowing but innocent" of the ways of the world. It was pure religious doublespeak. They were either all-knowing or they were not. You would expect a god to recognise the princes of darkness, even if they were in disguise, with the devil hidden in their hearts. Perhaps they knew but could not, like so many others, help being seduced by Mick's lips. Perhaps, as the devout believed in the One True Religion, they were warning us in their parable about the girl having the devil in her heart.

The Fathers, John and Paul, are warning their younger god, George, that she has got the devil in her heart and his reply implies he knows this but her lips they really thrill him. "Who else could this be about?" the religion asks. Well, this depended on your faith. If your faith was strong, then it was clearly about Mick, the devil with the thrilling lips. If your faith was not so strong you might point out that the song seemed to be talking about a girl and was not even written by the gods.

Even if this story of the older, wiser gods warning their younger idealist about the true nature of the Rolling Stones is true, it does not explain the next time Scripture refers to the help the gods gave the fallen angels.

It was a cold December day outside and we had a guest speaker from the little-known organisation – outside of devout religious circles – that was known as the D.I.A., the Demon Intelligence Agency. It was a secretive organisation set up to look into claims of demonic visitation. It originated in the New United States of America and seemed to have its roots in a former organisation set up just before the time of our Lords on earth in order to protect the old United States from threats from abroad. A reading of the history of this organisation seems to suggest that the main threat to the American way of life actually came from that organisation, a seeming law unto themselves, then known as the Central Intelligence Agency.

We all had to sign the Official Secrets Act before being introduced to Brother X (not his real name, we were unnecessarily told), who was then wheeled into the room. An old man with silver-grey hair, a former field agent, now retired to give lectures to devout organisations about the history of the occasional demonic visitation to the material world.

Like a lot of hard-to-believe aspects of religion, these demonic visitations, like the instances of those hearing the voice of God, or visitations by angels, mainly seemed to happen in the past and rarely in the present day. Most of the people who were investigated as potentially possessed by demons in the modern day turned out to simply be assholes or suffering from a mental health problem. The greater equality in the Beatle universe, the emphasis on the importance of love and nurturing of all children tended, unsurprisingly, to produce well-adjusted adults, and when people turned out mean or bad, some in society, especially the more religious, assumed there must be some demonic interference. The rest of society just assumed it was simply a part of the rich tapestry of life, that some people were a bit boring, some were kind, some were generous, some were mean and some were just plain unpleasant. The truth seemed to be that individuals could be all these things at different times. It went back to the age-old conundrum for religion, the problem of evil. That if God was all-powerful and all-knowing why would he allow evil to exist in the world he had created. Did he do it on purpose to amuse himself? "And on the eighth day God created assholes." Some argued it was a result of free will, the gift that God had bestowed upon us, which meant we had the choice to be good or bad. But why could he not in his wisdom have given us free will within the boundaries of goodness? I had a theory that the One True Religion was not comfortable explaining evil or bad behaviour so either ignored it or distracted our attention by referring to demons and fallen angels and telling us tales around the fireside in deepest winter about the original devils fallen to earth to battle against the rise of the Fabulous Four. And so we listened to Brother X, all in rapt attention, some in genuine fear of the existence of the dark side, others like myself because, after all, everybody liked a good ghost story at Beatlemas.

Brother X was telling us of some of the things he had seen in his career. He told us of a case where a group of people had started their own religious cult based on the teachings of Mick, Lord of Darkness. They wore daggers around their necks, a symbol of their dark lord, as Mick told people that a Jagger was a man who in mediaeval times was a knife man whose main job was stabbing people.

Brother X smiled. "We pointed out to them that in the past a jagger was actually someone who looked after pack horses, that they had been deceived by the Great Deceiver. They took this as a great honour, to be deceived by their master. It was then we realised they were harmless idiots. They accepted that the Beatles were gods and that the Stones were simply the antithesis of the Beatles, so were less blasphemous than those small sects that have grown up around other individuals and groups, that claim their particular icon is the true son or sons, daughter or daughters, of God. The Madonnaites, who believe in the 'Like a Virgin Madonna', who on closer inspection of the historical record was nothing like a virgin, the Presleyists, who believe he was more than the Baptiser of the Beatles, the Springsteeners, who worship the life of the working class and American cars, the Gayeites, a prophet assassinated not long after John the Father, who ask the fundamental question 'What's Going On?'. This false god was called Marvin and known to his followers as Marvin the Father. He was, somewhat confusingly, shot and killed by Marvin, his father! There were the Jacksonites, who claim their god was assassinated by the demons Propofol, Lorazepam and Midalozam and who is, of course, frowned upon by the One True Religion for displeasing Paul the Father for buying the sacred Beatle scrolls which Paul saw as rightfully his. Then there are the Beyonceans, who follow the teachings of the goddess Beyonce. Her followers point to the fact that she came to prominence in the group 'Destiny's

Child', that the clue was in the name, that she was indeed the child of destiny with her two disciples Kelly and Michelle before leaving and forming her own ministry. She went on to do good works with her vast wealth but it is of course ridiculous to see this singer as a god."

He paused and there was light laughter at these seemingly ridiculous sects who'd put forward their choice of god to follow. I wanted to ask why their choices were any more ridiculous than the four gods of the main religion but managed to hold my tongue as it was again the kind of question that could get a student expelled. There were many of these, usually, small sects and they were tolerated by the church as long as they remained small and no challenge to the One True Religion. Along with these cults who followed the various prophets who had been around in the time of the Beatles there was also the phenomenon of the Second Coming. It is written, almost as an afterthought in the Holy Book, hidden in a chapter full of other equally insane and unlikely prophecies, originally entitled "Prophecies", that the Beatles will one day return to earth in a second coming.

"After they all ascended into heaven, they sat two on each side of God the Father. It was known, although no words were spoken, that they would come again, to Earth, in their glory to judge the living and the dead."

There it was written in the Holy Book, so it must be true. This meant the devout were constantly on the lookout for the next John, Paul, George and Ringo and there was a continuous stream of charlatans, many claiming to be the newly risen John or Paul, quite a few claiming to be the reborn George and one instance of an individual claiming to be Ringo who was soon assessed by the Order of John the Father, to be suffering from delusions of whatever the opposite of grandeur was. Mixed in with this expectation of the Second Coming of the Beatles was the idea that the anti-Beatles would appear just before the Second Coming, presaging a great battle between the forces of love and peace and the forces of anarchy and chaos. So the devout were also on the lookout for any reprobate or seeming threat to society so they could proclaim them the anti-Beatles, partly in horror, but also in the hope that it meant the Beatles were on their way down from heaven. Most people took this prophecy with a large pinch of salt and got on with their lives, although it was a very popular concept in the New United States, who were much more devout than most. It served the purpose of keeping the devout busy looking for imaginary saviours and devils when they might otherwise be spending their time enforcing their ultra orthodox views on the rest of us. I had the feeling that the devoutest John in our class, "Pope John", suspected I might be an anti-Beatle, a spy in the house of God, sowing discord among the faithful.

Brother X was telling the age-old story of the Rolling Stones revealing their true nature. "Though they spread chaos wherever they played, with their concerts often ending in a riot, they managed to insinuate themselves into the fabric of society and, once they had done so, felt it was safe to reveal what they really were. In response to the gods who had once again wooed and wowed the world with their musical masterpiece in the year of our Lords 1967, the Rolling Stones responded with their own attempt to seduce the world with the album that revealed who they really were. 'Their Satanic Majesties Request'."

He paused, letting this evidence of their satanic nature sink in. He clicked a button and an image of the cover of that album came up on a screen behind him. It took all of my willpower not to laugh. He had shown us the image as evidence of their belonging to the dark side. Mick Jagger was sat with the other Stones, all dressed in faintly silly clothes, dressed as a wizard with a ridiculously large wizard hat, and any notion of them as a threat to society or anyone was immediately dispelled by this picture of five men dressed in silly clothing.

"This was the first time they revealed themselves but not the last time. If anybody was left in any doubt about their true nature they made it quite clear with their sermon 'Sympathy for the Devil', when Mick Jagger finally introduced us to who he really was. He asked us to guess his name but he had already told us in the title. 'Just call me Lucifer,' he says. The anti-Beatles of course will try to mimic the real thing, and John the Father in His wisdom believed this to be the case. He said, 'Everything we did, Mick does exactly the same. He imitates us.' And so I would introduce to you, these men of wealth and taste, their Satanic Majesties."

He swept his arm dramatically to indicate the picture behind him. I again stifled a laugh, and when I was in control of my face I could not help myself. I had to ask some awkward questions. I tried to put them diplomatically. Brother X nodded at my raised hand.

"Could I ask what you make of the gods sending the Rolling Stones what appears to be a greeting on the cover of their masterpiece? It not only says 'Welcome the Rolling Stones' but 'Welcome good guys the Rolling Stones'. I mean, how do you interpret 'good guys'?" I continued as innocently as possible. "I would, for example, think it meant they thought the Rolling Stones were good guys and not the princes of darkness. I mean, they use the actual word 'good'. Were the gods wrong, then? Were they bad judges of character? Could they not spot a demon a mile off? And to show their mutual appreciation, didn't the Rolling Stones, if you look closely, include pictures of the gods on the cover of their 'Satanic Majesties' album?"

Brother X gave me a shocked look that suggested I had gone too far and I could hear the tutting of the devoutest of the Johns, who was sitting in the front row lapping up the talk of the demon Stones. Brother X recovered himself and managed a false smile. "You are, of course, correct about the message, but the church believes it was a demonic invasion, put there without the knowledge of the gods, and anyway this was before the great reveal of the 'Satanic Majesties' and their announcement of where their true 'Sympathy' lay. And as for the faces of the gods on their own inferior attempt to copy Sergeant Pepper, well, we believe, in the DIA, it was part of an attempt to put a demonic charm on the gods, a failed attempt of course. The records show that after this time there was less cordiality between the two camps. John the Father started on His journey to show the world the way to peace and love and an end to war; the Rolling Stones carried on their dark path which eventually led them to Altamont and the ultimate in dark demonic acts, a human sacrifice."

He let that hang in the air and then carried on with his case against the Rolling Stones. "It is written in the Holy Book about the time when the Rolling Stones released their most diabolic sermon proclaiming 'Sympathy for the Devil', when Mick described all the horrors through history that he had been involved in. It was hidden on an album which included other sermons which amongst other things incited the people to riot in the streets and another stating their desire to sleep with underage girls."

He picked an ancient, leather-bound copy of the Holy Book from Brother John's desk and opened it at a page where he had placed a bookmark. He read, "And in the year of our Lords 1968, there was held a bacchanal by the devil and his demon friends to celebrate the release of their latest blasphemy. And so was gathered at the Vesuvio an assortment of sprites, hobgoblins, witches and mischievous spirits from the darkest cellars and underground dwellings in London, spewing forth from the volcano in a wild celebration of the dark arts. It was a scene of untold excess. Moroccan drapes were festooned on the walls, large pictures of the chief demons narcissistically arranged between the drapes. An endless supply of mescaline and alcohol were placed around in huge silver bowls, temptation abounded at every turn. And into this wild melee was added the mix of the Rolling Stones playing their new long-playing record. And the guests were said to be mesmerised, particularly with the song proclaiming that their true sympathy lay with the devil himself! And into this satanic revelry there appeared two gods. John and Paul, the Fathers, had heard of this abomination happening in their kingdom and decided to attend, unbeknownst to the devils no longer in disguise. And so Paul bravely approached the man who was playing the blasphemous songs of devilment and respectfully asked if He would play His own sermon. The man knew this would be against his master's wish but felt unable to resist the command of this man who seemed so familiar. And so He played the song of the Beatles and lo, there was silence for the next seven minutes and eleven seconds. And all the demonic spells were broken and many formerly fallen angels saw the light that night and repented and went on to live righteous lives.'"

He put the book down and gave me a meaningful look. I felt he was daring me to question the Holy Book. I held my tongue. I would have been on very dangerous ground. It was, of course, all nonsense. John and Paul did not sneak in, they had been invited, had actually enjoyed the music of their rivals. It was true they had played their new song and the guests had been mightily impressed. Who would not have been? And 'Hey Jude' did sound like another gift from God, so I could see how the story might arise, and it was, after all, all about the story. And so I wisely kept my own counsel. That if there was an orgy of indulgence that night, John the Father, according to the unofficial texts discouraged by the church, was indulging quite merrily himself and left with his eyes popping out of his holy head.

Brother X was giving his final evidence for the case for the prosecution. "And in that same year, the anti-Beatles filmed a show, their infamous 'Rock and Roll Circus' in which not only did they perform 'Sympathy for the Devil' but Jagger ripped off his shirt and revealed a picture of the face of the devil in his true form drawn across his chest. It is rumoured it was painted with the blood of a virgin. The powers that be decided this unholy film could not be shown on television for fear it would corrupt those that were unfortunate enough to watch it."

He did not mention that John the Father also appeared in this "infamous" programme or that the usual reason given for not showing it was that Mick Jagger felt they had been upstaged by the performance of "The Who", another group of young prophets around in the time of our Lords, who, of course, now had their own small religious cult following who talked a lot about wanting to die before they got old and not wanting to get fooled again. They even had their own cult within a cult called the Moonies, who believed in living lives of excess and silliness.

I put my hand up.

Brother X frowned and nodded at me. "Yes?" he said impatiently, eager to carry on his tirade of evidence against the Stones.

"Could I just ask why the powers that be would ban this film for being too demonic, yet years later they gave him a knighthood?"

"Yes, well, the devil works to inveigle himself into the corridors of power by flattery and subterfuge. He often moves in mysterious ways."

"I thought that was God the Father."

"Yes, he too sometimes moves in mysterious ways, but as we keep saying the devil is the great imitator."

I gave up; the man was clearly insane. He had the unseeing glint of fanaticism in his steely blue eyes. He had spent a lifetime dedicated to unearthing demons and devils and studying their history. Where I saw bad behaviour, he saw the influence of the devil; where I saw someone with mental health issues, he saw demonic possession; where I saw dark shadows, he saw dark shadows in the dark shadows. I was asking him to question this lifetime of dedication, a pointless task. I decided to sit back and enjoy the story.

"It was at this time that the Rolling Stones became involved with the occultist film maker Kenneth Anger. Mick Jagger provided the music for his film which was called"—dramatic pause—"'Invocation of My Demon Brother'. It was a short film with music by Jagger and starring Bobby Beausoleil. Does anybody know about Mr Beausoleil's other famous activities?"

As usual, given we were a religious community who spent our lives studying the times of the Beatles, examining every aspect of the time of their ministry on earth, nearly every hand went up. Brother X pointed to a front-row John.

"He was a disciple of the man many see as the true anti-Beatle, a man who managed to interpret the lyrics of the Lords in a manner most blasphemous and completely against their true meaning." He paused and almost whispered the name as if to say it too loud would summon up the darkness it represented to the followers of the One True Religion. "Charles Manson."

"Very good. So you have a connection between the anti-Beatles, imitating and insinuating themselves into the world of the Beatles in England, and the man, as you rightly say, who by the very evilness of his actions is held by many to be the true anti-Beatle."

Hang on. He had spent the last hour telling us that the Rolling Stones were the anti-Beatles and now he told us there was another one. How many anti-Beatles were there?

He continued. "The story of Manson the evil prophet is for another time. For now I will leave you with the facts of the events in the year of our Lords 1969, when the Rolling Stones committed the ultimate demonic act, a human sacrifice, in Altamont, California, exactly a year to the day of the release of their acknowledgement of their true nature, 'Sympathy for the Devil'. This time of year is known in the One True Religion as a time of darkness, when evil spirits come out to play, a time when I do not need to remind you of the terrible events that occurred over a decade later on December the eighth, the time of the Assassination. And who carried out this terrible deed? This blood sacrifice in Altamont? The people who had been hired by the Stones as their security, the Hells Angels. Yes, angels, not from heaven, but from the depths of hell itself. They sacrificed an innocent young man and at the same time released their new long-playing record entitled, in honour of their dastardly deed, 'Let It Bleed'."

He looked around the classroom with a look of triumph on his ancient face, his glance lingering on me, the Doubting Thomas of the class, daring me to refute the obvious evidence of diabolism he had laid out. I could have pointed out that they had held the free concert in the first place as a nice gesture to their fans, that they were horrified by the events at the concert, but I could see there was no point. Even in the history books they talked about the earlier concert at Woodstock representing the height of the flowering of the counterculture of love and peace, whereas Altamont signalled the end of it. I could have reminded him that the One True Religion did not believe in a place called hell, but the others seemed gripped by his story, so why spoil their fun? The truth was I enjoyed a good Beatlemas ghost story as much as the next man.

# Chapter Nineteen
## Happy Beatlemas. War is Over.

---

The train pulled into the station and came to a smooth stop. My ever-smiling mother was stood on the platform and seemed to be wearing reindeer antlers on her head. It turned out to be her Beatlemas outfit for the day. She loved Beatlemas. Her children returned and there were parties and get-togethers and singing and dancing and general merriment. I had the feeling my father disliked Beatlemas for all the same reasons. I pressed the button, the train doors swooshed open and I stepped onto the platform. My mother rushed over and gave me a crushing hug. She stepped back and looked me over.

"Happy Beatlemas," she said.

"War is over." I gave the expected reply.

"Is that all you've got?" she said, nodding at my small bag.

"Oh, yeah, imagine no possessions and everything."

"Yes, of course." She paused and then said. "You haven't gone all religious, have you?"

"You do know where I am when I'm away?"

"Yes and we're very proud of you and we love our Fathers who sing in heaven but we don't want you to spend your life chanting and living in a cave."

I laughed. "Is that what you think we do? I think you might be getting me mixed up with bats. We do spend time in contemplation occasionally but there's not much chanting and I haven't spent any time in a cave yet."

We were making our way through the spotlessly clean station building. There were plenty of people milling about, passengers from my train and people leaving to go wherever they were going for the Beatlemas holidays. It was a relatively large station but there were hardly any staff around. Everything was automated. The government had a policy of doing away with as many menial tasks as possible. The Beatles had believed in doing something they loved, which for them was making music, and the life lived ordinary was something they had only briefly experienced and discovered it was not for them. Each god had worked briefly with his hands to show they were attuned to the lives of the masses but they soon turned to their more important task of being gods.

As it turned out not everyone was a creative genius (or a god) and some people genuinely loved trains and enjoyed working in and around them. And customers liked to see other human beings to ask their questions. The trains themselves were driven by automatic pilots but there were always staff available. It had always been a question for egalitarian societies. Who would do the menial and crappy jobs? Presumably this had been asked by the more well-off who were worried about who would wait on their tables and clean their streets and so on. The answer was that a lot of the menial jobs could be simply done away with, automated by new technology, and the rest were done by people who actually enjoyed doing them, some like the rail staff almost on a volunteer basis. As they were largely unnecessary, they were paid a minimum wage which was supplemented by the basic income that the government paid that ensured that everyone had a good standard of living. Those jobs that were menial and crappy but essential were simply very well rewarded. This contrasted with the bad old days when these jobs were usually done by immigrants who were, at the same time, usually ill-treated because they were immigrants in a double whammy of unfairness. Because of the policy of equality in all countries in the sphere of the One True Religion, immigration was no longer based on economic necessity but rather curiosity about the world.

We had reached my mother's electric car in the car park. I threw my bag into the back seat and climbed into the passenger seat. My mother got into the other front seat and drove off. She did not really need to drive; she could have just put the postcode in and let the car automatically drive there. But she did not trust the car and so always drove manually. Unfortunately she was a terrible driver and the car was covered in scratches and dents from her numerous mishaps. Luckily the many safety features in the car tended to prevent any serious accidents. Technology had not in fact advanced all that much since the time of our Lords. The time before the rise of the One True Religion was so taken up by the wars that raged around the world that most of the advances were concentrated on the development of more effective weapons. After the slow but inexorable rise and spread of the One True Religion, the advancement of technology slowed to a snail's pace. This was for two main reasons. Firstly, as part of the beliefs of the new system it was ordained that science and technology should be directed towards the purpose of improving the life of people and saving the planet. This replaced the previous emphasis which was driven by the profit motive. This meant there would be a pointless new version of a piece of equipment every year with "new" features that the multinationals, with their powerful advertising departments, would convince us were absolutely essential. People would upgrade their phones and entertainment systems on an annual basis. For example the Apple corporation, who had cleverly appropriated the name that the gods had chosen for their own venture, doomed to failure in their own time due to being ahead of its time, had by the time of the start of the new religion just released their iPhone 250. This insanity had stopped, along with the nationalisation of social media, a pernicious twenty-first century development that had led to the spread of nonsense on a global scale and the making of billions for individuals who had had the good fortune of having one good idea. The state had nationalised and then released the many forms of social media under strict restrictions, realising the danger of the state being in control of such a powerful medium.

If the first reason for the brakes put on technological advancement were political, the second reason came directly from the Greatest Story Ever Told, the story of the Beatles. John the Father, a god who loved gadgets and new technology, was sent a warning, so the Holy Book tells us, by God the Father, in the form of a mischievous sprite called "Magic Alex". He was a young man from Greece who held the gods, especially John the Father, in his spell for several years. He impressed John, the Fire God, with his "Nothing Box". What did the box do? Frankly, the clue was in the title. It was a box with a set of lights that blinked randomly. Seemingly on the basis of this electronic wizardry and various claims he made about the gadgets he would invent, he was installed as head of "Apple Electronics". But he comes later in the Great Story. Suffice to say that the One True Religion has taken his appearance in the lives of the gods as a warning against the claims of scientific and technological progress. Quite a lot of people, especially scientists and inventors in general, have argued that rather than a warning against science and technology, it should be a warning against listening to charlatans. The church thought this would attract attention to the fact that the gods, generally thought to be all-knowing, had been duped by a man who had hypnotised them with a box of flashing lights, so instead made a big thing of the experience being a warning against technology itself.

"So, have you met a nice young woman?" My mother asked the same question she always asked when I came home for a visit. She tried to keep the desperation out of her voice, but it had got worse since the last time I had been home.

"No, funnily enough, I haven't met a young woman in the all-male religious college I attend."

"Well, you are allowed out aren't you?"

"Do we have to go through this every time I come home?"

"I just want you to be happy. And I thought it was a religious duty to seek love. After all, the second commandment is 'All You Need is Love'." I saw her looking out of the corner of her eye. She looked pleased with herself at this new approach in her long campaign to see me "happy", which meant, to her, being in a relationship.

Maybe she was right. I thought about it. I was human, I felt lust. I just had not met anyone yet. I could not work out whether I was a romantic, looking for the perfect partner, or simply lazy. Including other people in your life was hard work and looked quite complex. I had my books and my friends, but I still thought about it. Others in the Lennonary had girlfriends and boyfriends; there were no rules against it. As my mother had said, it was almost a religious duty to love in the eyes of the One True Religion.

"I'm fine, Mother."

"There's always the relationship centre."

I raised my eyebrows. The relationship centre was a modern day version of the old job centre. Instead of jobs which were plentiful and easy to find, often guided by the government department for work and pensions, this centre provided people with options for finding partners in love. So central had the notion of love become in the One True Religion, there was a whole government department dedicated to the finding of true love or something quite close. In the old days we had been concerned by the numbers of unemployed; now the main concern was the numbers of unattached. The Prime Minister had even come up with a new term for the policies involved. She had called it Emotional Socialism. It was put forward that left to the market, there was an unfair distribution of love in the world and that it was necessary for the state to help out as much as possible.

There were those who thought we should be free to be lonely and unhappy and saw this as yet another example of the state interfering in our lives, but the truth was it was really only there for those who needed it. There was no question of it being made compulsory to be in a relationship. There was just a lot of help offered to find love. From an early age we were offered advice and guidance on relationships and sex. We were told of the bad old days when women were treated in unacceptable ways, suffering sexual harassment and rape. The rules around consent were made very clear and there was much discussion around domestic violence. Psychologists talked to us about how our instinctual behaviours might not lead to happiness, that men were overly forgiving of a pretty face and that women were overly impressed by confidence and status and that although these might explain attraction it did not necessarily lead to lasting love. Each person was allowed to be who they felt they were in terms of their sexuality. No longer was a person made to feel any less of a human simply for being who they were, with the only exception those who had a proclivity for children.

One of the great government departments was the Department for Happiness, which was dedicated to providing the pillars of happiness for each individual. John the Father is famously quoted as saying, "When I was five years old my mother always told me that happiness was the key to life. When I went to school they asked me what I wanted to be when I grew up. I wrote down 'happy'. They told me I didn't understand the assignment, and I told them they didn't understand life."

This is the quote above the entrance to the fabulous building that houses the Ministry of Happiness. Some academic scholars have pointed out that there is no source for this quote and therefore we cannot guarantee that he ever said it. Some religious scholars have pointed out that he wrote a sermon called "Happiness is a Warm Gun" and that we should study the message of this song for the meaning of happiness. Luckily this has not happened apart from a few diehard fundamentalists who have driven themselves half crazy by trying to untangle the meaning of this song. Not only does it seem to be split in three parts, with the first two parts showcasing John the Father at his playful, indecipherable best, the third part is either a not-too-well-hidden comment on sex or is informing us that happiness is based on the feeling of a warm gun – that is, a gun that has just been fired. This seems to go so much against John the Father's general teachings about peace and love that it is only taken seriously by a very few fundamentalist Johnnists who believe that the word of God is the word of God, however mystifying, and therefore must be given due attention. Sanity has prevailed and instead the quote he quite possibly never said has become the basis for many government policies.

The pillars of happiness tended to change with different governments but there are five pillars that tend to remain the same. The five pillars were a loving relationship, good family ties, meaningful employment, a decent place to live and a decent social life, or the pillar of friendship as it was also known. Different ministers try to make their name by adding new elements that they believe lead to happiness, sometimes successfully, sometimes verging on the ridiculous. The latest Minister for Happiness, for example, has decided that an element to achieving happiness was "helping others" and has come up with a reward system that rewarded people for acts of kindness. There was an intense argument going on at the moment between the minister and the advisor who had come up with this idea, who was arguing that the minister was missing the point by actually rewarding people, that the act of kindness leads to a good feeling that was a reward in itself, while the minister, a practical man and a politician who wanted to be seen doing something, argued how could you encourage people to do more acts of kindness without rewarding them? And so the madness went on. But I could see it was a harmless madness. Coming up with policies to get people to be kind to each other sounded like the definition of insanity but it also sounded similar to the kind of mad, utopian, idealistic idea that John the Father might come up with, particularly in what has become known as the time of his "Peace Ministry". At the end of the 1960s John the Father stayed in bed for peace, planted acorns for peace and put up posters telling the world war could be over, if only we wanted it to be. So seemingly mad ideas, if their hearts were in the right place, were often taken on. The populace would smile and shrug their shoulders.

"I don't need to go to the relationship centre. I'm perfectly happy. Where's Dad?" I asked to change the subject.

"Oh, he's in his shed, as usual. I told him last week that he loved that shed more than he loved me."

"What did he say?"

"He said of course he didn't, while looking longingly at the shed."

"I suppose it could be worse. He could be spending his time with another woman."

"I think I'd rather be spurned for another woman. How would you like coming second to a shed?"

I laughed. I am fairly sure she was joking. "What's he doing in there?"

"The Lords alone know. He's taken up looking at the stars, bought himself an expensive telescope. He keeps going on about how the stars are aligning."

"Really? Does he think something momentous is going to happen?"

"No, he's a scientist. I think he literally means the stars are aligning. Some large stars are aligning and appearing as one."

"Well, doesn't that usually portend some great event? Weren't the stars said to have aligned in July 1957, when the two Fathers met?"

"Well, if you believe in that sort of thing," she said and then looked at me and laughed, presumably remembering her son was a second year student at a religious college who might be expected to believe in exactly "that sort of thing". "Oh, it's the Beatlemas Fayre this evening, at Saint Peter's Church."

I groaned. The Beatlemas Fayre was a tradition in our family. A celebration of Beatlemas with stalls that sold refreshments, singing and dancing, silly games and which usually ended with a service and the singing of Beatlemas carols. All the proceeds went to improving the church, a wonderful old building which was a replica of the church in Woolton where it had all begun all those years ago. It received an annual grant for repairs which was never quite enough. This year storms had damaged the roof and the parish priest had deemed the Fayre the "Beatlemas 'Fixing a Hole' Fayre". I had loved the Fayre as a child, had eagerly looked forward to it as a magical and exciting evening, but the sheen had worn off as I got older and it was now something to be reluctantly endured. What had seemed magical now just looked ordinary through my adult eyes.

I looked at my mother's expectant face and knew there was no getting out of it. She loved it. My father, who felt similar to me, had taken to inviting me to his shed before we left and offering a variety of alcoholic drinks, some of which he had made himself in the famous shed which doubled as a small brewery and now apparently trebled as an observatory, in order to soften the edges of the evening to come.

Two hours later and I was sitting in one of the two chairs in my father's shed. With the emphasis on sustainability, society had gone through a number of materials to use for construction throughout recent history. This had included using something called cob, sheep's wool, cork, recycled steel, hay bales, rubber and so on. My father's shed was made of wood. There were sustainably managed forests and people liked the look of wood. Indeed studies had shown that being surrounded by a natural material like wood significantly increased an individual's feeling of wellbeing. The Department of Happiness soon got involved and there had been a spate of policies to encourage people to buy wooden houses and other buildings. Because of the influence of the One True Religion, Norway had become the tree-growing centre of the world. Forestry had always been a traditional and important industry in Norway and now it was *the* industry. It allowed people to say their building was made from Norwegian Wood, which people believed brought a blessing upon the place.

My father was standing in front of the door, blocking my escape, grinning like a madman. In one hand he held a small glass with his homemade vodka made from his home-grown potatoes and in the other was a taller glass holding a dark swirling liquid that seemed to have a life of its own. I had been given the same and took a sip of the vodka. After I had stopped coughing and I could once again see through my watering eyes, I looked up at my still grinning father.

"Good stuff isn't it?"

"John almighty, Dad. That really stings the back of your throat."

"Sign of a good vodka."

"According to who? How much of this stuff have you made?"

"Oh, you know, a few gallons."

"Gallons? What are you going to do with all that?"

"Well, between you and me, I thought I'd drink it." He took a sip and coughed a little and a few tears welled up in his eyes. "It certainly warms the cockles of your heart."

"It's the lining of my stomach I'm worried about." I took a sip of the stout. In truth it was not too bad so I put the vodka down and took sips from the stout to take the taste of the vodka away. It was all very well being alcoholically fortified for the Beatlemas Fayre but I wanted to be able to stand up. Alcohol was not illegal as such but it was extremely highly taxed because of its links to problematic behaviour. The church supported this, often reciting the experience of John the Father's lost weekend, which lasted for eighteen months and saw him drinking to excess and occasionally making a fool of himself. They put this forward as a warning about the dangers of excessive alcohol use, that he went through this experience in order to help us understand the dangers, to suffer for us so we would not need to.

Scripture even provides a nice little story to excuse the behaviour of the Fire God. He was said to be inconsolable after being separated from the love of his life, Yoko, Ocean Child. He took to drinking to numb the misery, and there is even a story of the miracle of John the Father turning milk into brandy. It is told that he was drinking a glass of milk one evening while thinking of his lost and distant love and his tears fell off his face and into his milk, turning it into a delicious drink of milk and brandy which he continued to drink until he was reunited with Yoko.

Although alcohol was not illegal, just very expensive because of the high taxes, the making of alcohol without a government licence was against the law and so my father, my gentle, well-meaning, eccentric father was an unlikely fugitive from the law. He never sold any of his booze, just drank it himself and gave it to his long-suffering family members, so under normal circumstances he was pretty safe from the authorities. However, he was not the only person who had a shed and a homemade distillery, and one of the problematic behaviours that had been related to alcohol use in the bad old days was intimate partner violence. When there was the occasional outbreak of domestic violence the police would always search the shed first and if enough home distilleries were found it would lead to a round of random shed raids.

My father did not drink very often and neither did he become aggressive when he did. It was just another one of his many hobbies. When he drank he became a little more talkative and then usually fell asleep. He now turned to his latest hobby and directed me to take a look through his new toy, an impressive looking telescope that was pointed at the night sky, which seemed a good start. I looked through the eyepiece lens at the clear night sky. I saw a million stars in the sky. I straightened up and looked at my father. His face had a look of excited expectancy on it. I gave up.

"What am I looking at?"

"It's the night sky."

"I see you've done your research."

He ignored my sarcasm and told me to have another look. "Can't you see the planets are aligning?"

I looked but there were just a lot of twinkling stars in the sky. "Mother said it was the stars that were aligning."

"Well, it sounded better when I was telling her; she likes a good story and stars aligning sounds better than the planets aligning. But it's the planets and it only happens once in a blue moon."

"What does it mean?"

"Mean? It doesn't mean anything, it's just exciting because it happens so rarely."

"What is the difference between a planet and a star anyway?" I foolishly asked, as I should have known that my father, a scientist and an enthusiastic follower of the useless fact, told me the differences.

"Of course, by definition a star is a celestial body that emits its own light whereas a planet gets its light from a star. The earth is a planet and it gets its light from the sun, a star. So which is bigger, a planet or a star?"

"I would have thought a planet."

He looked at me with a look of small triumph. "No, a star is much bigger than a planet."

He went on to tell me about the other differences, which included their shapes, their temperatures and the matter they were made of. After five minutes I was reaching for the homemade vodka and my coughing and spluttering finally silenced my father's lecture.

"So, anyway, if you look closely you can see two planets aligning and they seem to have reached perfect alignment tonight. I think it's Jupiter and Saturn."

"But it doesn't mean anything?"

"Why does everything have to mean something? Sometimes things just happen for no reason and we should appreciate them for what they are."

Without realising, he had just dismissed fifty percent of all religious belief with his implication that the world might just be filled with random meaningless events. I had come to realise that I was essentially a contrarian and liked to argue with people whether I agreed with them or not. In the Lennonary I was surrounded by believers and therefore found myself questioning their every belief and statement, and now in the outside world I found myself questioning my scientist father.

"I can't see the planets aligning because I don't know what I'm looking at, but what about the planets involved? Wasn't Jupiter the king of the gods?" I was not even sure what point I was making. It might have been the vodka talking.

My father looked at me blankly and then, perhaps like my mother, remembering where I was when I was not at home, he seemed to try and humour me.

"Yes, and Saturn gathered together the unruly peoples under his jurisdiction and gave them laws, and under his reign were the golden ages that men tell of, he ruled the nations in perfect peace," he said, quoting from some obscure source. He nodded thoughtfully as if he could see that perhaps the alignment of the planets could indeed be seen as something that signalled good tidings. And then, being my father, he ruined it.

"Oh, and he was said to eat his sons so they would not usurp him."

"Nice, let's hope he hasn't given you any ideas. What about that really bright star in the sky?"

"That's it, that's the two planets in conjunction. Some people call it the Star of Liverpool, said to have appeared over the city of Liverpool the night before the historic meeting of the two gods. There's a few people who call it the Star of Bethlehem, based on some old story about guiding kings and shepherds to the birthplace of the son of God a long time before the actual sons of God appeared."

"Right. Do you think He will be hoping for a daughter next time?"

My father looked thoughtful and then said, "I suppose it depends on who writes the story."

I had thought my father was a religious man, not particularly devout, but certainly a believer. He had now, perhaps with his tongue loosened by the firewater he had made, after suggesting the world was a place made up of random meaningless events, suggested that religion was a story. I suppose it was. The fact was that a story could be true or fictitious.

I took another look through the eyepiece of the telescope and stared at the brightest star in the sky. It seemed so close to the earth that its downward beam of shining light seemed to reach all the way down to the ground like a high-powered spotlight, and it seemed to be shining on my small town. I decided not to drink any more of my father's vodka.

\*\*\*

It was a cold, clear night. The sky was cloudless and the stars were visible but seemed dwarfed by the bright star that I had come to think of as the Star of Liverpool, although my pedantic father kept reminding me it was actually two planets in conjunction and not a star. We arrived at the church hall at just before seven. It was early and there were not many people there yet, but my mother had promised to help with setting up the stalls and the readying of the stage for the entertainment later on. She herded me and my father through the door and gave us various instructions. They were mainly around the theme of not sneaking off early and a particularly stern order to enjoy ourselves or else.

She wandered off to offer her services and before she could offer ours as well, we scurried off and found a semi-hidden corner where we sat down on some boxes. My father produced a small hip flask and two small steel cups and poured us both a drink.

"Cheers," he said and downed the contents in one. His coughing fit and leaky eyes told me what was in the flask, so I decided to sip mine.

My father was telling me about his new stargazing hobby and was describing to me what a comet was. I was not sure why, I had certainly not asked, but by now his tongue was moonshine loose and the facts were flowing like a recently undammed river. He had moved on and was saying, "Good question, the difference between an asteroid and a comet…" although I had no recollection of asking that question, when we were mercifully interrupted.

Ivana was an old school friend, part of a tight circle of friends who had thought themselves dangerous rebels against the world of adults. In retrospect we were just another group of friends and despite our firm belief that we were virtual outlaws, it was all in our youthful heads. I could not think of anything we did that was dangerous or really rebellious; it was all talk. As we got older we were all pretty much integrated into the traditional bastions of the system. I was in a religious college and Ivana was in her last year at university, where she was studying the New Classics. This was the study of those two great empires of the far past that included the time of our Lords. The empires of Great Britain and the old United States. It was a course which looked at the literature, history, philosophy and languages of the ancient British and American worlds. A religious and a classics scholar!

Ivana, tall and untidy, looked the part of absentminded scholar with her short, messy brown hair and her seemingly thrown-together outfit of baggy jumper and jeans. She solemnly greeted my father and politely listened to his stories of the stars and then dragged me away, telling me there was someone she wanted me to meet. We made our way to the other side of the hall towards a group of young people who were standing around the church piano, a sacred instrument in the One True Religion largely because John the Father had written "Imagine", the Lords' Prayer on it. Someone was playing a tune and they clearly knew how to play. We reached them and I leaned over the piano player's shoulder to watch her fingers move gracefully over the keyboard. I recognised the tune in the deep recesses of my mind but could not put a name to it. It felt like a tune that was important and historical and I also felt it usually had words but the player was not singing. A line about being too tired flashed through my mind but then was gone. As I leaned over she stopped playing and looked at me over her shoulder.

"Paul almighty," she said, smiling up at me. "I am getting wafts of alcohol from someone here, that's making me feel quite giddy."

There was some familiar laughter and I looked up to see my sister Linda was a part of the group. I looked around me at other familiar faces from the neighbourhood, the three King sisters from next door and the two Shepherd brothers from across the road and my sister Linda, and then my gaze rested on the young woman sitting at the piano.

She looked a couple of years younger than me with short blonde hair cut into a traditional Beatle bob. She was wearing a black polo-neck jumper with tight-fitting black trousers and black suede boots. At first I thought she may have been a devotee of Saint Astrid, but Ivana soon disabused me of this notion with her introduction.

"This is Paula. She's an old friend from college. She's in her second year now in the Order of Paul the Father."

I must have looked aghast because Paula laughed and said, "Don't worry, I love all the gods equally, as I'm sure you do. You must be John. I've heard a lot about you."

I tried to formulate words but they did not seem to want to come out in the right order. I thought it was the result of the virtual ambush of my friend and sister to deliver me into the orbit of a mortal enemy, a devotee of the other Father, the second Father, the least popular of the gods in our order. When I had thought about the question of why Paul was treated with disdain in our order, I'd realised I had no idea why. In fact, the more I thought about it the more I understood there needed to be a Paul. I simply could not imagine four Johns; all that fire could only have led to a massive conflagration. It needed Paul, the Water God, to put out all the little fires started by

John. When I asked my fellow students why they were not so keen on Paul, the other Father, they would look around them cautiously to check no one was around (you must remember that officially all the gods were sacred and equally loved) and nod wisely and give their various reasons. None of them made sense to me. He was too ambitious, too driven, one of them told me. This seemed a strange criticism, especially of someone they accepted was a god. Others said he disliked Saint Stuart, constantly made fun of him and his terrible bass playing. This was a cardinal sin for the Johnnists, who knew Stuart was John's best friend. But Stuart *was* a bad bass player and if Paul was jealous of Stuart, did that not show that he loved John? The rest of the comments seem to coalesce around the idea that he was too nice, as if this was a crime, that there was something essentially suspicious about this. When I say that this is often the way Ringo, Our Starr in Heaven, is portrayed, as a nice guy and that this is seen as positive, they will reply, "Oh, well, that's just Ringo."

Perhaps that goes to the root of the matter. Ringo was just Ringo. Paul, on the other hand, was a worthy rival of John the Father. Having thought about it for some time I came to the conclusion I had nothing against Paul the Father and secretly admired him. I just went along with the general disregard in the Lennonary because it seemed politic to do so. I was also careful never to praise him in front of my Stuartite friends who, understandably, held him in an extremely low regard and never mentioned his name if they could avoid it. Then there was the feelings of John the Father about Paul. The scriptures tell us about the brotherly love, the sacred connection between the two. The last ten years of John the Father's mortal life is a tale of initial bitterness between the two. Paul would make attempts to connect with John and they would occasionally meet. The bitterness began to fade as he came to the last years of his life. That sounded to me like the trajectory of a love affair that came to an end. The greater the bitterness, the greater the love, and John the Father was clearly very bitter.

And there I was in the presence of a disciple of Paul. I had been brought up with a Paulist sister so was used to the petty bickering that the two camps tended to engage in. But this follower of Paul was a smiling assassin, with her perfect teeth and blue-grey eyes containing no trace of animosity. She radiated friendliness. I thought of all the put-downs and witticisms I had taunted my sister with through the years, all the reasons why most of the students in the Lennonary were secretly against Paul, the other Father, and eventually came out with:

"Nice to meet you."

She smiled and turned back to the keyboards where she played an old favourite Beatlemas song, unsurprisingly Paulist, "The Pipes of Peace". The others joined in the singing. I stayed for a few choruses and then made a hasty retreat, feeling as if I had received a severe shock. I found my father still hiding in the corner and asked him some more questions about the stars. His tedious answers seemed to work. The rapid beating of my heart seemed to abate after a short time.

We were later joined by Paula, who had wandered over with the three King sisters.

"We come bearing gifts," the oldest King sister, Olivia, said. They had brought some hot mulled wine, a popular Beatlemas drink, although no one seemed to know why. No one had ever been able to connect it to the Beatles.

As the evening grew more lively with a variety of performers on stage and dancing in the middle of the hall, the others drifted off to join the fun and I found myself alone with Paula. She talked a lot about John the Father with a surprising amount of in-depth knowledge. She even quoted large extracts from his two books, sacred texts to the fundamentalists, a bit of a laugh to the more sane. She read her audience, who happened to be me, so read the stories in the sense of them being funny, even quoting her esteemed Father, Paul, who wrote the introduction to John the Father's first book and instructed us, "None of it has to make sense and if it seems funny then that's enough." She said these words in a way that seemed to suggest it could be a philosophy on life itself.

If she had set out to impress me then she had succeeded. I did not let this show outwardly but I could not help thinking that she seemed to mirror a lot of my own thoughts and feelings about John and Paul and the One True Religion. We were finally interrupted by the Shepherd brothers who came along and marvelled at the birth of this unlikely friendship and they said, with only a little mockery in their voices, "Glory to God the Father in the highest and on earth peace, goodwill to all men and women."

# Author Profile

Born in Somerset in 1967 to the tune of "Strawberry Fields Forever", the author is now working on the Second Book of the Beatles. He now lives in Brighton.

What Did You Think of
*Love Them Do: The First Book of the Beatles?*

A big thank you for purchasing this book. It means a lot that you chose this book specifically from such a wide range on offer. I do hope you enjoyed it.

Book reviews are incredibly important for an author. All feedback helps them improve their writing for future projects and for developing this edition. If you are able to spare a few minutes to post a review on Amazon, that would be much appreciated.

## Publisher Information

Rowanvale Books provides publishing services to independent authors, writers and poets all over the globe. We deliver a personal, honest and efficient service that allows authors to see their work published, while remaining in control of the process and retaining their creativity. By making publishing services available to authors in a cost-effective and ethical way, we at Rowanvale Books hope to ensure that the local, national and international community benefits from a steady stream of good quality literature.

For more information about us, our authors or our publications, please get in touch.

www.rowanvalebooks.com
info@rowanvalebooks.com

www.ingramcontent.com/pod-product-compliance
Ingram Content Group UK Ltd.
Pitfield, Milton Keynes, MK11 3LW, UK
UKHW041940130225
455056UK00004B/109